# When the Lights Go Out

## CARYS BRAY

PENGUIN BOOKS

PENGUIN BOOKS

UK | USA | Canada | Ireland | Australia
India | New Zealand | South Africa

Penguin Books is part of the Penguin Random House
group of companies whose addresses can be found at
global.penguinrandomhouse.com

Penguin
Random House
UK

First published by Hutchinson 2020
Published in Penguin Books 2021
001

Typeset in 10.9/15.9 pt Sabon LT Std
by Integra Software Services Pvt. Ltd, Pondicherry

Printed and bound in Great Britain by Clays Ltd, Elcograf S.p.A.

The authorised representative in the EEA is Penguin Random House
Ireland, Morrison Chambers, 32 Nassau Street, Dublin D02 YH68

A CIP catalogue record for this book is available from the
British Library

ISBN: 978–1–786–09109–3

www.greenpenguin.co.uk

MIX
Paper from
responsible sources
FSC® C018179

Penguin Random House is committed to a
sustainable future for our business, our readers
and our planet. This book is made from Forest
Stewardship Council® certified paper.

For Matt

... every time it rains
You're here in my head
Like the sun coming out

Kate Bush

How dreadful knowledge of the truth can be
When there's no help in truth!

Sophocles

The generations of men run on in the tide of Time,
But leave their destined lineaments permanent for
ever and ever.

William Blake

# PART I

# The End of the Day

# 15 December

## AND IT CAME TO PASS

He looks like a prophet, arm extended in exhortation as he stands beside the war memorial. Emma comes to a halt across the road, umbrella clutched in one hand, the other supporting a stack of books wrapped in brown paper and string. Should she—? If she—? The books tilt and she supports the tower with the umbrella pole. He is speaking but she can't hear him over the sound of the traffic and the Salvation Army band playing carols on the corner of Neville Street.

A double-decker stops at the lights, obscuring Emma's view. While the bus waits, she salvages the stub of her previous thought, which was to do with the weather and the music. *Snow had fallen, snow on snow* – the words of the carol are incongruous. The rain falls and falls. Pouring down roofs and hurrying along gutters. Skimming windows and diving off sills. Collecting in divots and rolling away in search of its level. At first it was inconvenient. Then irritating. Now it's intimidating: a reminder of water's powers. Of its ability to loosen soil and cut stone, to slip into wall cavities and under the lips of doors. Even when the clouds are wrung out, the air holds wet memories and damp steals into houses, hitching rides on clothes and shoes, and in the segments of folded umbrellas.

It has been years since it snowed. Emma remembers testing a drift beside the back door with a 30-cm ruler, barely discovering the ground before its whole length disappeared. Those were the days. Those days – she thinks of Dylan and James's reception class nativity when she hears that. *And it came to pass in those days ...* So began Dylan's part when he was Narrator One, years ago, perhaps even during the year of the snow. Emma doesn't remember what came next, but the way he said *those days* seemed very knowing. Afterwards, they would say it when something went wrong: *And it came to pass in those days* that Dylan forgot his lunchbox; that Dylan had to stay in at break time; that Dylan's teacher sent another note home. And, as Emma waits for the stationary traffic to shift on this wet Saturday morning in December, she thinks: *And it came to pass in those days, that Emma went forth to town for some Christmas presents and, while walking past the war memorial, beheld a man pointing to heaven.*

The bus coughs; then it pulls away, and she can see him again. Yes, a prophet, she thinks. All he needs is a staff. And a robe. A robe of righteousness – has she made that up? She doesn't think so; it's got a decidedly Biblical ring. A sandwich board stands beside him, covered in a series of exclamations: 'RECORD RAINFALL EVERY WINTER FOR YEARS TO COME! BRITISH CITIES MOST THREATENED IN EUROPE FOR FLOODING!

SEA LEVELS TO RISE BY 1.2 METRES! CLIMATE CHANGE THREATENS FUTURE OF GOLF!' Too much information, Emma decides. And the exclamation marks are misjudged.

He gestures right, the thrust of his hand pointing past the arcades and ice-cream shops, beyond the carousel and Silcock's Funland, over the hump of the Marine Way Bridge and on to the sea. She suspects he is talking about the tide. Last year, the sea occasionally burst over the wall and on to the road, as if it was playing peek-a-boo. Perhaps he is envisioning a stage beyond games, when the sea lifts its skirts, steps over the wall and tramps along Marine Drive; when empty shells line the road like ears, listening for the next incursion, and the next.

Meanwhile, in parks and play areas, puddles collecting in the grassy landing spots under climbing frames and swings are spilling into ponds. The fields beside parks and the rugby and football pitches at the schools are newly formed lakes – Emma has seen ducks swimming on them. There is water everywhere and temperatures are mild, meaning the mosquito eggs that lie waiting in the moist, frequently flooded soil will survive the winter and wake when covered by spring and summer rains.

Emma watches as people pass him. She has no idea whether he usually stands in front of the memorial on a Saturday morning or if this is a one-off. She tries not to use her car where possible, which means she rarely shops in town. Someone stops to take his picture. He doesn't appear to mind, but he must. How could he not? The photograph will probably end up online where he will be misunderstood. His clothes are wrong: the safety boots, combat-style trousers and checked shirt might look perfectly reasonable if he was, say, digging a trench or mowing a lawn. But here, in town, his clothes seem aggressively outdoorsy – he has the look of a professional protestor, more firebrand than friend. And where is his coat?

There is still so much to do. The food and the final presents. The wrapping. The decorations. And she needs to decide about a tree. Last year's repotted spruce sits on the patio in a horrible stasis, her ministrations – she has fed it vodka, lemonade and dissolved aspirin – have so far failed to either cure or kill it, and she won't buy a plastic tree or one that has been grown as part of a monocrop and sprayed with glyphosate. The spruce can have another week, she decides, not willing to write it off quite yet.

The traffic moves again, and Emma waits a while longer, until she is convinced she has seen the worst of it. He is not frightening or accosting anyone. People are ignoring him with the equanimity they afford chuggers, Mormons and *Big Issue* vendors. Though it is hard to tell from this distance, she suspects he is shivering. Or maybe he is feverish with purpose, vitalised by an opportunity to alleviate some of his own fear by passing it on to other people. But that is just speculation and can be put to one side in favour of what she knows: he is wet and cold; he is beset and troubled. His name is Chris, and he is her husband.

# A FLOOD OF WATERS UPON
# THE EARTH

The rain falls like stair rods, long bolts stabbing the van. Chris glances down at a pair of cardboard carriers in the passenger footwell before returning his attention to the road, which appears in frames as the wipers whip back and forth and the windscreen is speared then cleared, speared then cleared.

Every morning when he wakes, Chris listens for the rain. The drunk 'let me in' kind that batters the skylight like fists. The blasting Blitzkrieg kind. The splatting and pattering kinds. The trickling and plopping kinds. Always rain.

Every morning while James is out delivering newspapers, and Emma is busy rousing Dylan, Chris types a message in the local Buy, Sell & Swap Facebook group: 'CHRIS ABRAM, AVAILABLE FOR GARDEN DESIGN, MAINTENANCE AND ODD JOBS – TODAY!' The take-up has been poor. He usually gets a 'like' or two before his words are pushed down the page by someone selling a bin bag of baby clothes, a saggy second-hand sofa or an antique fax machine.

At this time of year, he should be trimming manicured lawns, pruning hard fruit trees, planting bulbs and clearing leaves. There are sheds to treat, blown-out fence panels to replace and damaged trees to tend. Instead, he unblocks gutters, pressure washes driveways, bails excess water from ponds, and waits. For the phone to ring. For the rain to stop. For the first frost. He used to love winter. Crisp ground and sparkling fields; the whole world sharp and shiny.

When jobs don't come in during the week, the boys go to school, Emma goes to work, and if Chris has nowhere to be, he can linger in the kitchen, reading up on rain gardens and tinkering with accounts that have never been so up to date. Saturdays are different – worse, though today is less so, he decides, glancing at the cardboard carriers in the passenger footwell as he joins the Formby bypass. But Saturdays, in general, are difficult. A few weeks ago, he was supposed to be repairing a shed roof, but it was bucketing down, and he'd had to postpone. He put a message on the Buy, Sell & Swap page and, rather than sit at home awaiting a response in full view of his family, Chris drove into town, where oily buses, full to the gills, crawled through puddles, and shoals of pedestrians dived in and out of shops. Irritated, he turned on to the coastal road and headed to the northern end of the beach. He parked and waited. After an hour, he gave up and headed home.

On his return, he reversed the van into the garage. The sandwich board was in its usual place, leaning against the wall. He spread it open and stared at it for a while.

Having come across a series of landscape scenes shaped as letters of the alphabet on the British Museum website, Emma had suggested making him a sign he could leave on customers' driveways while he was working. Not everyone would notice his van, she said. She, for one, never noticed vehicles, but people might look twice at an interesting sign. She found the board in the antique shop on Shakespeare Street, sanded it, painted it white and then, after some musing, drew his name. 'C' was a garden hook, 'A' a pair of rakes leaning against each other, 'M' two pine trees supported by angled stakes. It was the optimism of it that got to him on that inclement Saturday afternoon; the memory of Emma crouched on the patio, in the sun, as she pencilled an outline, his knee pads strapped to her jeans with gaffer tape. The board was a symbol of her faith in him and the business – how easy it is to accept kindness when you feel deserving of it.

Chris opened a tin of white paint and unearthed a brush. One stroke, and he was committed. He thought about the people in town, with their golf umbrellas and fancy coffees, their loaded shopping bags and their sea-level houses and, later, he returned to the garage with a packet of James's Sharpies and made a list of things he imagined might trouble them. Then he made a deal with himself. If he had no work on Saturday mornings, he'd stand beside the sign in town while awaiting messages and calls. In the moment, it made sense; his pluck would be rewarded. He was daring himself. Daring the weather. The deal was a form of inoculation: a jab of discomfort to protect him from a bout of disappointment.

There's movement in the carriers as Chris approaches the traffic lights at the end of the bypass. He directs a shushing noise at them, following it up with a couple of the tongue-clicks he makes around horses, hoping one or other of the sounds will soothe the fidgeting animals to stillness. He has not discussed livestock with

Emma, though he has opined on cheap home-grown protein and the benefits of adding animal pellets and urine to the compost heap. As far as Emma is concerned it has been hypothetical. She is amenable to chickens or bees but this, he concedes, is different. Still, it's easier to ask forgiveness than permission. He will seek absolution for the carriers, for the hay bales and the hutch lying in the back of the van and, eventually, for the sandwich board.

When his mobile rings Chris indicates, mounts the kerb and jabs the hazard light switch. He digs under a canvas bag on the passenger seat, snatches the phone and flips open the case. The number is unfamiliar. Let it be work, he thinks.

On answering, he is greeted by an elderly voice asking for help with a flooded lawn. Having explained there's very little he can do until the rain stops, Chris attempts to end the call, but the man says *please*, and since the address is nearby and he has nowhere else to be, Chris agrees to pop round.

The man is waiting at his gate, mushroomed by an enormous umbrella. He leads Chris down the side of his house to the back garden; the near part a quagmire, the far corner entirely submerged.

'Best to stop right here, today,' Chris says, resting a hand on the old fellow's arm. 'We'll only cause further compaction. Once all this rain's stopped and some of the water's evaporated, give me a ring and I'll bring boards and a fork. Get the air circulating. Then, if you like, I'll come back, wash down the patio, and have a go at improving your soil structure.'

'With compost?'

'Yeah. See where it's worst, down by the fence, in the far corner, where there's a bit of a dip? It's a nice shady spot. I could make you a bog garden. That might help. Plant some nice hostas. Sleeping Beauty – that's a good one, and it's slug resistant – marsh marigolds, Japanese iris, creeping jenny ...'

'Would *you* have a bog garden?'

'No, it wouldn't really suit my—'

'What've you got, then?'

'An acre. At the edge of the Moss.'

'Grass?'

'Some, but—'

'And you're keeping off yours, too?'

'*I* am,' he says. 'But I've got two big lads. Can't keep them indoors all winter.'

'Look at the state of it,' the old fellow says. 'It was like this last winter, too.'

'You should think about future-proofing. I could build a berm. It'd break things up nicely. Or you could try a tapestry lawn. They're perennial and don't need much mowing – half a dozen times a year should do it. And they attract insects and bees. Better for the environment all round. More importantly, in your case, they're supposed to absorb up to fifty per cent more rainfall than grass. Most people aren't keen, though. If they've got a lawn, they like it green and uniform.'

'And what's in one of these tapestry lawns?'

'Thyme, buttercups, clover, pink daisies, sweet violet – you choose. Plant in patterns, if you like. Make a sort of mosaic. I could show you some pictures, on the internet.'

'And it'd be all right to walk on?'

'Absolutely – keeps everything low-growing. And, depending on what you've planted – let's say you've gone for some Corsican mint – it'll smell nice when you step on it.'

'Well. That's something to think about, isn't it?' He turns to Chris, brighter now. 'Just dig a soakaway, to be going on with.'

'It won't work,' Chris explains. 'It *might*, if the soil was heavy; if it was clay ... but it isn't.'

'Just a test hole?'

'There's no—'

'Why don't you give it a try?'

'If I dig a hole, it'll fill with water from the bottom up.'

'Let's see, shall we?'

Chris fetches the Cornish shovel from the back of his van.

Arm trembling, the old fellow attempts to hold the umbrella over the pair of them. The wise man and the foolish man, Chris thinks. And, sure enough, as he slides his shovel into the saturated ground, the rain comes down and the floods come up.

The world was always going to end. Chris sees that, now. As a boy, he believed it was his great misfortune to have arrived on the planet just as things were winding up, and while it gave him an excuse to disregard the bits of school he didn't enjoy – it wasn't as if he'd need algebra in the end times – he was burdened by the knowledge, anticipating pestilence, plague and famine. Forever on the lookout for wars and rumours of wars; for desolation and signs and wonders.

Chris checks his mirrors and pulls away, raising a hand to the old fellow who stands forlornly at his gate. He drives through the estate and back to the main road where the drains are gagging, spewing water on to the pavement. He thinks of the story of Noah, and of his father's belief that the Flood caused the extinction of the dinosaurs. The dinosaur encounters of Chris's boyhood – a class project on Jurassic carnivores, the prehistoric playset in the Year 2 classroom and a favourite T-shirt – were reminders of God's penchant for genocide. He pictured diplodocuses knocked off their feet by muddy torrents, their long necks reaching for the surface like periscopes. Tyrannosauruses trying, and failing, to counter currents with their tiny arms. Pterodactyls landing on the last treetops of the last hills before taking to the skies and eventually falling out of them, exhausted: plop, plop, plop. His father did not discourage such imaginings. St Paul may have appealed for congregants to think on whatsoever things are pure and just, but his father's personal frequency remained tuned to matters of gore and dust.

It had come as a relief, in his late teens, to uncover a deep seam of scepticism and, while embarking on an NVQ in Horticulture (and retaking Maths GCSE), Chris abandoned his old imaginings and leaped, like the lame man at the gate of the temple, into a whole life: one that had the potential to reach a deliciously mundane conclusion; illness and old age were his new prospects and he embraced them. Relieved from the anxiety of premature death – not just his own, but that of everyone and everything around him – Chris had learned to live.

Now, he sees those happy years for what they were: an interlude. And, as he turns on to the coastal road, the rain finally easing, he longs to return to that halcyon time: falling in love, finding the house, creating the garden. Emma wanted a meadow, a vegetable plot and grass where their future children would play. He started with the meadow, cutting the patchy grass and removing the clippings; working up the soil with a rake before blending wildflower seed with yellow rattle and sand, then scattering the mix like magic dust. Sometimes, when he was at work, Emma buried bulbs among the seed, no scheme or pattern in mind, just an array of surprises. She could quote great chunks of poetry and happily recount the plots of novels she'd read years ago, but she had no knack for remembering plant names: 'What's this one, again?' she'd say. 'What's that one?' He had supposed her initial enthusiasm would fade but it didn't, and he remembers the summer solstice when, six months pregnant with Dylan and proud of their outdoor endeavours, she invited their parents for a picnic tea. Emma's mother, unwilling to sit on either the grass or a picnic blanket, hovered on foot, bemoaning their lack of garden furniture as her father gamely remarked on the weather. Chris's father offered thanks for the homegrown food in an uninvited and unnecessarily long prayer that referenced each stage of the water cycle, and his mother, while *helping* in the kitchen, saw a container, lid-side down, which she 'righted', only to upend the cake Emma had carefully iced that morning.

Guests finally departed, they lay side by side on the grass, chuckling – oh, they were so pleased with themselves: the rational, reasonable progeny of risible parents.

He leaned across and kissed her. She straddled him, sundress spilling over her stomach and on to his as she rocked her hips and kissed him back.

Afterwards, Chris dozed off.

When he woke, Emma was standing in the wildflowers, head ringed by a daisy-chain crown. The light felt like a gift and he could almost believe it had broken curfew purely for his pleasure.

'Welcome back, sleepy head! Did you have a *most rare vision*?'

'A what?'

'You, lying there, made me think of Bottom.'

'Who?'

'From *A Midsummer Night's Dream*.'

Emma launched into a bewildering tale of lovers, fairies and magical juice. She followed it with one of her own: a midsummer night during which she and a group of friends left a post-exam party and, having 'borrowed' a copy of *A Midsummer Night's Dream* and several cans of cider, gathered at the bandstand in town where they stumbled their way through the play.

He lay watching her talk, thinking how much pleasure she took from things: her pride in the vegetables she'd picked and prepared that morning; her delight in her expanding stomach; her lazy smile as she'd straddled and subsumed him.

Having reached the end of her story, Emma turned on the spot, taking in the garden.

'Isn't everything beautiful?'

He agreed that it was.

*'The world was all before them, where to choose their place of rest, and Providence their guide.'*

'Shakespeare?'

'Milton,' she said, and then, pointing at the yellow flowers that almost reached her knees, 'These tall dande-lions are *so* pretty.'

'They're cat's-ear.'

'These long spiky things. I thought they were a bit boring, but the tips – look, they're flowering.'

'Purple toadflax.'

'What about these pinky ones, with little faces?'

'Red campion.'

And as the light finally faded, Chris lay on the cooling grass, naming everything, like Adam. His clever wife, his beautiful garden, and the world all before him.

Chris decelerates as he approaches the roundabout at Pontins, taking it slowly, one eye on the road, the other on the curve of the holiday camp's exterior wall, the cheerfulness of the bright fence panels undermined by a series of flags dangling from their posts like sodden ponytails.

A few years ago, during the then wettest December on record, this road was closed for eleven weeks due to flooding. The dune slacks filled with water which, instead of running out to sea, poured on to the road, along the footpaths and through the golf course. Channels and pipes in the area hadn't been maintained and gullies hadn't been cleared of leaves. It was rumoured that the outfalls of some drains couldn't even be found and retired council workers were contacted to locate them. He wonders how many more long-forgotten drains snake along this essential road? How many pipes are silted up? How much water would it take for the slacks to spill beyond the road and the footpaths and past the golf course before trickling into town?

He adds these worries to others that plague him: increasingly extreme weather events, the decline of wildlife populations, political inertia and, closer to home, the gradual collapse of the lawn-care scheme that used to be the backbone of his business.

Customers started switching to pay-as-you-go last winter. And who could blame them? Chris promised they'd get their money's worth, eventually. But who wants to make monthly payments to maintain a lawn that's under water? Then came the heatwave. It didn't rain in June. Not once. The rest of the summer wasn't much better. Every night on the news it was 'hosepipe ban this, hosepipe ban that'. Customers called and said, 'No point in you coming out, mate. Let's leave it for now. Oh, by the way, I've cancelled my direct debit.' And in the midst of this, his father died. Rudely, without notice. Chris has since learned there was a spike in deaths coinciding with the high temperatures. Hundreds more than expected. Another thing to blame on the weather – the *climate*. He doesn't exactly miss his father. It's more that he can't help noticing his absence. There's an empty space on the horizon, as there was after the town's gas holder was demolished. Chris had liked knowing where he was in relation to the tower; it had been a place-marker, something he looked for on his way home.

Disoriented and gloomy, Chris did what he could in the boiling weather. When he cut grass, he kept enough length to offer the soil some shade and left the cuttings in situ, hoping they'd also provide some cover. Customers on meters worried about the cost of watering. Others recycled bath, sink and washing-up water, but the ground was so dry, the water rolled, settling at the lowest point. There was nothing to do but leave the grass to recover, and it mostly did, after a few weeks of regular rain. In the meantime, Chris mulched borders and got on with hedge trimming and bed work. He had a decent clearance job, so he wasn't unoccupied. But the regular money he could count on each month was shrinking again; he knew things would tank if there was another wet winter.

And here he is, tanking. Here he is, back to his beginnings: the interlude of his happiness a distant realm, a *most rare vision*. Here he is, waking each morning listening for the rain, plagued by a fresh dread of the future which now includes Emma, Dylan and James; the house; their land. And he is already grieving. Imagining the loss of everything he holds dear. Just as he imagined the obliteration of the dinosaurs when he was a boy.

# MERCY KILLING

When the shower is over, the sky sapped and pale, Emma steps on to the puddled patio. The house squats behind her, a 1970s dormer bungalow with brown double-glazing units and ugly corrugated roof tiles. It has low ceilings and thin walls and is prone to damp. The dehumidifier runs at all hours, a mechanical dowsing rod, detecting water wherever it is employed. She had dreamed of a Victorian house in town: terrace or semi, two bedrooms or three – she was flexible, and prepared to accept some dilapidation in exchange for a large garden. But the combination of antiquity and acreage proved well beyond their means. Their house-hunt took place in the spring, and thoughts of high ceilings and period features vanished when, having driven to the very cusp of the town, they followed the canny estate agent, not through the front door, but through the wooden gates at the side of the house and into the garden. The acre of scrubby pasture sold the place to them. Infected by nostalgia, Chris for his early childhood on the farm, Emma for summers spent with her grandparents in Cornwall, neither truly considered the upkeep of the house or imagined times when the weather would force them indoors, and anyway, on the day they looked round, the interior, though basic, dated and empty of furniture, was bright and clean, the walls scrubbed and whitewashed. Months later, mould crept out from corners, blooming along skirting boards, contouring window frames and speckling the ceilings.

Chris divided the land into three, laying turf at the near end, which he keeps short for the boys. Behind the lawn is the space they call the meadow and beyond it, beside a row of fruit trees at the boundary, is the vegetable garden, relegated to the back of the plot to spare the greenhouse and young plants and trees from the boys' balls. On a Saturday afternoon in a month or two, Chris will climb a stepladder and, muttering about colony collapse and neonicotinoids, he'll fertilise the early-flowering plum trees with a tiny paintbrush. Subsequently, as the rest of the garden wakes up, Emma will come out in the afternoons to count bees. It won't be a representative sample, of course, but she hopes her reported sightings will make Chris feel better.

She splashes across the patio to the garage. If they'd built it themselves, they'd have arranged things differently. It was here when they bought the house, nestled alongside the boundary fence and within swinging distance of the wooden gates that open on to the driveway. Wide enough to contain two vehicles, the previous owners described it as a 'workshop', though as far as Emma knows it was only ever used to store old furniture and garden tools; unsurprising, perhaps, as 'work' requires light and whoever built the structure didn't think to intersperse the concrete sections with any windows. Not long after they moved in, Emma and Chris had the up-and-over opening replaced with a pair of steel doors, making the building more secure for Chris's van and tools.

Between the boundary fence and the exterior of the garage, a gap, barely a passageway, acts like a black hole, collecting fallen leaves and garden rubbish. Chris usually clears it in the winter, but this year he hasn't, so Emma will do it herself. Perhaps the physical exertion will help to dispel thoughts of him standing beside the memorial, soaked and scruffy. The shovel blade scuffs the concrete hardstanding as she scoops a pile of saturated leaves. Squeezed between the fence and the concrete wall, she backs out of the narrow passageway and transfers the mess to the green wheelie bin. She thinks of Chris and works harder, repeating the movements, until the wood of the shovel's shaft grows warm against her supporting hand and her head is empty of everything except the sound of her coat sleeves brushing her body and the beat of her breath.

She is almost halfway through the job, about to scoop another shovel of muck, when a frog crawls out of the rotting leaves, twitching and bleeding. Emma closes her eyes for a moment, an involuntary response when the boys are hurt or there's violence on television. She takes a long breath and opens them again. The frog is badly injured. She must have caught it with the blade. Her hands tighten around the shovel. She is armed, and it is her unpleasant duty to end the suffering she has caused. And she will. After three. She counts, and nothing happens. She tries again, unable to determine whether the insubordination originates in her brain or arms. A breather, she thinks, a moment to collect herself before she delivers the blow.

She backs out of the passageway, passes the garage doors and comes to a stop on the puddled patio. If she pops into the house for a glass of water, the frog, with any luck, will be dead when she returns.

'You haven't cleaned the sandwich maker, Mum,' Dylan complains as she steps through the back door.

'Neither have you,' she replies.

James sniggers and pats her on the head. 'Good one, Emma-Jane,' he says.

Emma is ambivalent about this recent use of her full name. Only her mother addresses her that way, and it's hard to tell whether James is motivated by camaraderie or a desire to undermine her.

She removes her sodden trainers, awkwardly, without undoing the laces, and as the boys butter the outsides of their sandwiches and lock them in the toaster, she tells them about the frog.

'You kill spiders,' Dylan says.

'Only massive ones with hairy legs. And faces.'

They laugh at her.

'What? They've got faces; they *have*. And I mostly don't kill them.'

'No, you get Dad to do it. You're, like, an accessory.'

Emma wipes damp hair from her forehead. She pulls her phone out of her back pocket and types 'humane kill frog' into the search engine.

'I can put it in a Tupperware box and stick it in the fridge. It'll fall asleep, and then I can shut it in the freezer and it'll die.'

Except she would have to pick up the frog, somehow. She could use a piece of kitchen towel so as not to touch its mucusy skin. But it might wriggle or groan, and the thought of it, agonised and struggling, makes her feel queasy. She lifts the lid of the slow cooker and checks the curry before taking a glass from the dish rack and filling it with cold water.

'Stop procrastinating – you know what you've got to do,' Dylan says.

'Do you think *you* could—'

'*I'm* not doing it!'

'How much would you pay me?' James asks.

'I'm not *paying*.'

'In that case' – James extends an arm and points at the back door – 'get out there and finish him off, Emma-Jane.'

Emma downs the water and places the empty glass on the worktop. She returns her phone to her pocket, wriggles her feet back into her trainers and steps outside. The shovel is propped against the wall, beside last year's moribund Christmas tree. Emma grabs it and, with her spare hand, retrieves one of the bricks Chris uses for propping the wooden gates that open on to the driveway.

She hurries down the partially cleared passageway and covers the frog with the brick. Then she stands on it. After a few moments, she steps off and scrapes the brick with the shovel, trying not to look at the paste on its blade. Shovel aloft, she reverses out of the passageway and squelches away from the garage, through the boggy lawn and into the meadow.

When they first bought the house, she thought of this place as 'the countryside', a natural landscape, forged in slow time and silence. Of course, she was wrong. In times past, this was the shore of Martin Mere, formerly the largest body of fresh water in England: a vast sheet, silvery in the sun, black in the shade, widening in wet weather and tapering in the dry. She has tried to imagine it as it was, hundreds and hundreds of years ago. A treacherous wilderness, covered in deep pools of acidic water and bog, blurred by lingering fogs and mists. A place ancient people skirted while hunting for food and collecting peat for fuel, the ground so flat it was probably difficult to discern the water's edge. The mere used to reach as far as the primary school where she works as a welfare assistant, and the house where she grew up, not much more than a mile away, in High Park. As a child, Emma was familiar with the Moss, the flat plain of farmland that bordered the town, but she had no idea what it was *before*, no idea about the lake. She found a book on local history and realised the words had been there all along: some of the older generation didn't say High Park, they used the name their parents had used, Blowick, an Old Norse word, meaning Dark Bay. She discovered that people had been trying to drain the mere since the late 1600s. Eventually, in the mid-nineteenth century, steam pumping led to effective drainage and the soil offered up its treasures: spearheads and palstaves, red deer and aurochs bones, and an ancient canoe that lay across the first-floor landing of the Botanic Gardens Museum like a felled tree.

The drained landscape is one of ditches, tracks and dog-leg roads; of remote farms, knots of trees and dark, fertile soil. Not a natural landscape at all, but a complex product of human intervention. Beautiful, all the same, Emma thinks, sadly, as she tips the shovel and wipes the blade on the soggy, rain-flattened vegetation. *Beauty is truth, truth beauty* – the phrase echoes from long-past poetry seminars. But truth is often not beautiful, she decides, feet wet, pieces of frog smeared on the ground in front of her. Presently, her life is full of unbeautiful truths, the foremost being that she is a coward.

The back door opens, and Dylan and James bolt out. 'Did you do it?' they yell.

Emma nods as they jog across the puddled patio and on to the sodden grass where they each commandeer a goal. She knows the drill. They will fire long balls at each other in a game designed to improve Dylan's shooting and James's goalkeeping, each hitting the deck when the ball comes back to them – their clothes will be filthy.

'Let me get out of the way, before you start,' she says, hurrying back to the house.

The atmosphere indoors is dense and earthy: a musty mix of wet washing and the ionised air from the dehumidifier, which is stiff and sharp, like crisp sheets and metal. Emma makes coffee and watches the boys. When she hears the familiar rumble of the van's engine she steps into the hall and waits for Chris to appear. She needs to see him, to marry the man beside the memorial with the husband in the hall and confirm they are the same person. There was a time in their marriage when talking, like sex, was recreational, a chance to rub their ideas up against each other and experience some relief in the sharing. Now, she can't fathom how to talk without making things worse. There is an inevitability about their conversations, as if they are trapped in an Edgar Allan Poe story where all interactions are a gateway to the protagonist's worst fears.

Emma has tried to digest the news and then, like a mother bird, present Chris with safely regurgitated bits. But every hopeful comment has a rejoinder.

'There are moths that eat plastic,' she told him, a while ago.

'Know what else they eat? Wax,' Chris said. 'And guess what bees use to make their honeycombs? Yup. Not so good now, is it?'

She hears the gates open, the drag as the swollen wood scrapes the driveway. He has gone straight round the back. She returns to the kitchen and spies him on the patio, a cardboard carrier in each hand. The image of him standing beside the sandwich board recedes, and she watches, full of the waiting feeling each of his new ideas triggers: is this the step too far? And if it is, what to say?

## SIGNS OF THE TIMES

The lads stop playing football on the puddled, churned-up grass and stroll over, elbows and knees caked in mud.

'They're not pets,' Chris says, indicating the carriers. 'They're for farming. We're going to be farmers.'

Emma steps out through the back door, clutching a mug of coffee. He wonders how she spent the morning. There's usually something on a Saturday. Last week it was a coast and countryside clean-up at Rimrose Valley Country Park and the week before she was nurdling at

Blundellsands, picking tiny pieces of plastic off the beach after an especially high tide for some national survey or other. He won't ask in case she returns the question.

He places the carriers in the garage where it's dry and Dylan and James help with the hutch. They're almost as tall as him now, all arms and legs, twiggy: a pair of saplings. The hutch is a two-storeyed affair. The first floor houses semi-detached living quarters, each with a ladder leading to its respective ground-floor run. Ideally, they'd place it on the grass, but it could be spring before the ground dries and so, for now, they position it on the patio.

'Well, this *is* a surprise,' Emma says. 'I'm not sure why ...'

'I've been thinking about it for a while.'

'You never said.'

'Rabbits are easy to dispatch,' he explains.

'Oh? Where are you sending them?'

Emma sips her coffee, and, with the lower half of her face hidden by the mug, it is hard to read her expression. There are lines around her mouth. He doesn't know when they first appeared; they've sneaked up on him. 'Wipe that smile off your face,' his father used to say. Impossible for Emma: the skin that brackets her lips is stamped with the creases of every smile she's ever made.

Before the boys were born, they used to go walking at the weekends and, on the way back from Pendle Hill, Whernside Peak or wherever, Emma would lounge in the passenger seat, trainers off, feet propped on the dashboard while she read to him: short stories, novels, poetry – she kept a stash of books in the car, some in the glove compartment, others stuffed into the pocket of the door. He wasn't much of a reader; he'd never read any poetry unless he counted the Psalms, but there was a poem Emma liked about getting old. Maybe it was the way she read it that appealed to Chris: softly, pausing in places, like a prayer. Or perhaps it was the fact that its contents were so far removed from their present – oldness was abstract back then and prompted thoughts of possession rather than decline: Emma would be *his* until the end of everything. He remembers only one line: *And loved the sorrows of your changing face*. The words come back to him as he looks for anger or disappointment in the corrugations of Emma's forehead.

She lowers the mug.

'So, you *do* mean they're easy to kill?'

It's his cue to make nice and request forgiveness. Yet why should he? This year's harvest was poor – the courgettes and runner beans were decent enough, as were the early potatoes, but the carrots split, the leeks bolted, and the Brussels sprouts keeled over. It was already wet when he dug up the remaining potatoes. Now, they're festering in the storage bin, waiting to be exhumed by an unsuspecting Emma. Above them, the onions, strung from the roof of the shed like gold and red Christmas decorations, are decaying from the inside out; a gentle squeeze is enough to send a pulpy heart sliding through each neck. And, once again, thanks to the rain in Spain, there are gaps on supermarket shelves where there should be lettuces, broccoli and spinach. It's not as if things are going to get any better. What does Emma think she's going to eat?

'Who gets to name the rabbits?' Dylan asks.

'It's best if we don't. They're for meat. We'll look after them and then—'

'We'll slaughter them!'

'It's not funny, Dylan. They'll have a nice life here. Shelter. Food. Some babies. And after that …' Chris shrugs and then, mostly to Emma, and all at once, like tearing off a plaster, he says, 'We'll go for three litters a year. Once the babies are eight weeks old, they're fryers. You should feed them extra protein if you want to dispatch them any time before three months; otherwise they aren't worth it. From three to six months they're roasters – that's what we'll be looking at. Post six months they're stewers.'

'We talked about *bees*,' she says.

'Did I tell you about the hives in New York that produced this poisonous green honey? Guess what the main ingredient was? Antifreeze.'

'Well, that's New York … I don't see what it's – I don't know anything about rabbits. How to look after them or—'

'It's easy as pie.'

'Rabbit pie,' James interjects, laughing.

Emma nods. 'Right,' she says and, turning, steps back into the house.


Chris reverses the van into the garage. When he opens the driver's door he is assailed by the comforting smells of oil, creosote, Jeyes Fluid and seasoned wood. He takes the knee pads out of the pouches in his trousers and chucks them on the dash before grabbing the multi-packs of baked beans from the canvas bag on the passenger seat and adding them to the towers of tins in the far corner. The baked beans are for himself and the boys. He is storing pinto, cannellini, kidney and black beans for Emma who, unless she changes her mind about eating meat, is more likely to suffer from appetite fatigue in a food shortage. According to his calculations, survival on basic rations for fifty days requires 14 kg of rice and 14 kg of beans per person. This translates to approximately fourteen 4-kg family bags of rice and 150 tins of beans. He wishes rice came in tins, too; he worries about whether the clip-lid dustbin where he stores the bags will prevent damage from heat, moisture and pests.

The back wall of the garage is lined with the old metal shelves he rescued from his parents' garden shed before they sold up and went to live in the static caravan. Emma sanded the shelves and painted them with bottle-green Hammerite. They hold essential foodstuffs: sugar, vanilla extract, salt, vinegar, brandy and vodka, as well as half-used tins of paint, tubs of nails and screws, balls of string and twine, twist ties, loppers, bow saws, hedge shears, secateurs, fifteen hessian sandbags and a small bag of sand.

As Chris turns, he accidentally nudges a cluster of broom handles and they clatter to the floor. He bends to pick them up. They used to be topped by signs. Emma had a collection – she could have staged an exhibit: 'Emma Abram, My Life in Protest'. Individually, the signs were a testament to her persistence and optimism. Collectively, they were a catalogue of disappointment.

Chris went with her to a protest once. Drove her because it was drizzling, and he didn't like the thought of her lugging her homemade sign to the station almost two miles away. It had been a roadside fracking protest. Most motorists beeped in support of the protestors, or protectors, as they preferred to be called. A few, all men, Chris noticed, rolled down their windows, made obscene gestures and yelled, 'Fuck off,' and, 'Get a job.' When this happened, Emma laughed and blew kisses. Chris had only ever seen minute-long clips of protests on the news, portraying them as exciting and action-packed. God, it was boring. There'd been some bad singing and a chorus of half-hearted slogan chanting which seemed to embarrass Emma, mainly, he suspected, because he was there to witness it. *What do we want? No fracking! When do we want it? Now!* A little farther down the road a group of scruffy young people in camouflage gear congregated around a green and black flag. An elderly lady in a yellow bobble hat followed Chris's gaze. 'They like to stand there,' she explained. 'They do their own little protest. Because they're anarchists, *bless their hearts*.' Then she offered him a homemade, dairy-free fairy cake.

Not long later, Emma threw in the towel. Ever the recycler, she dismantled the signs, stacking the broom handles in the garage where they would no doubt come in handy and, the following spring, she used the corrugated plastic boards to cover and warm newly planted seeds as they dawdled in the still-cool ground. Every time Chris

went to check on the potatoes he was badgered by a row
of remonstrations:

HONK YOUR SUPPORT!
SAFE FRACKING IS A FAIRY TALE
NORTHERN ~~POWERHOUSE~~ SHITHOUSE!
#RESIST!
FRACK OFF!
THERE IS NO PLANET B
SAVE AINSDALE LIBRARY!
SAVE BIRKDALE LIBRARY!
SAVE CHURCHTOWN LIBRARY!

'Why don't you keep them safe somewhere?' he asked,
fed up of seeing them. 'You might need them again, one
day. Not the library ones, but the others ...'

She wouldn't, Emma insisted. It had all been a complete
waste of time. No one in power cared about literacy and
community. Or air pollution and rising global temperatures. They weren't bothered about the risks of poisoned
water, birth defects and cancer clusters. 'We're the *desolate
north*,' she said. 'We're nothing to them. We might as well
be insects.'

Emma's giving up niggled at him. Her dropping of
everything: the environment, peace, the preservation of
public services – it was as if she had unclipped an eighty-
litre backpack, chucked it on the ground and walked away.
What could he do but pick it up? That's the way marriage
works, isn't it? There are ecological structures to preserve.
If someone takes the bins out for ten years and suddenly

stops, the other someone has to do it. While Emma had been doing the worrying, protesting and preparing, he hadn't had to. Once she stopped, it was up to him. Of course, if she'd taken it more seriously, spent less time on fancy signs, he'd have realised sooner. But he's got the 'backpack' now. He's better equipped to carry it. Stronger, more determined. And he's filling it with new worries every day: telemetric readings of concerning activity in the Yellowstone caldera, ice melt in the West Antarctic, the number of harvests remaining – somewhere between sixty and a hundred, depending on what you read.

Chris gathers the broom handles and leans them back against the wall. They feel cold. Not damp, though. He eyes the builders' bag of wood. Please not damp.

'Keep it up,' Chris calls, glancing over his shoulder.

Dylan's face is scrunched and angry. James is less scrutable, thanks to his sports goggles that look, with their protruding, tinted lenses, like a piece of retro-futuristic technology.

Misty rain hangs in the air like a ribbon curtain. The road, one-track in places, barely two-track in others, is flanked by deep, open drainage ditches brimming with mirror-dark water. The landscape is a splay of plain, occasionally interrupted by clusters of trees that stand like pieces on a chessboard, and telegraph poles, leaning at various angles thanks to the subsidence of the peat soil. The fields are waterlogged. Recent weather has not been kind to the Moss. Thanks to twentieth-century farmers, there are very few hedgerows, and during the dry summers unopposed winds blow away the topsoil. Water from the ditches is pumped on to crops, reducing the water table under the peat. The ground is a metre lower than it was in the 1960s and two metres lower than it was in the 1690s. While the land levels are increasingly lower, and therefore more susceptible to flooding, despite pumping, the tracks and roads, reinforced with hardcore, are becoming incrementally taller.

In the distance, Chris sees a car. He slows, and the lads follow suit. There is no retreat. Where the hardcore ends, the saturated slope of the bank begins. They jog on the spot in single file, heads bobbing like whack-a-moles. Chris starts to say so but stops – Dylan and James won't laugh because to laugh would be a concession, an admission that this isn't so bad after all, and they won't give him that. They are united against him. Earlier, as he passed the porch where they were bent over, tying their laces, he overheard their treacherous grumblings and it pleased him. Chris remembers the moments when he shared a one-for-all feeling with his sister: the mutinous pleasure of being united against a common enemy. He has little choice but to force the lads into this. So many of their friends are unfit, overly attached to their phones and consoles, with little idea of what it is to pit oneself against the world in a physical way. There is no evidence that, left to their own devices, people instinctively do what's best for them. After Great Uncle Harold had his foot amputated, he persuaded hospital visitors to wheel him outside for a smoke and a Mars Bar. If humans can't stop guzzling sugar and nicotine to stave off diabetes and early death, how can they be expected to have the self-control and prescience to save the world?

Chris carries on running. With the car gone, he can imagine it's just the three of them out here beyond the last of the streetlights, the plain of the Moss stretching ahead, the steady turbining of the lads' breath behind him. And for a moment, he is not sure whether he is running home or running away.

## A TIME TO REND, AND A TIME TO SEW

Emma never planned to have a sewing room. When they looked around the house, she and Chris noted the downstairs bathroom and imagined they would eventually convert the smallest of the three upstairs rooms. But they grew used to the existing arrangement and as neither of the boys, though they occasionally moan about sharing, is prepared to downsize, Emma has, by degrees, adopted the third bedroom. It is not a patch on her grandmother's sewing room – large and airy, it smelled of lavender and a brand of washing powder Emma, despite her best efforts, has been unable to locate. This room, like the other upstairs rooms, has sloped ceilings and a skylight. At the apex, a bookcase holds stacks of fabric neatly wrapped around magazine boards. Egg boxes cradle ovals of left-over wool. Recycled jars full of buttons float in a row, their lids screwed to the underside of a shelf. And a length of blue velvet dangles from a hanger. The room houses the ironing board and two tables; one is topped by rulers, tailor's chalk, scissors, a 'self-healing' cutting mat and a rotary fabric cutter; the other is for sewing. The machine is her grandmother's, the same 1975 Singer 533 Emma learned to use when she was seven years old and was staying with her grandparents in Cornwall for the first time.

Up until that summer, her grandparents had felt like strangers. They came north for occasional weekend visits, arriving wrapped, like a pair of presents, in quilted coats, scarves and pullovers. There were even two pairs of fluffy slipper-socks in Grandma's handbag. 'I know you like your carpets,' she'd say while she and Grandad made a production of removing their outdoor shoes. As each layer came off, Emma knew she was getting closer to the prize, a paper bag of boiled sweets or liquorice torpedoes, hiding in one of their many pockets. The house struggled to contain them. Grandad longed to be useful and sought out jobs in the back garden. Once, he forgot to take off his shoes when he came indoors and got mud all over the cream carpet. Meals were followed by walks, in all weathers. The boot of their car contained jackets (with sleeves and without), wellies, golf umbrellas, hats, a pair of binoculars and other paraphernalia to aid them in their pursuit of fresh air. Their visits concluded with Emma's mother muttering, 'Thank goodness,' as she waved them off, and the argument that always followed her father's, 'Oh, come on, they're not so bad.'

Emma didn't want to go away, but her mother needed a break. It was the school holidays and Emma thought they could have a break, at home, together. But it turned out that it wouldn't be a break if she was there, so Grandma and Grandad drove up and packed her into their car, where she spent seven hours sitting between a pair of fold-up chairs, her legs balanced on a wicker picnic hamper.

Grandma and Grandad's house was old. The windows had to be dragged up and sometimes they'd slide down again, as if staying open was far too much effort. The bare stairs were painted red and most of the rooms were carpet-less. Floorboards objected to feet with groans and occasional squeals. There was no central heating. Instead, on rainy, chilly days, which were plentiful during that first summer, there were open fires and hot-water bottles. Beds were made with sheets, blankets and floral bedspreads, and at night Emma lay with her feet in the toasty stamp of the hot water bottle, bedspread arranged so only the cold tip of her nose poked out. The bathroom window was perpetually unlatched, leaving the toilet seat so cold it stung the backs of her thighs when she sat down. No two dining chairs matched, and cushions, throws, curtains and rugs were a cacophony of colours and prints. The kitchen floor tiles were a kind Emma had previously only seen outdoors. There were peaks and troughs in that floor, matching the hilly landscape behind the house. Battered pots and pans hung from a rack on the ceiling. The cooker was fat and old-fashioned. Beside it was Aslan's dog basket. Whole walls were covered in picture frames of all different shapes, colours and sizes. At the top of the stairs was an aerial photograph of the house. Grandad pressed his finger to the glass; 'You are here,' he said. Every time Emma passed the photograph, she stopped to look. Its very existence made her feel better about being away from home. To see the place she inhabited from above, to mark the back garden, to trace the curve of the road and the humps of the hills, was to better understand where she was.

Grandma and Grandad lived a different sort of life. At first, Emma didn't know what to make of it. Her grandparents seemed careless, and her own, centrally heated, carpeted, always-tidy home stood in her mind, for a time, as a reproach to their creaky, well-worn shabbiness.

In between walks with Aslan, gardening and baking, Emma was taken up to the sewing room. She and Grandma were to make an owl. Emma chose material from a box of scraps. One shade of purple for the owl's top and another for his bottom. They placed the pieces back to back and sewed around the outside, leaving a small opening. He was turned inside out and given a pair of solid plastic eyes with shanks – clip, clip. Grandma stuck a funnel in his opening, and they filled him with rice before sewing him up. Emma named him Fat Freddy. He had a comforting, just-right heft, and she carried him everywhere. At night, she placed him on her forehead, pretending she was ill and her mother, keeping watch at the bedside, was gauging her temperature. 'I'm all right,' Emma mouthed, bravely, the press of the imagined hand resting on her head like a blessing.

Emma returned home with three jars of blackberry jam, Fat Freddy and an inkling that, in the difference between her mother's present and past lives, lay a message to her grandparents: by choosing her own way of living, her mother was effectively ruling out theirs. This was accompanied by the realisation that she wasn't supposed to like Grandma. That love, like pie, was a finite resource and in loving Grandma, Emma was stealing a slice that belonged to her mother. She has since wondered how it might feel to be mothered by Grandma, a woman who never said, 'You're welcome,' when she was thanked but rather responded with, 'Yes. Well,' as if she didn't believe you, or wanted to discourage further pleasantries. But, at a distance of a generation, parenting failures are easily recast as foibles.

Emma's parents moved to the Cornish house six years ago.

'But you hate it there,' Emma had exclaimed, at the time.

'I never said that,' her mother replied, which was true, but was, Emma felt, against the spirit, if not the letter, of her mother's erstwhile sentiments.

Emma claimed the aerial photograph. It hangs on the wall of her sewing room and Fat Freddy lies on the top shelf of the bookcase, beside an almost heart-shaped stone which Chris found during a garden clearance. He sanded and polished it before using a point chisel and hammer to write 'LOVE ME' on its back. There should be a comma between the words, but instead his sign-off resembles a command which, like other injunctions, is written in stone.

Emma lifts a tissue-paper bundle from the cutting table. Inside is a knitted christening shawl. She'll take it to the Post Office on Monday, after work. '*How* many hours' labour?' Chris will ask, if he sees it. 'And the wool was *how* much?' In the evenings, she often knits for a couple of hours while watching television or listening to an audiobook. It's as much a way of relaxing as anything, like mediation or adult colouring. If she could be sure Chris wouldn't take it as a criticism, she would inform him that this year her knitting and sewing has covered the cost of Christmas, both boys' birthdays and new school shoes.

Emma slips the blue velvet off its hanger. It's cut from a pair of curtains one of Chris's old ladies gave him back in the summer. It mustn't be pressed; crushed pile never recovers. She has been making bags since she inherited the machine. The loss of her grandparents – first her grandmother and, days later, as he'd always hoped, her grandfather – was followed by the loss of her job when the library closed. It was not how these things were supposed to happen. Great sadnesses should arrive one at a time. For them to come all at once felt remarkably unfair. How Emma missed her grandmother's abrupt, interrogative phone calls, and the knowledge that though he rarely added anything to the conversation, her grandfather was listening on the upstairs phone, like God. And how she missed the many different aspects of her old job: organising reading groups, showing older people how to use the internet, visiting schools to promote the Summer Reading Challenge and, most of all, studying people's symptoms and prescribing useful books.

Emma likes to say she started sewing bags because they're easy to make and good for the environment. Mostly, though, it was because using the machine made her feel close to her grandmother. This blue velvet bag will house a newly purchased copy of *The Monster Storm*, a picture book Dylan used to love. She'll sew a pair of yellow button eyes above the bag's front pocket and a series of white felt triangles will poke out of the pocket's lip, like teeth. It's a Christmas present for her nephew Elijah, who is a bit of a monster.

Emma measures and cuts a pair of handles, folds them in half and, holding the iron a couple of inches above the fabric, blasts each strip with steam. She folds again and pins the handles, ready to sew.

Behind her, the door opens. She turns; Chris fills the doorway, hair damp, face shiny, a white, pink-eyed rabbit in his arms.

'It's the boy one. Hold him.'

'I'm busy.'

'Just for a moment, to get a feel for it. You'll need to—'

'Not here.'

'Come down, then.'

Emma sighs. Chris smells sludgy, a combination of dirt and sweat. And the heels and toes of his socks are darkened where water must have leaked through his boots.

She leaves Elijah's bag pieces for later and follows Chris to the kitchen where he places the rabbit in her arms.

'Hand there,' he says. 'Like that. Then he won't struggle. That's right. Gentle, but firm.'

Emma can feel the rabbit's insides: the motor of his heart, his pumping lungs, the chassis of his ribs. She glances at Chris. The middle years, marked by anxiety, self-doubt and a growing awareness of one's mortality are, she recently read, the unhappiest of one's life. She won't characterise Chris's unhappiness as a mid-life crisis. To speak of it as such would be to invite jokes and questions about whether he has bought a motorbike or started going to the gym. And how would she respond? 'No, he is stockpiling food and foraging on the beach.' Chris has hit his forties like a rut in the road and rather than accepting he has likely had half his life, and, for him, the world will one day end, he appears to be worried that unless he does something about it, the world will end for *everyone*.

The rabbit flicks his ears; they are veined and translucent, delicate as petals. It occurs to Emma that the purpose of handling the rabbit now is to make it easier to kill him later, and it feels as if they are in a Brer Rabbit story and Chris is the stupid bear or fox, certain to be outwitted by this quivering creature.

## MADE OF MEAT

It's easy to open the understairs cupboard and flick the consumer unit's main switch. Chris does it one-handed while the boys watch television and Emma sets the table. A moment later, he's assailed by complaints.

'Chris! The electric's gone again.'

'Dad! The telly's off.'

If decarbonisation happens, people will be more dependent on electricity. Eighty per cent of power outages are due to erratic weather, and it's not like the weather's going to get less erratic, is it? Preparation is key. If it weren't for the freezer, Chris would cut the electric for a whole weekend and see how they cope. But they would lose Ziploc bags of pitted cherries and stewed apples, blanched spinach and peas, chopped chillies and rhubarb, slow-cooked red cabbage, ice-cube trays of carrot-leaf pesto and much more. They are too dependent on the freezer. Emma is happy to make jam, but she won't learn to can food because she once read a novel in which a woman accidentally poisoned her mother-in-law with a jar of home-preserved runner beans. 'Imagine if I *killed* your mother,' she says whenever he encourages it.

Chris is doing his best to prepare them. He read that turning down the thermostat by one degree can save almost a hundred pounds a year, which gave him the idea, back in the autumn, to switch the boiler off altogether. It's been a mild winter so far. And when it's been cold, they've managed. The shower and cooker are electric, and Emma boils the kettle to wash the dishes. There's an open fire in the lounge, though Chris prefers to save the wood for emergencies. He makes subtle comments during the news: 'What would happen if we were in a hurricane?' or, 'How would we cope without water?' He chooses television programmes that include survival and has solicited family involvement in the creation of bug-out bags. He holds fire drills and frequently reminds Emma and the boys that bad things can happen at any time.

Last year he had a customer, Arthur Thursby, who'd lived in Cockermouth when Storm Desmond hit. Chris managed to convince Emma to have Arthur and his wife Shirley round for tea, during which he'd hoped to be treated to a full account of the horror of the floods. He assumed Arthur and Shirley had been married for years, but widowed Arthur had met divorced Shirley during the clean-up.

'That flood was the best thing that ever happened to us,' Shirley said fondly, thwarting Chris's plan.

No matter. Talking about possibilities and listening to second-hand stories can't come close to personal experience, and that's what this is. He waits a few seconds before calling, 'I'll just see what's up ...'

He is noisy, now, jiggling the contents of the cupboard – the hoover and the boxes that house Christmas decorations – while lifting the unit's lid and allowing it to knock shut.

'Nothing doing,' he calls.

'*Rage, rage against the dying of the light,*' Emma shouts back good-humouredly. 'Candles, then,' he hears her saying to the boys.

'I'll walk down the lane after tea and see if it's just us,' he calls.

'It won't be, though, will it?'

'Isn't usually,' he lies.

The kitchen smells of coconut and coriander. Tea has been sweating in the slow cooker since morning. Emma serves the curry in bowls; then she sits heavily and smiles. Her concerns seem to be shrinking like Russian dolls, each smaller than the next. She reduces waste by preparing the broccoli and cauliflower stalks alongside the florets, whisks the accompanying gunk from tins of chickpeas into meringues, and trawls charity shops for second-hand wool and fabric. Meanwhile, he's left to worry about phosphorus depletion, mass extinction and wildfires in Chile: the world is burning, and Emma is smiling at lit candles and curried vegetables.

They're supposed to sit and talk to each other at the weekends. Weeknights are busy, interrupted by James's hockey practice and Dylan's football training, and by Dylan's mates slipping in and out of the house as if they own it.

'The solar charger's on the windowsill, if anyone wants it,' Chris says. 'And the wind-up torch, too, for when you need the loo. Where are the matches?'

'In the cupboard,' Dylan drones.

'The candles?'

James points at the lit pair on the table.

'The rest of them?'

'In the cupboard, too.'

'The batteries?'

'In the garage.'

'The car inverter and the lantern torch?'

'In the van.' James starts to laugh. 'With the LED beanie.'

'Oh God, not the *LED beanie*,' Dylan jokes. 'It really would be the end of the world if someone had to wear that.'

'Glad you find this so funny.'

Three candlelit smiles capsize, and everyone looks at their food.

'Are rabbits nocturnal?' James asks eventually.

'They're crepuscular,' Chris says. 'It means they're most active around dawn and dusk.'

'Do you think they know they're rabbits?'

'That's an interesting question, James.'

'Thanks, *Emma-Jane*.'

'You mean Mum,' Chris says, unable to tell whether James's recent habit of addressing Emma by her full name is intentionally disrespectful or a poorly executed joke. Either way, he doesn't like it, but perhaps she isn't bothered – he really should ask.

James grins and continues, 'Also, do they know we're human?'

'I don't know,' Emma says.

'And do they know they live in the world?'

'I think it's only humans who have an idea of the whole world, as opposed to, say, a field, or a pond ... but then, I suppose migrating birds must have an immense sense of space and place. The pink-footed geese that arrive in the autumn come all the way from Iceland and Greenland. They only stop here for a few weeks before carrying on to Norfolk. And dolphins and whales travel hundreds of miles. What do you think?' Emma addresses the question to everyone, but Chris has nothing to add.

'Do you think they can remember stuff?' James asks.

'Maybe,' Emma says.

'Do you think their mum told them stuff before they left? Like, have they heard any stories about rabbits – you know, adventures, and what good rabbits should do; stuff like that?'

'No,' Chris says.

'Zebra finches sing to their babies while they're still embryos. I read that, Dad.'

'Birds sing. Who knew?'

'And when temperatures climb above a certain point the finches make a special warning sound which helps prepare the eggs for the warmth.'

'Can you remember where you read that, James?' Emma asks. 'I'd like to have a look, it sounds really—'

'This is real life, not Beatrix Potter. The rabbits are *animals*. They're made of meat.'

'So are we,' Emma counters.

Chris glances down at his arms. The rolled-up sleeves of his checked shirt expose bunched muscle, weathered skin and a dusting of dark hair. He recalls the sense he sometimes had when he first stopped believing in a life after this one – that he no longer resided *in* his body, but was, rather, the sum of its parts; that his skin was, at once, both his and *him*.

'*I'm* not meat,' Dylan protests.

'Well, there's a story …' Emma begins.

'Here we go.' Chris drops his spoon in his bowl and leans back in his chair. Emma has a story for everything.

'It's basically a conversation between two aliens who can't get over the fact that humans are made of meat. They've picked up several people from around the world and probed them, just to make sure.' Emma chuckles in that way of hers – part laugh and part nudge, an entreaty

47

to join her. 'It's funny because they describe human speech as *meat sounds*. And they say humans sing by squirting air through their meat.'

The boys laugh at this, especially Dylan who says, 'Their *meat*, ha-ha! Squirting through their *meat*!'

'Anyway,' Emma continues, 'they're so disgusted by us, they decide to ignore the radio signals coming from earth. And that's why we *seem* to be alone in the universe, because the other life forms don't think we're worth knowing. To them, we're just meat.'

'That's it?' Chris is disappointed. 'And the moral is …?'

'There doesn't have to be a moral.'

'The point, then. Or is it a *pointless* story?'

'Are you two arguing?' James asks.

'No,' Emma says. 'We're having a discussion. Who'd like more curry?' She pushes her chair back and grabs a tea towel before lifting the stoneware bowl out of the slow cooker and on to the table. 'So … rabbits,' she says, casual and light, in a back-to-the-matter-in-hand manner, as she spoons more curry into Dylan's bowl. 'Who's going to do the *dispatching*?'

'Me,' Chris says.

'Really? I can't imagine …'

'Oh, I think you can – Emma-Jane killed a frog today.'

'You mean Mum.'

'It was an accident.'

'No, it wasn't,' Dylan says.

'It was, at first. Then it was a mercy killing.'

'You did it, then?' Chris asks.

Emma nods miserably.

'First she disembowelled it with her shovel then she crushed it to death with a brick. Like something out of *Horrible Histories*.'

'Well, I couldn't use the shovel again. I couldn't make myself take aim. It was easier to gently cover it with a brick and stand on it.'

'Hey, Mum. What was the last thing that went through the frog's head?'

'I don't—'

'Its brain!'

'The key is to be quick and efficient,' Chris says, fed up of the boys' silly comments and Emma's squeamishness. 'So I'll be using the broomstick method.'

'Oh, the broomstick method. Right. Good.'

'It works like this,' he continues, ignoring Emma's determination to make this awkward. 'The rabbit sits on the floor, on all fours – as they do. You put the long part of a broom over its neck. You stand on the broom, securing the rabbit, then you lift the rabbit's back end up until you've folded it over the broom. Snap. Dead.'

'It doesn't struggle or anything?'

'Not in the video I watched. This American woman, she just positioned the broom and *snap*! You cut the arteries in the neck straightaway and it bleeds out quickly.'

'The video was recorded in America, though? Is it even legal here? Have you checked? There's probably a government white paper on appropriate ways to, you know, *dispatch* animals.'

'I'll check,' he promises. But he won't. Who'll know? It's not as if he plans to sell the meat.

'And if the rabbit struggles, you just … what? Wrestle it to death?'

Dylan snorts.

'You'll have to learn how to do it, too,' Chris tells Emma. 'It's no use shaking your head. What if something happened? If a fox got to one of them and it was still alive? It'd be cruel not to.'

'I couldn't. And I wouldn't know if it was a fatal wound. I'd take it to the vet, first.'

'You'd know,' Chris says, remembering his father killing animals, on the farm. 'I've seen it, with piglets.'

'But it was a dairy farm?'

'There was always a sow, for bacon. Sometimes she'd tread on a piglet or there'd be a birth defect, something terminal, and Dad would …' Chris raises his hand and swoops it through the air, concluding the movement with a whip of his wrist while simultaneously clicking his tongue against the roof of his mouth.

'Sorry, he'd what?'

'Pick them up by their back legs, and *whoosh*.' Chris makes the swoop and the clicking noise again.

'*Whoosh*, what?'

'*Whoosh*: head, meet pen.'

'Whoosh,' Dylan says, whopping James on the forehead with the flat of his hand.

'Dylan! But that was a long time ago. More than thirty years. I'm sure it's not how things are done today …'

'He used a bolt gun for bigger animals. Put it right in the middle of the forehead.' Chris makes a gun with his fingers. '*Click*. Straight through the brain. You can stick a nail in the hole afterwards, if you like, to make sure. Pith it.'

'*Pith* it?'

'It's optional. The pithing.'

Before bed, Chris slips back into the understairs cupboard and flicks the switch. The microwave beeps, the television starts talking to itself and – *Let there be light* – the house is no longer in darkness.

'Thank goodness,' Emma calls from upstairs. 'I was worried about the freezer.'

Good, Chris thinks, glad to have disturbed her equilibrium.

'I'll be up soon,' he calls. 'I'll just catch the forecast, now the telly's back on.'

He always watches the weather. Growing up, the forecast was as much a ritual as prayer or church: a prophecy to be acted on with waterproofs or jumpers, a flask of soup or a carton of juice. Overnight, it will rain. Tomorrow, it will rain – he doesn't care about that; tomorrow is Sunday. But, he learns, there will be rain the next day, and the next. Every day in the foreseeable future is marked by rain; it's just a matter of how much. Of whether the cloud graphics sport one drop or two. If Chris were delivering the forecast, he'd talk about climate as well as weather. The forecasters don't seem to care about climate, though. They're too busy outdoing themselves with descriptions: the rain is coming in spates, volleys and torrents; it is falling at a rate of spits and spots, dribs and drabs, and cats and dogs. Cloud, which was formerly either heavy or patchy is now a nuisance: nuisance cloud here, nuisance cloud there.

He stays for the local forecast hoping, by some miracle of microclimate, to discover a different outlook on the zoomed-in map. He listens as the smiling presenter delivers the same bad news, but with added local detail.

'The A555 Manchester Airport Relief Road remains closed after the equivalent of half a month's rain fell over the course of the weekend. Lancashire Fire and Rescue Service continues to deal with widespread flooding in towns and properties. The Environment Agency has a number of flood alerts and warnings in place. Have you been caught up in the deluge? Do tweet us your photos and stories.'

Tutting, Chris turns off the television and heads upstairs.

In the bedroom, back to the mirror, Emma glances over one shoulder at her reflection. Dressed only in her T-shirt and knickers, she clutches a medallion of buttock in each hand and doesn't see him for a moment. When she does, she lets go.

'It's all downhill from here, right?' she says. 'Literally. Down-leg, at least.'

'Looks good to me,' he says, because it does, and, more importantly, because it's the right answer. It's Saturday night and Dylan and James have already been corralled to bed. These things exponentially increase his chances. Married sex is sex; it remains as much about a welcome glance at the curve of Emma's arse as it ever did, but it is also a matter of cooking and of washing up, of saving money at the supermarket, of who taxied the boys where, and of the need for a good night's sleep. Which reminds him of the canvas shopping bag he neglected to bring indoors, earlier, after he removed the baked beans.

'Just popping out to the garage,' he tells Emma, suspecting he's missed his chance when she says, 'OK,' flings back the duvet and flops on to the bed. By the time he gets back she'll probably be dead to the world.

On his way out, he grabs a torch. While he's at it, he'll check the wood. The possibility that it may be getting damp has been niggling at him all afternoon.

Chris places the torch on the floor beside the builders' bag and kneels next to it. He lifts a piece of wood. It feels dry and solid. He removes another piece and, holding one in each hand, lets them dangle before knocking the ends into each other. When wood is wet, the thud is dull. But this collision sounds dry. He does it again; yes, there's almost a ring to it.

Before he returns to the house, he opens the back of the van, just to see. He knows what's there – he's only checking, like Emma studying her backside in the mirror. Yes, there it is: the sandwich board, collapsed and defaced.

Many years ago, on his dad's bi-monthly Saturdays off, they'd join like-minded friends and stand beside a wallpaper table topped by a collection of leaflets with titles like 'JUDGEMENT IS COMING, ARE YOU READY?' (Chris wasn't.) Most people didn't stop for long enough to hear about the problems with the world, never mind how to fix them, and those that did stop for a moment mainly looked pityingly at Chris, the only child. Passers-by seemed happy, but Chris knew they weren't. They were ignorant and damned, and it was almost embarrassing for him, in all his specialness, to be present – though there were, much to his shame, moments when he didn't feel very special at all. In an effort to draw a crowd, the adults took it in turns to stand on the wrong side of the table, pretending to be interested members of the public. Chris liked to stand behind the table, if possible. Occasionally someone brought stools, the low, three-legged camping kind, and Chris sat down. Those were the best days. The pavement was speckled with chewing gum; you could draw invisible lines from spot to spot, identifying shapes and constellations – he knew because he spent most of the time looking down.

Afterwards, there would be a treat. An ice cream from Rossi's or a sherbet fountain. He'd sit in the front of the car and his father would talk to him. If there was any greater pleasure than his father's full attention Chris couldn't imagine it. 'I wouldn't say this in front of your mother,' his father would say, and, 'Don't tell your sister.' Sentences opened with, 'You know, Chris …' And what could a boy do in the face of that but say, 'Oh, *yes*, I know.'

Those were days of love and terror. God loved the world and killed everything; his father loved him and whacked him with a belt. Things were either right or wrong, good or bad. There was always a winner and a loser. Even tickling was a zero-sum game. His father would tickle his victim until they cried and only then, having won, would he stop. Chris was often in trouble. Occasionally deservedly so, but also for the smallest and most unexpected infractions. Like the time his mother discovered he had been overheard saying he was only 97 per cent certain of Jesus. After his sister Ruth's bedtime, Chris had to go to his parents' room to *discuss his behaviour*. How he hated it when that happened. The way the door closed behind him. The way there was nowhere to sit: to walk around the bed was to be trapped in the far corner beside the wardrobe, but to stay near the door was to remain at close range. There was never an actual *discussion*. His father did all the talking, summarising as he went, like a judge, while his mother looked on, head inclined, listening attentively. It was like being stuck in the head teacher's office beside a fellow pupil, a snivelling little snitch who was about to learn, for the umpteenth time, that telling tales is not a shortcut to approval.

'Why on earth did you say it?' his father asked, when what he meant was, 'Why did you embarrass me by saying it in front of someone?' Doubt was forbidden, and his father sensed a 3 per cent stash of it might lead to an escape hatch that must be battened immediately.

'Who are you, the thought police?' That's what Chris said afterwards, to himself, when he revisited the scene, braver and gobbier. What did he actually say? Nothing, to his father. He attacked his mother instead. 'Why are you so worried about it? *You* never come with us to town. *You* never witness.'

She made a noise, strangled and disbelieving, the sort of sound that might escape a person who had been hit. His father reflexively shielded her with his bulk. 'Look what you've done,' he shouted. 'Get out!'

Afterwards, his mother accompanied them on Saturdays for a while, hands shaking as she proffered the pamphlets. Chris thought, Serves you right. And he thought, You don't deserve this. Serves you right; you don't deserve this. Serves you right; you don't deserve this. His feelings for her have always been partitioned accordingly.

In those days, Chris had been spreading the Good News. Now he is spreading the Bad News. It is easy to dismiss his initial pique, recasting his petulance as principle. In so doing, his Saturday-morning vigils become courageous. When disasters happen, there are always people who can't accept something catastrophic is unfolding. Their response is one of incredulity and they continue with everyday routines, unable to adapt and make new decisions, incapable of any deviation from their usual behaviour. There's a name for it: normalcy bias. Standing beside the sandwich board, he is disrupting normalcy by telling the truth.

No one cares, though, do they? Chris's piqued self re-enters the fray, not so easily dismissed after all. He has watched scientists being interviewed on the television, earnest men and women wearing their smartest jackets and ties, or blouses, while sitting in front of a visual of the city of London (an appeal to business – 'It's in our best financial interests to do this'), or in front of some kind of weather, a flood or a blizzard (a plea to parents and carers – 'It's dangerous to ignore us'), or in front of a wall of books in an office at a university somewhere ('Listen to me, I've read a lot more than you'). But they don't look panicked, do they? These reasonable, well-dressed scientists prepped for the cameras, their powdered foreheads deflecting the light, are restrained and logical, brimming with probabilities and majority consensus. 'Ninety seven per cent of us agree,' they say. And *there's* the escape hatch for contrarians. Three per cent – too large for his father back in the day but, if he was still alive, just about big enough now.

Chris grabs the shopping bag from the passenger seat of the van and removes a towelling sweatband. He slides it over his head until it sits around his neck, soft and snug against his throat. He leaves it there for a moment. Then he stretches it, pulling this way and that. Eventually, he takes it off and stuffs it in his trouser pocket.

When he steps outside, he thinks the rain has stopped, but he is mistaken. He feels it on his neck as he turns to lock the door. And he hears it, as he crosses the patio in the dark, whispering softly behind his back.

## NIGHT THOUGHTS

Emma is a newcomer to this hour. Of course, she used to wake in the night when the boys were small, but always in the enclosed cocoon of the bedroom. This venturing downstairs, and sometimes outside, is a recent thing, caused by Chris's snoring. She can hear him now, through the ceiling, breath sawing back and forth, catching in the folds of his throat. He isn't overweight, doesn't smoke and hardly drinks. She expects it's his age. The skin of his face is lately baggier; a slight landslide, nothing serious – if anything his topography is more interesting. It's what happens to men: they get interesting.

For a while, she lay beside him, eyes squeezed shut, trying to breathe herself back to sleep. But the noise. The lathering draw of each inhalation. The ensuing *click* as exhaled air snagged on the dry ridges of the roof of his mouth. Gargle, *click*. Gargle, *click*. Gargle, *click*. Eventually she gave up, felt for her phone on the bedside table, slid out of the covers and stepped around the bottom of the bed. Guided by the phone's lit screen, she reached the doorway and then caught the outline of something unexpected on Chris's bedside table: a white towelling sweatband complete with black Nike tick – a further addition to the mountain of absurdities, newly topped by the rabbits and the amended sandwich board.

Wide awake now, Emma forces her feet into the trainers that live beside the back door. She unfastens the lock and slips outside. Here on the Moss the night has breadth. When the clouds are low the dark tucks itself in, and it is impossible to see where it meets the sheet of the bare fields. But, for the moment at least, there is no cloud. The moon is a full-faced night clock, the sky behind it wheeled by stars. The scene should be stark, laced and lit by frost, but it feels as if the seasons were suspended during the mulch of mid-autumn and now the wind has died down, the mild air smells of mud with a twist of brine.

Emma steps out to the edge of the patio, where it meets the sodden grass. Behind her, the house hunkers, its unlit windows blind. The rabbits sit in their semi-detached quarters, noses twitching. Emma can only hope Chris won't abandon them when fresh worries strike, as they surely will. She supposes it is her presence that has woken them. Like James, she had imagined them to be nocturnal. Despite instructions to the contrary, the boys are already calling them Boy Rabbit and Girl Rabbit. Chris should have known better than to forbid it. The impulse to name is at least as old as Adam; older, of course.

Emma won't eat rabbit. It's not that she objects, morally. She has seen the T-shirts and car stickers – 'IF YOU LOVE ANIMALS, DON'T EAT THEM'. She isn't that sort of vegetarian and has always kept her own counsel when friends or colleagues rant about people who can't be trusted because they don't love cats, or dogs, or animals as a homogenous group. She has never had a pet, though she did, her grandmother assured her, have a share in Aslan, the blue merle Border collie. Grandma had been operating on the assumption that *all* children want a pet – she had very fixed opinions about what *all* children wanted. But Emma felt no desire for a pet, and it occurred to her that Aslan, who had a very high opinion of himself, would have been extremely insulted by the notion that he was part-owned by someone as insignificant as her.

Emma stopped eating meat a few years ago, when she first attempted to restrict her worries about the world to things only she could address. She couldn't un-birth the children, un-earth the disposable nappies or un-plumb the white goods. It was a matter of finding something to lay on the altar of her guilt, a thing that wouldn't inconvenience anyone but herself. She still cooks meat a couple of times a week for Chris and the boys. In the beginning, she had imagined she might be tempted to steal a strip of chicken skin or rip the crisped fat from a rasher of bacon when no one was looking. But it has been horribly easy, which means it wasn't a sacrifice. So she volunteers. Turns up for buckthorn clearance and beach clean-ups. Takes part in butterfly and amphibian surveys. She can see the appeal of religion, the list of rules that must be followed to achieve virtue. But she is searching for a different kind of goodness. There are websites that expose the unethicality of her whole life, alphabetically, from Adidas to Zurich. Every decision can be scrutinised, from what you eat to where you go on holiday; what you wear, to what you throw away – and, of course, ultimately, there is no 'away', no vanishing spell: everything, including humans, remains on the earth in one form or another. Emma is trying to make things better. Chris is preparing for the worst. Between them, she once thought, they might just have it covered.

Emma steps back into the house where, thanks to the drawn curtains and closed blinds, it is darker than outside. She stands motionless for a moment in the night kitchen.

The refrigerator hums and the clock ticks. Underneath those sounds she can just about discern the soft mechanical hiss of the dehumidifier sucking water from the air behind the closed lounge door. Every time she wakes in the night Emma thinks of other houses, clustered in the town and dotted across the Moss: occupants prone, clothes removed, eyes closed. What luck to be born at a time and in a place where one can take safe sleep, if not sleep itself, for granted. Yawning, she flicks the light switch, appreciating the instant light after the evening's power cut, though its brightness stings her eyes. The mop leans against the worktop where Dylan must have left it once he tired of chasing James around the house, shouting, 'Submit to the broomstick method!' She opens the breadmaker and fills its metal bucket with flour, oil, yeast and tepid water. Stirs in a spoon each of cinnamon and nutmeg, adds two cups of raisins, and sets the timer so the loaf will start cooking later. The smell will waft up the stairs while James does his paper round, eventually tugging Dylan out of bed by his nose, like a cartoon hound.

She peers into the fridge and momentarily considers cutting herself a slice of cheese. In the freezer, she spots the trotters, piled in a transparent Tupperware container. Flat side down, they resemble tiny, prostrate pigs, each pair of toes poking up like ears. The boys laughed at them, but they'll accede to Chris's demands with their usual have-a-go ease. Emma won't. She may be handy with a needle, but she won't indulge Chris's apocalyptic fantasies by practising sutures on pieces of dead pig. She closes the door and yawns again, eyes watering, until, emptied of air, she feels she might melt in a puddle on the kitchen floor. If she doesn't go back to bed now, she'll start finding other things to do and, by mid-afternoon, she'll be good for nothing. In the past, she has tried to sleep on the sofa – straight on the cushions, as to activate its bed mechanism is to create a tremendous creaking noise. But the sofa is never as comfy as she imagines: the leather holds no heat and, wrapped in a blanket, she slides into the dip where its seat meets its back.

She creeps back up the stairs and pauses on the landing, which smells different in the dark: dense and yeasty, inspissated by unabashed mouth breathing and the bellows of three pairs of lungs. Chris is still snoring. Quieter now, a low rattle. She steps into the bedroom, crouches, and nudges his hip. If she can roll him on to his side, the snoring usually stops. But he is surprisingly rigid in sleep. And he is heavy, too.

'Chris,' she whispers.

'What?' he mumbles, as he always does, even though she only ever wakes him to make this request.

'Turn over.'

'What?'

'Turn. Over.'

'Oh, sorry.'

He rolls towards her, settles briefly but then flings back the covers. 'Toilet,' he mutters as he feels for his phone and staggers to his feet.

Emma walks around the bed and slips under the covers, thinking of the remaining Christmas preparations, the most enjoyable of which will be baking for the Christmas Eve party. At least she doesn't have to buy anything for Chris this year. They agreed not to exchange presents, though on discovering a two-year-old AA Road Map of Great Britain in Oxfam, she couldn't help herself – he can keep it in the van, a failsafe in case he's ever without GPS.

Chris likes utilitarian gifts. He'd rather buy fresh blades for her rotary cutter or a magnetic pincushion than flowers. On her last birthday he took her to her favourite restaurant, Master McGraths. There had been no sign of a present, and she wondered whether he was economising and the meal itself was her gift. Not that she minded, but it would have been nice to know beforehand. She could see he was watching the bill, adding it up as he went along. He even tried his 'You won't be wanting a dessert?' trick when she ordered a starter, and she bristled, wishing his frugality extended to the 'essential' survival purchases he was making online.

Still, a couple of glasses of wine doused her irritation and when she went ahead and ordered dessert, he didn't bat an eyelid.

'Em, you know women and girls are more likely to die in natural disasters?' he said while they waited for her apple tart.

She nodded and, nicely tipsy, knocked back the last of her wine.

'In 1991 there was a cyclone in Bangladesh. A hundred and thirty-eight thousand people died. Guess what proportion were women?'

'I don't know.'

'Ninety per cent. The thing about natural disasters is they exacerbate existing inequalities.'

Those weren't his words. He'd read them somewhere. Emma glanced at the jacket he'd hung on the back of his chair. Its pockets were big enough to conceal a book. Something about feminism and the environment, perhaps. She'd have preferred a frivolous gift, but he couldn't help going practical, it was in his DNA.

The tart arrived. Chris rested a hand on her thigh as she ate. The boys were babysitting their cousins and would be dropped off later. With the house empty, there was a good chance he would attempt to sweep her off her feet and carry her up the stairs, something she almost always put a stop to, afraid he might trip and land them both in hospital, the unwitting subjects of a junior doctor's anecdote. Or maybe they wouldn't make it up the stairs, she thought, licking a glob of crème anglaise from her spoon.

'I've bought a coastal survival course.'

She put the spoon down and removed his hand from her thigh.

'For me?'

He nodded.

'A coastal survival ...'

'You'll make a shelter—'

'Myself? I'll make a—'

'Shelter—'

'Out of what?'

'—where you'll spend the weekend.'

'In a *homemade* shelter?'

'And you'll learn to make lobster pots and fishing nets.'

It wasn't as if she had expected anything spectacular. In fact, having noticed among friends and colleagues that husbands and boyfriends who bought over-the-top gifts often seemed to be compensating, she was suspicious of grand gestures. Extravagant presents seemed like apologies – no, she decided, not apologies but statements of intent: I'll keep buying fancy presents and you'll continue being a dogsbody.

'Will there be a toilet?'

'They've got a compost toilet on site. And if you like the toilet, I thought we could try—'

'Oh, I don't think so,' she replied, signalling for the bill.

The journey home was quiet. By the time Chris pulled on to the drive she felt cold sober, and when he cut the engine she stepped out of the car and carried herself up the stairs.

Emma hears the toilet flush, and then she hears Chris padding up the stairs. He steps into the room and stands beside the bed, candle-like, head and shoulders lit by the light of his phone. When he puts the phone down, he lifts something to his face. The sweatband. And in the moments before his screen fades to standby, Emma watches as he pushes his bearded chin into the towelling loop, arranging it like a pair of headphones with a chinstrap.

'Hope-it'll-keep-my-mouth-shut,' he says, the words bumping into each other as the material squeezes the hinge of his jaw.

The bed dips as he gets in and rolls on to his side. They lie face to face in the darkness. She can't see him, but she imagines him, face wrapped like Marley's ghost. He presses the tops of his big, always-cold feet to her calves. She lets him and, moments later, he is asleep. Her husband. The man who is attempting to silence his baggy throat with a Nike sweatband. The man who is lately worried about starvation; who is going to breed and kill rabbits in their back garden – and though she hasn't asked him not to, she wishes he wouldn't.

Emma closes her eyes. To date, she has adopted the role of spectator, as she does when the boys get giddy, watching while anticipating the crossing of a line, the ending of a tether, telling herself that Chris will feel better in a few weeks when it's lighter and drier and he isn't chasing work; when there is more to his days than low-maintenance landscaping and he isn't coming home with chilblains and chapped skin.

She closes her eyes and waits for sleep. There is a clicking in Chris's throat. As if a latch is being lifted to let each breath out. Click, click, click. Like the cocking of a gun. Emma anticipates the next click, and the next. And it's no good; she can't bear the profligacy of lying awake when she could be up and doing.

Rain patters on the sewing room's Velux window. Emma turns off the light and unhooks the blind. The weather has changed. Where there were stars, there is cloud. She unlatches the handle and arranges the open window so it is level, protecting her head from the rain like the peak of a cap.

Sometimes, when Emma looks out of the skylight, she feels helpless. Nero fiddled while Rome burned; she will sew while the polar ice melts and the seas surge. It was this view of the Moss that gave her the idea for a quilt. A fabric map made of time and geography: nine blocks, beginning with this land as it was eighteen thousand years ago when a vast ice sheet receded, and water filled a depression in the glacial drift. She has started work on the central piece: the Moss, as it looks in present-day aerial photographs. An appliquéd Tetris jumble of triangles and rectangles, parallelograms and squares, in a variety of earthy colours and corrugations. The quilt won't be finished for a long while, but in these uncertain times there's something comforting about holding its middle. *You are here*, she thinks as she does. Connected to all that came before and all that will come after.

Here, she feels afloat on a sea of fields: *water, water, everywhere*. To the east, hidden by the darkness, is the plateau of the Moss and, eventually, Martin Mere, now a wetland nature reserve. To the west the dark is perforated by the amber dots of the town's streetlights. Beyond them, lurking in the shadows, is the sea. It is easy, in the face of its relentless rhythms, to imagine it as immutable, but the Wirral and Sefton coasts were once linked by plains: a few miles southward, and the tide still exposes preserved hunters' footprints in the mud. Later, the seemingly shallow sea and treacherous sandbanks resulted in perilous shipping conditions that led to the establishment of the world's first lifeboat service. Out there, in the muddy, shallow coastal waters, are the skeletons of more than three hundred ships that were wrecked along the coast, their rusting ribs periodically buried and uncovered as the winds and tides shift.

It seems the water will return. How quickly, is a matter of some dispute. Emma discovered an online tool allowing her to move a cursor, and consequently the sea level, up by one foot, two feet, three feet, and more. It is her fault Chris also discovered it. He plays with it, raising the oceans by so much, so much, and so much, and, as the green pixels of the Moss are first speckled and then drowned by blue, he reminds her that climate change will wreak havoc on the British coastline; that more than half of the best agricultural land in the country is found at five metres or less above sea level; that the local authorities with the largest populations of pensioners are all beside the coast. And she reminds him that the tool is just an internet gimmick; that there's no reason to believe it's any more accurate than Find Your Celebrity Look-alike or Discover Your IQ. But Emma wonders. Does the tool rely on old altimeter measurements and digital elevation model maps from aerial photography? Or is it up to date and calculated by GPS? And if it's GPS, are the town's building tops skewing the data? Might a future incursion be worse than predicted? Or better, perhaps? When the tide is out, the sea lounges up to two miles from the shore. How many cubic metres of water would it take for the sea to go beyond its occasional invasions and stage an occupation? To roll over the unintentional, accreting wilderness of marram grass and marsh marigolds that grows along the northmost stretch of beach? To hoist itself over the coastal defences at the town's centre? To conquer the bulwark of the dunes to the south? And what about the rise and fall of the water table? The weather. The estuary. The water-ways and canals, and the meander of the River Douglas? How to find out for sure? Emma has browsed university websites, searching for a likely expert and, periodically, rehearses correspondence in the shower:

*My husband is very worried about rising sea levels – he is also worried about the bees, the soil and bands of marauding scavengers, etc. But on the matter of sea levels, I am hoping you may be able to convince him that we are unlikely to be flooded out of our home in his lifetime. And it would be helpful if you could suggest our sons may also avoid this fate. Or at least imply that, after our deaths, there may be enough time for them to sell the family home to some poor schmuck(s). A few words from you on this matter may save my husband a lot of worry. I, on the other hand, already feel terrible for Mr and Mrs Schmuck who almost certainly have children of their own and will have nowhere to live if and/or when the water comes. If you could let me know whether you think the water will encroach slowly, allowing the Schmuck family enough time to run, or drive their (electric?) car away from the flood zone, I would appreciate it.*

Of course, she has never written such a letter. And what could she do with an answer, anyway? Chris would not believe reassurance and she would not promulgate anything else. When Emma worked at the library, she supervised Song and Rhyme Time, leading choruses of 'There's a Hole in My Bucket', 'The Farmer's in His Den' and 'Michael Finnegan'. Endless demands and questions: *The farmer wants a wife!* and *With what shall I mend it?* – followed by the inexorable return to the beginning of the song and the original dilemmas: *Poor old Michael Finnegan, begin again!* The children laughed as the songs restarted, each iteration faster than before. That's what it's like with Chris: There's a hole in the ozone layer, dear Emma, dear Emma!

Emma closes the window but leaves the blind up. She switches the light back on and lifts a fold of fabric from the bookcase – a Christmas duvet cover, bought for a couple of pounds in the January sales. She cuts along its seams and then places the top piece on the cutting table where she spreads it flat. She draws around a small cardboard stocking template. Again, and again: five, ten, twenty. Then she cuts. She'll fill the stockings with treats and give them out on Christmas Eve. In both of her families, the one into which she was born and the one into which she has married, Emma is the middle-woman: a fastener, a link. Growing up, she learned to smooth things between her mother and grandparents. Like a zip, she remained attached to both sides, forever ready to lock them together. She attempted the same for Chris and his family. Each Christmas Eve his parents had arrived full of God and thunder, and they left, somewhat tempered by non-alcoholic eggnog, carols and home-made treats.

The light is changing. Before long, it will uncover the morning. She folds the remains of the duvet cover and neatens the cut-out stocking pieces. There are times when, having been up for most of the night, she slips back to bed for thirty minutes. At this hour Chris's breath sometimes reverts to a low tide of draught and draw. And there are other times when she stands at the skylight and watches the milky dawn pour into the glass bowl of the sky. She glances out of the window. This morning's pitchy sky may eventually lighten to battleship grey; it's not worth witnessing.

Out on the landing she can smell the first tendrils of cinnamon and nutmeg. In the bedroom, the dark hulk of the wardrobe is revealed to have handles and detail on its doors. She steps around the bed, careful not to disturb Chris who is lying on his side. When Emma got married her mother said, 'You've made your bed. Now you can lie in it.' What a poor way to convey foreboding. Who purposely makes an uncomfortable bed? She slips into her space and tucks her right arm under the pillow.

Here she lies, in the bed she has made. On clean sheets and a mattress that is neither too hard nor too soft, but just right. In a house that is built on the shore of the drained bed of an ancient lake. Her hand hovers over the knuckle of Chris's shoulder.

'I saw you. By the memorial,' she whispers. 'I'm worried about you.'

There, she has said it. And she feels lighter. Speaking to a sleeping person is, she imagines, like offering a prayer. There is a comfort in owning the words, in uttering them without any expectation of response.

Chris places a heavy hand on her thigh. Though fast asleep, he must, on some level, be aware of her presence. Emma lies still and stares up through the ebbing darkness at the ceiling. She remembers the summer after finals; she spent it at home, in the back garden, in a bikini top and a pair of denim cut-offs, lying on a folding aluminium lawn chair, the crisscross plastic strapping sticking to the backs of her legs as she alternately read racy romance novels borrowed from the library and reacquainted herself with the favourite classics of her adolescence. 'What can you *do* with an English degree?' her mother asked. 'Have you considered a PGCE?' Emma hadn't, but she picked up a prospectus and circled several postgraduate courses, thinking it might be easier to learn something new than decide what to do next. Then Chris appeared in the back garden wielding a chainsaw, wearing what appeared to be a pair of chaps over his work trousers, a harness fastened tight around his waist and thighs. He'd come to cut down the eucalyptus tree, a job her mother had been asking her father to do for months.

'Shall I whack it a few times and then shout timber as it falls on to next door's greenhouse?' her father joked whenever her mother mentioned it.

'I'll lop off the three branches at the fork, fell the trunk and treat the stump,' Chris said, staring at Emma.

'I felt it the moment I saw you,' he told her, months later, with an openness she'd come to expect – she imagined it came from his parents, who were forever declaring their love of the Lord, and though Chris didn't believe, he had inherited that faculty for feeling and declared himself

72

without shame, not appearing to mind whether he was alone in his affections. The fact was, she had felt something too as she stared at the young man in the tight T-shirt and chainsaw trousers, but her first feelings could have sprung straight from one of the smutty books she was reading and, initially at least, resided more in the vicinity of her knickers than her heart.

The favourite fictions of Emma's adolescence – Jane Austen's novels and Shakespeare's comedies – and the racy romance novels she devoured that summer all concluded with marriage. Happily ever after was also The End. But how might it be, Emma wonders now, if marriage was not The End, but was, instead, conducted in five-year increments like a mortgage, with appraisals and extension discussions: 'Would you like to continue at this interest rate?' 'Are these repayments manageable?' 'Have you been thinking about switching provider?'

Chris sighs and rolls on to his back. The movement dislodges the sweatband which comes to rest on the pillow beside him. Emma closes her eyes. If she can just hurry herself to sleep before the snoring resumes.

Moments later, she loses touch with her surroundings and is dreaming, hard. She dreams she hears the sewing machine's rattle, the dip and draw of the needle, the twirl of the cotton reel. Yanked back to the sewing room by her subconscious, Emma discovers the stocking pieces, sewn together in her absence, like the cut leather in 'The Elves and the Shoemaker'. But her pleasure is muted by the realisation that the whomping sound isn't coming from the machine. A woodpecker, she thinks, opening the skylight, but the noise intensifies and breaks the dream, and Emma lands back in her body, one arm under the pillow, her half-open mouth leaking spit. She is flattened by tiredness, practically ironed to the mattress. There is no machine. There is no bird. Just Chris beside her, air soughing up the spout of his throat. The outline of his neck is like a pipe in the shadows and she wonders whether it would break under a broomstick.

# PART 2

# The End of the Tether

# 22 December

## THERE'S A GREAT DAY COMING

Each morning Janet stands in the kitchen, Ruth's old computer open on the worktop beside her, reading stories about militant secularists and the persecution of Christians; about gay marriage and acceptable demonstrations of patriotism; about the closure of abortion services and suggested prayers in response to school shootings, all taking place in towns and cities that felt far away when she first began to explore the World Wide Web, but now feel so familiar and near that she has, more than once, imagined her five grandchildren in their various class-rooms, standing, hands on hearts, chanting, 'I pledge allegiance ...' And then she has to remind herself that she lives in a different world from the one she observes through the window of the old laptop.

It was probably easier, Janet thinks, to believe in God when the earth was at the heart of everything, floating in space like a cosmic bullseye. Now, there are no bound-aries, and as the universe gets bigger, He inevitably gets further away. Perhaps that's why it is so difficult for her children to believe. Even before she was married, she imagined her children: upgraded Janets, optimistic configurations of her best bits. But while it may be reasonable to expect to own a better car than your parents, it is, Janet has learned, entirely unreasonable to expect to produce better children. Her legs, for example – she had been certain any daughters would inherit them. And musicality – every child of hers would learn to play the piano. But you get what you're given. Ruth and Chris are built like their father: tall and trunky. They inherited Frank's ears, too, of course. And as for music: whenever Janet tried to play the piano, they surrounded her, battering a bass and treble counterpoint, until she stopped playing altogether because to sit down on the stool was to invite their unwelcome accompaniment.

Janet imagined her children's spouses, as well. Sober and upright. Decent, solid, people with God in their hearts and Psalm stanzas on the tips of their tongues. They would be regular visitors to the home she and Frank would one day own, something large and airy – a converted barn, say – and she would be at the centre, beacon-like as the family matriarch, lit by a warmth she has never managed to kindle, but possesses in her dearest imaginings.

Chris, her firstborn, was also the first to go astray. Janet was shocked when he stopped attending church in his late teens. But no matter, she knew that he, like the Prodigal Son, would one day return and apologise. Of course, there were women. Chris never said, but Janet isn't stupid. She watched him, strutting about, all pleased with himself. She spotted the tattoo peeping out from under his shirt-sleeve. As his mother, she wanted people to think highly of him but how could they, with *that* on his arm? He needed no adornment besides that which God had given him. Janet and Frank prayed for Chris to be miserable in the lifestyle he was living. Then Emma appeared. Oh, the way she looked at Chris! The way she touched him when she thought no one was paying attention! The way she sat on his knee, regardless of whether there was an empty chair at his side! Janet and Frank tolerated her, believing she, unlike the tattoo, was temporary.

Small and soft, her round face perpetually flushed like a Pink Lady apple, Emma was pleasant enough in the moment, but it was apparent that she, like the fancy jumpers she knits, would come out baggy in the wash. Emma would age badly – it was written in her aspect: the meat of her cheeks would subside into jowls and her neck would thicken. She wouldn't wear pregnancy well, either, Janet predicted. And, sure enough, Emma was not a woman who blossomed. She unashamedly went to seed, her face puffy and sweat-sheened, her ankles braided by creeping veins – not that Chris seemed to mind.

Acceptance came when Emma was approached at Frank's birthday party by Janet's so-called friend Miriam who asked, 'What if the baby has its dad's ears?'

Bewildered, Emma had replied, 'What's *wrong* with Chris's ears?'

And Janet finally gave in. Oh, all right then, she thought, I wouldn't have picked you, but you'll have to do.

Keen to let her light shine in the social media age, Janet posts heart-warming articles on Facebook and copies and pastes inspirational quotes from Billy Graham (rest in peace) into friendly little emails with, 'Thought you might like this,' or, 'Interesting!' in the subject box before sending them to Emma. If Janet can convince Emma, Chris will have to listen. If Chris listens, Ruth may listen, too. It's important for Janet to take every opportunity to share the good news. This may include (but is not exclusive to) seasoning her conversation with gospel truths, imparting stories of how God has worked in her own life, asking the children what they'd like her to pray about on their behalf, and asking them to pray for her. The last two make Janet's insides shrivel. She has always believed that prayer, much like keeping a diary, should be an entirely private matter, though during that first awful winter in the caravan she made an exception by acceding when Frank introduced daily couples' prayer. Each morning they knelt, side by side, heads bowed, eyes closed, listening as each other's words fell flat against the thin hardboard walls. It was not, Janet felt, prayer in a traditional sense. Not communion *with* God, but rather communion *via* Him; God as a telegraph machine, a way of sending emergency dispatches to each other: 'Please help Janet to feel better about living here,' and, 'Please help Frank to find a way to occupy himself, such as spending time out-doors, walking.'

It isn't clear to Janet whether the children's desertion is a test or a punishment. She knows she is also at fault. There have been times when she has lacked faith. Times when she has prayed with rote words and without either discipline or belief. Sometimes, people don't know how to come back to God. This idea is posited in many of the articles Janet has read. In order to avoid embarrassment, it may be best to discuss the way back to God while on a car journey, during which both people can look ahead rather than directly at each other. But Janet doesn't drive. And since she is now eligible for a bus pass, it is difficult to think of valid reasons to ask either Chris and Emma or Ruth and Rob for lifts.

Until this summer, Janet's life was governed by Frank's movements. Each morning he'd go out for a walk. When Janet heard him, pausing at the door to scrape the soles of his boots on the 'WELCOME' mat or knocking them together to dislodge the mud, it was her cue to pour water from the recently boiled kettle over a pan of eggs. Then she would open a new tab on the computer and type '5 minute timer' into the search bar. The countdown started immediately and while the numbers descended, she got the plates out, made tea with what was left in the kettle and dropped two slices of white bread into the toaster. Eventually, Frank would emerge, cheeks flushed, his remaining hair pressed flat in the shape of his hat. He would put his coat away and step back into the kitchen for breakfast: eggs on toast, sprinkled with salt and pepper, the yolks sticky at the edges and runny in the middle. It looked like she had been busy while he was out. Frank had no idea how long these things took. He had never made breakfast. Not that she'd minded, of course. She had never taken out the rubbish or wielded a screwdriver, and nor had she wanted to.

During breakfast Janet used to close the computer and give Frank her full attention. The Bible divides women into Marys and Marthas. Men might think they prefer

Marys, but what would happen to the world if women sat around all day listening to their husbands, sons and fathers? What men *really* want is a woman who can inhabit both archetypes; it's just that they require the Martha part – careful, troubled, and occupied with anything other than them – to remain invisible. Jesus was, after all, a man.

Saturdays are especially empty since Frank passed. On decades-ago Saturdays, Janet used to wash the children's hair and cut their nails. After the two of them were scrubbed pink and de-clawed she would cup their ears and position her nose right next to their scalps. Oh, the smell of their clean heads! On less distant Saturdays, after Frank returned from his second walk, Janet would boil the kettle again and pour the hot water into a Tupperware bowl as he sat heavily and placed both hands around each calf, lifting until his ankle rested on its opposing knee. That was how he removed his socks: slowly, carefully. The GP had advised fewer walks as there was some wear and tear in his right hip. When Frank ignored the advice, shorter walks were suggested, as a compromise, but of course he wouldn't be told. Once Frank's feet were bare, Janet placed the bowl on the floor ready for the trimming of his toenails and the sanding of his corns. She knelt at his feet. Like Mary Magdalene but with short hair, she once said. Frank didn't find her comment amusing, so she never repeated it, and the memory joined other thoughts a more forgiving soul would have long since discarded. Sometimes, Janet would type '*Un bel dì vedremo*' into Ruth's old computer and click the 'play' icon. Frank didn't like opera. Well, Janet had never been keen on Frank's feet. At one time, decades ago, his hairy toes had been a source of laughter, and she couldn't imagine deliberately handling them. It seems only moments since the summer when the pair of them sat beside an irrigation ditch during Frank's lunch breaks, eating meat-paste sandwiches, her feet covered by the nylons she refused to remove (while outdoors, at least), his hilariously bare. This younger Frank and Janet will have a hastily planned October wedding – Chris is on the way. The following spring, days before Chris's arrival, the Frank who sits beside the ditch on one of the empty hessian feed-sacks he brings in place of a picnic blanket will fall off the roof of the barn. He will survive the subsequent head injury. It will be a miracle. A miracle that will feel like an awful lot of work with a tiny baby and a newly uncoordinated and restless husband to care for, but a miracle, nonetheless. For a time, Frank will be more not-dead than alive; haunted by what happened, or rather didn't happen, when he lost consciousness. He will become obsessed with near-death experiences, always wondering why everything went dark before he reached the end of the tunnel; why the light shrank to a point and then switched off like the bulb of an old television set. Whether the difference in him afterwards resulted from the injury or that experience, Janet never knew. But they made sense of it, together. Like Ebenezer Scrooge, Frank had seen what *might* be, if he didn't change. And so began a search for God that lasted a lifetime. Frank found a congregation, they settled down, made friends, offered service, and then a problem arose: a questionable interpretation of scripture, an irreconcilable matter of doctrine, an inexorable falling out, and Janet had to gird her loins (did women have loins?), leave, and begin again.

Janet knows she needs to look forward, not back. Nostalgia gets you nowhere – look at Lot's wife! But it is hard. Still, she might swap a wish to change the past for one to direct the future. She plugs in her keyboard to practise for the Christmas party. Emma adopts an eclectic approach to Christmas celebrations. She likes a little bit of everything but is especially fond of nostalgia, the songs everyone knows because they sang them in school: 'Little Donkey', the 'Zither Carol' and 'Walking in the Air'. Heavy on whimsy and light on doctrine, that's Emma for you. This year, Emma has requested the 'Calypso Carol', which Janet has been practising with an accompanying bossa nova drumbeat. She would prefer to play the 'Hallelujah Chorus', which she has also been practising. During the writing of the 'Hallelujah Chorus', Handel is said to have declared to his manservant, 'I think I did see all heaven before me, and the great God himself.' Perhaps the music will evoke similar feelings in Emma who will pass them on to Chris. Or in Ruth's husband Rob, who at least believes in *something*, though it is so cordial and agreeable as to be unintelligible to Janet.

It is Janet's dearest wish to have a *family Christmas*, this year. What she means by *family Christmas* is somewhat nebulous, but she can imagine herself saying it to people, her so-called friend Miriam, for example. In Janet's *family Christmas*, all grandchildren will enthusiastically participate in a nativity play. There will be candles, prayers and traditional carols, with Janet adopting a supervisory role, though her preferences will be shared by all and therefore remain implicit. In mood, a *family Christmas* resembles the Norman Rockwell painting of a mother, father and three children arriving at Grandma's house: all wrapped in coats, hats and gloves, grinning as Grandma's dog, a red bow tied around his neck, jumps up and greets them. Janet ignores the substantial front door, wide open as cold air blasts down the hall. She overlooks the poorly positioned holly branch which is sure to catch the oldest grandchild's leg as he steps into the house. And she pays no mind to the youngest grandchild, whose wellies have trailed snow on to the red carpet, and who has a round, piggy face and a chasmal, shouty mouth into which one might feasibly cram an apple.

Last week, Janet walked to the Spar shop and photocopied the 'Hallelujah Chorus' lyrics. Oh, she can already picture herself surrounded by a choir of family! Yes, music is a way into people's hearts. How Janet loves a rousing hymn. Back in the autumn, she was practising 'There's a Great Day Coming' on the keyboard when Chris and Dylan popped round with a bag of mulch.

'That's a good one, Nan,' Dylan said as she finished. 'It's like a football chant or a rap battle – the other side will be defeated. Boom!'

'Oh, I think "Who is on the Lord's Side"' would be better for that sort of thing,' Janet had replied, lightly, in case he was teasing her – it's hard to tell with Dylan. But he opened Ruth's old computer and found a rendition of 'Who is on the Lord's Side?' on YouTube and after they had listened to it, he helped her make an account, so she could join those who, below the video of the choir, had written: 'I am on the Lord's side!' And, for several weeks afterwards, Janet watched videos before breakfast and joined people from all over the world affirming the hymns' words in the comments:

'It *is* well with my soul!'

'What a friend *I* have in Jesus!'

'I *will* sing the wondrous story!'

Most people live as if they will not die, blithely making modifications to the world that they may not be able to enjoy. After Chris and Dylan dropped off the mulch, Janet planted a cherry tree in the small garden beside the caravan. Best to carry on regardless; best to try, anyway. She remembers moments of panic when the children were small and she allowed herself to believe in their eventual old age. What a horror it was to imagine them altered beyond recognition, their perfect skin mottled and baggy, their vital bodies hunched and plodding, and with no mother to care for them. Ruth, in particular, had a sensibility that made it easy to envisage her as the ancient and garrulous occupier of an austere room in a second-rate care home.

Now, she wakes in the night to the thought that she is not the mother she might have been and instead of resorting to her usual rejoinder – nor are the children the offspring they might have been – Janet has, in the dark interval between dreams, discovered a watertight compartment at her centre where reserves of love are heaped like a butter mountain. All this time she has been holding something back – she is like the time machine in the programme Dylan and James were so obsessed with when they were smaller: bigger on the inside! What to do with these reserves? Where to spend them? On her grandchildren, of course. She has finally grasped how hard it is to spoil a child. Childhood is over in such a short time and it is surely better to regret coddling than stringency.

And there remains a surplus of love which she must bestow on her children. How to dish it out at this stage? Just you wait, Frank liked to say – in recent years he'd meant it nicely: just you wait for heaven, everything will be perfect, there. He'd quote Revelation: *God shall wipe away all tears from their eyes; and there shall be no more death, neither sorrow, nor crying, neither shall there be any more pain.* And Janet would think: What tears? What sorrow? What crying? We've had a good life. Haven't we? It was one thing for *her* to have regrets, but what had *Frank* got to complain about? She remembers the greenhouse they built at Victory Avenue. They managed to grow a potted peach tree. Peaches are best eaten immediately after being picked but Frank put the two fruits in a bowl where they could be admired. He saved them until, skins wrinkled and flesh soggy, they were inedible. All that waiting. All for nothing. Perhaps she has also waited too long. But she must do something with these leftover feelings. They mustn't go to waste.

This, Janet suspects, is the five-minute timer segment of her life. A last chance to act while the seconds run out. In addition to the new softness at her centre, there are other feelings, harder and less equivocal than those she

87

usually allows. Long-sunk thoughts are bobbing up like corks. An internal voice whispers snappy observations through sharp little teeth making her wonder whether, over the years, she has mistaken her own silence for agreement.

How easily she had nailed her loyalty to the mast of Frank's marvellous project: they would train up the children in the way they should go, and when the children were old, they would not depart from it. The formative years were hers and with distance comes perspective; she can recognise her failures: the missed teaching opportunities, her occasional impatience, and the many times she relinquished the responsibility of discipline. It had been so much easier to leave it to Frank. *Wait until your father gets home* – that's how it worked. But Frank was no King Solomon, and while his adjudications made him a figure of fear, the resentment cultivated by the children during the hours between crime and punishment was Janet's alone.

There's nothing like an ending to concentrate the feelings. When Frank told her they were leaving the farm, Janet felt a new and unexpected fondness for the cold cottage. And it was the same when he told her they were leaving the terraced house on Victory Avenue. How easy it is to summon love when you know you must leave. Frank was always better at endings. He was a drawer of lines, a builder of walls, a closer of doors. One day, Janet used to think, the world would end and, on finding himself alone in a field of stubble, Frank would dust off his hands and say, 'Well, that's that, then.' As it was, Frank left before the end. And it may be that she is not far behind him.

Janet moves through life slowly now. Accompanied, in her mind, by Elgar's 'Nimrod'. There is something heroic and weighty about actions backed by Elgar. Three weeks ago, hospital appointment letter folded neatly in her handbag, Janet processed to the bus stop where she caught the X2 to town and then the train to Liverpool. At the Walton Centre, the BBC News was playing on a big screen in the waiting room. Janet watched as bats fell from the sky in the heat and iguanas fell from trees in the cold; there were mudslides, floods and fires; it was like witnessing the Plagues of Egypt.

The doctor was young, as they mostly are, now. Jet-black hair, tight trousers and large, thick-framed glasses that reminded her of the ones her father used to wear.

'Where are you from?' Janet had asked.

'Bristol,' he said.

'Originally?'

'Um, Bristol.'

What a beginning. She wasn't sure whether she should apologise or explain that, momentarily carried away by imagination, she had been picturing his mother in a distant kitchen, so proud of her doctor son (clean-shaven, and not a tattoo in sight). But perhaps an attempt at explanation would make things worse: his mother might be from Bristol. She might be a doctor, too, Janet realised. Oh, she felt old and stupid.

He made notes as she listed her symptoms: headaches, nausea, occasional dizziness and problems with concentration. It had started the previous winter, she explained. She'd felt much better in the warmer months, but now it

– whatever 'it' was – had come back. How needy she felt as she spoke; she who had always approached illness like a spider in the corner of a ceiling: ignore it, and it will go away.

There were animal pictures to label (a rhino and a lion), and there was a dot-to-dot puzzle that alternated between letters and numbers. Janet had to name the day, which she managed, and the date, which she didn't.

'I often lose track of the exact number,' she confessed feebly. 'But I think that's quite normal, isn't it? My husband was better with dates.'

'You're on your own, Mrs Abram?'

Janet described the morning, six months ago when Frank, always an early riser, had failed to materialise. He'd seemed tired, so she left him to rest. It had been so hot, and while they had a fan, Frank didn't like to use it. Electricity is routed though the caravan park's own supplier, meaning it's not possible to compare prices and switch to a cheaper tariff, as recommended in the adverts and, worried they were paying over the odds, Frank was forever rationing their use; propping windows open in the summers and using a portable gas heater in the winters. It was always a relief to stay at Ruth's, after Christmas, during the park's annual closure: yes, it was noisy and chaotic, and Rob was rather too flippant for Frank's liking, but six weeks of unlimited heating was a treat. Eventually, Janet stepped into Frank's bedroom. During the night, flies had come in through the open window. The combination of their buzzing and Frank's absolute quiet alerted her to what had happened even before she edged around the bed and saw his suspended face. She had not really believed in his mortality. Any talk of death usually concluded with reassurances from Frank; she mustn't worry, he'd be fine after she passed. He imagined himself, like Job, in the throes of a knockout battle in which he would be last man standing. Consequently, in addition to shock and sadness, Janet also felt a pang of something else – embarrassment. It hadn't occurred to Frank that she would see him like this, body discarded like an old overcoat: he'd have hated it. Silly man, she thought in a rush of tenderness. Silly, silly man.

Janet isn't sure how much of this she said to the doctor. Quite a lot, she suspects. She was explaining Chris's insistence that Frank's unexpected death had been one of hundreds, coinciding with the unusually high temperatures, when the doctor nudged his cuff with the tip of his finger in order to peak at his watch face, and she trailed off, humiliated.

'I'm sorry for your loss, Mrs Abram,' he said sincerely, but with a proficiency that made her feel it was something he probably said at least a few times a day. 'Shall we continue? Do you know where you are right now?' he asked, and Janet felt a stab of panic. Fancy not being able to answer that!

'Did you get lost on the way here?'

'No.'

'Do you know why you've come?'

'Yes.'

'How are you sleeping?'

'Not well.'

When Frank was alive, he'd inadvertently wake her from the adjacent bedroom as he cleared his throat and knocked his pillow back into shape. Now, night after night, her sleep is disturbed by squalls of driving, diagonal rain needling the aluminium exterior of the caravan.

'I want you to say every word you can think of beginning with the letter "F".'

Janet opened her mouth and a vast white expanse filled in her head. If only she could cut a hole in it and catch some words. 'Fishing …' she began.

'That was terrible,' she moaned when he called time.

'You got nine.'

'*Terrible.*'

'The average is eleven.'

'But there were gaps. Moments when I had no words.'

After he had finished with her, Janet changed into a gown and climbed aboard an MRI scanner. Once she had stuffed her ears with the hospital-issue plugs, they placed a cover over her face and in she went. The scanner groaned and knocked. Gusts of wind blew down the tunnel in which she was trapped. You are lying on a very noisy beach, she told herself. What a refreshing breeze! But it was like a coffin, wasn't it? Like moving down the conveyer belt at the crematorium. Could they tell from the noise? she wondered. Were the sounds different depending on the density of what was being penetrated? Was it like lining up bottles of water and blowing in them?

As Janet left, the nurse presented her with a slip of paper. 'If you don't hear within four weeks, call the number,' she was told, and then, accompanied by Elgar, she processed to the bus stop, where she waited, wondering whether the results would arrive more quickly for something or for nothing.

Each morning since, she has told herself she would have heard if the news was bad. And yet, if it was good, they would have surely dashed off a quick letter to that effect.

Yesterday, she walked to the site office to check for post and the letter was there. She picked it up and carried it home. But when she got back, she found she didn't want to open it. While the letter was closed, all possibilities were open to her: a dignified decline, a remarkable recovery, and an uneventful old age. She remembered Emma's disappointing admission that she sometimes bought a lottery ticket. Not with any expectation of winning, Emma maintained, but as a licence to daydream. 'It's only a couple of pounds. And for a few days, while the ticket's sitting in my purse, I decide how I'll spend the jackpot.' The letter on the worktop is also a licence to daydream.

Janet plays the opening D major chord of the 'Hallelujah Chorus'. No, it sounds wrong. She decides against 'Trumpet' and selects 'Organ 2' before beginning again. As the little finger and thumb of her left hand climb the octave quavers, she thinks about non-believers betting on the horses or the football; on the results of general elections or white Christmases; on scratch cards or those awful fixed odds betting terminals. Janet bets on God. What does He want? Frank was always very sure about it. Janet is less certain, though she suspects He would like her to enjoy a *family Christmas*. She catches something out of the corner of her eye and stops playing. Water, on the floor beside the kitchen units. Just a spot, she thinks. But as she watches, it grows. A splash. A blob. A small puddle. Bigger now. Until its outer reaches discover an incline and it slithers towards her, like a creature in search of company.

## WARNING EVERY MAN

In olden times Chris might have covered his head in dust and ash or donned gloves and a black hatband as a manifestation of his innermost feelings. Today, he stands beside the steps of the north-east colonnade in the relentless, filmy rain. Most people glance at him and look away. Some have a sneaky second look, to make sure they've got the gist of the sign, thinking, Chris imagines, that none of it applies to them, and someone else will do something about it.

Here, beside the memorial, he is just a few hundred feet from the MP's office. Not long ago, a photograph of the MP was posted online. Super-imposed on to a landscape image of the beach, he looked wedding-ready, in a suit jacket and tie. The accompanying text induced residents to join him in making the town plastic-free. Emma, briefly excited, wondered how she might get involved in such an ambitious project. But the MP was merely advertising his attendance at a beach clean-up, something local volunteers had been doing for years without making fancy posters of themselves dressed in unsuitable workwear. The MP doesn't live in the town, but should he pass by on his way to his office, Chris would like to know what, besides self-promotion, he has planned.

There's a pleasure in this public expression of sadness. It's a relief to let his shoulders sag and face drop. Like taking off his boots at the end of a long, wet day. His past presence on the street with his father was an outward expression of an inner faith. This is an outward expression of an inner despair. No one wants to think about death. When do people even see it, nowadays? Animals are killed behind closed doors and sick people are taken to hospital or carted off to homes, their bodies eventually hidden in mortuaries. When death is so unrehearsed is it any wonder people hide from it?

Finally, a bloke stops. 'The climate's changed before,' he says, face emerging like a periscope from a circle of nylon blend and faux fur. 'Scientists! They can't even get the weather right, can they?'

Chris glances skyward. A bleary bank of cloud lies beached on the building tops, its misty tendrils leaching salt and brine.

The bloke looks up, too, squinting at the dank haze.

'It's all about adaptation, isn't it?' he says. 'Survival of the fittest. Darwin, and that. Before long we'll be growing gills again.' He awaits a response, grinning in anticipation of some sort of accord.

'Structural adaptations take generations.'

'Aw, lighten up,' he says, and slopes away.

Chris steps from foot to foot. It's not cold. Not really. Just wet. And gloomy. Even though it's only lunchtime, buses and cars are using their lights. On the other side of Lord Street, people collect under the covered walkways as rain trickles down the sloping glass roofs of the cast-iron Victorian verandas and the Salvation Army band play carols.

There hadn't been anywhere to park on Lord Street, so Chris left the van at Central 12 Shopping Park instead. And when he went to pay, he discovered he only had enough change for an hour. Still, an hour – minus time spent carrying the sandwich board down to the memorial and back – is enough time in the rain. And his phone might ring. It probably won't. But it might.

When Chris sees his sister Ruth and her husband Rob across the street, he turns away. But, moments later, as the pedestrian crossing finishes a bout of beeps, they're standing in front of him, expressions perplexed as they take in the sign.

Rob extends his usual greeting: 'Chris, *mate.*'

Chris nods. He is not Rob's mate.

'How's Emma? And the boys?' Rob asks, stepping closer to angle the umbrella over Chris.

'No point in sheltering him,' Ruth says, glancing up at the umbrella's ribs. 'He's already soaked.'

'No point in him getting wetter, either,' Rob replies mildly.

Ruth places her hands on her hips and, like the picture of the old crone who is also young, she is at once a woman in a coat with a velvet collar, and the girl who, hands on hips, solid half-moons of her knees poking out from under her dress, delivered instructions for the many invented games to which Chris was conscripted. Bossy Ruth. *Assertive*, Emma would insist. Chris remembers his delight at discovering the word 'ruthless' and fathoming its power to drive his otherwise goody-goody sister to excessive acts of anger and revenge: Chinese burns, wet willies, horse bites – she became proficient at them all. How Rob made it past Ruth's brook-no-bullshit glower is a mystery to Chris. Rob has the demeanour of a youth minister: rosy-cheeked and earnest, brimming with dad jokes and desperate to be down with the kids. Emma likes him, of course. 'You're embarrassed by his friendliness,' she complains. 'You don't know what to do with it.' It's not that, though. Rob is too eager; he's like a children's entertainer attempting to establish rapport before the jelly is lobbed at him. 'Hey, guys!' – that's how he greets James and Dylan. He wears his religion with all the poise of a politician in a backward-facing baseball cap. And it's a soft-soap spirituality: middle-class parents warbling patriotic hymns and volunteering with the Scouts. Where's the difficulty in that? Where's the striving? Rob's brand of Christianity is a kind of identity politics: I identify as saved, therefore I am saved. He may have talked Ruth into giving their three boys Biblical names, but has Rob ever read the Old Testament? If God exists, which He doesn't, but if, for the sake of argument, He does, and

He is standing at the entrance to heaven like a primordial hippy, greeting newcomers with 'Hey, guys!', Chris won't be able to bear it.

'Is that your old work sign?' Ruth asks.

'Yes.'

'The one Emma did for you?'

'Yes.'

'She must be disappointed you've painted over it.' She glances from Chris to the sign. 'Badly,' she adds.

'It's all about renewables, isn't it, mate?' Rob says. 'We've got the wood-burner and the solar panels now. That should cheer you up. No?'

'You're causing air pollution with your stove. And the refining of the rare earth metals they use in solar energy produces radioactive waste. So …'

Rob frowns. 'How about this, then? Why does Father Christmas have three gardens? So he can ho ho ho!'

Chris's shirt pocket vibrates. Saved by the bell. But when the screen lights up, it's Emma. He dismisses the call and returns the phone to his pocket.

Rob tightens the Velcro fastener on the neck of his cagoule and nods at the Salvation Army band. 'Oh, I like this one,' he says and sings along in a falsetto voice, 'Glor-or-or-or-or-oor, or-or-or-or-or-oor, or-or-or-or …' finally stopping when Ruth places a restraining hand on his arm.

'What are you doing, Chris?' she asks. 'Haven't you had enough of this sort of thing? You used to *hate* it.'

Chris isn't sure what to say. When you stand in front of your parents or siblings, you're there with all the other versions of yourself, and you may not like some of them, especially the ones that contradict you in the moment of your new certainty. He will have to tell Emma about this, he realises. Ruth and Emma aren't friends, as such. But they are sometime allies, and if he doesn't tell Emma what he has been doing, Ruth might just get there before him.

'Are you all right?' she asks.

Chris nods.

'Emma told me something back in the autumn,' Ruth says. 'About the potato lorries. She said when they leave the farms, they turn right at the roundabout. The one at Moss Lane and Roe Lane, beside the spot where library used to be?'

'I know it,' Chris says drily.

'It's a tight turn, isn't it? And when the lorries pass, some of the potatoes tumble off and land in the road and on the pavement.'

'That's right.'

'She said you park up by the bakery and collect the potatoes.'

What is there to say? Would Ruth rather he left them in the street to rot?

'It's a hunter-gatherer thing, isn't it, mate?'

Chris smirks. This, from a man who wouldn't know a Maris Peer from a Melody; a man whose hunting ability extends to checking the recommended offers on a wine app. As *if* Rob would retrieve windfall potatoes.

'There's nothing like the great outdoors!' Rob adds.

Chris laughs; the *great outdoors*, and look at Rob, all covered up, his keen, rosy face poking out of the bottle-neck of his cagoule.

'Are you busy at work?' Ruth asks.

'Not especially.'

'Did you tell Emma what I said about coming to do some cleaning?'

'Yes,' Chris lies. 'She said thanks, but she hasn't got time.'

'You know, if you need—'

'I don't.'

'OK.' Ruth shrugs. 'And *this*? Haven't you got anything better to do? I mean, it's *Christmas*.'

'Merry Christmas,' he says. '*Peace on earth, goodwill toward men*. And women,' he adds, not to be inclusive, but to remind Ruth that no matter what it says in the trendy version of the Bible they use at Rob's church, she wasn't included in the original.

Ruth gives him a hard stare.

'Well, the boys are at my mum's,' Rob says. 'We'd better go and rescue her. See you at the party. We're looking forward to it, aren't we, Ruth?'

She nods her agreement, lingering for a moment as Rob strides away. 'Sometimes, you're very like Dad,' she mutters, and Chris, uncertain what to do with her observation, pretends he hasn't heard.


The van is parked outside a large unit which was empty for months but has been jammed full of junk in time for Christmas: ropes of tinsel, light-up window decorations, fibre-optic Christmas trees, life-size reindeer and inflatable snowmen. Chris sits in the driver's seat, head tipped against the rest. He pulls his phone out of his shirt pocket. Emma has left a message.

'Where are you? The boys are waiting. And your mum's been on the phone. She didn't want to bother you because she knew you'd be busy, and she was upset because I didn't answer when she tried me, earlier. I said I'd been picking James up from hockey. And I said you *should* be busy. *Here*. With us, making food for the party. She went quiet, like she does when you don't say exactly what she was hoping to hear. I just – I haven't got time to stay on the phone while she gives me the silent treatment. Can you speak to her before she calls back?'

Chris deletes the message and, instead of calling his mother, tries Emma.

'Where are you?' she asks.

'In the van, outside that awful place that's just opened.'

'Chris, you promised—'

'I'm just taking care of a few things. I bumped into Ruth and Rob.'

Water trickles down the windscreen; already his breath is misting it up. He turns the key and puts the fan and wipers on.

'There's two enormous speakers just inside the entrance of whatever-it's-called – they haven't even got a sign. No, wait, they've sprayed the name on one of the windows: "XMAS LAND", that's what it's called. God. And the speakers are blasting out your least favourite Christmas song. Should be "Baby It's Wet Outside" this year.'

Emma makes an agreeing noise.

'*I'll hold your hands, they're wet, I bet,*' Chris sings and pauses in anticipation of a laugh that doesn't come. 'It's the Anthropocene, right?' he continues. 'And the place is bursting with plastic – floor to ceiling. I can see it all from here. They've got crap packed so high you'd need a ladder to reach the top.'

'I know. I walked past last weekend and thought how much you'd hate it.'

'You were in town? You never said … Why are they making all this stuff? The sea's full of it and by Boxing Day everyone's bins will be full of it. It's going to stick around forever. I'm sitting here thinking: *Anthropocene* – it's not a great word, is it? This should be the *Plasticine*. Right? It's a much better description.'

'Very funny.'

'I thought hockey was cancelled?'

'They had the pitch deep-cleaned yesterday. I told you, remember? The sand was full of moss and algae and that's why it wasn't draining properly. Chris, you promised you'd be home by now. The boys are waiting. And you need to call your mum.'

'So, while I've been in town—' he begins.

'Tell me later,' she replies.

He sits there for a while after she hangs up, watching the rain dribble down the windscreen. He should have told her about the sandwich board. There's a gap now, entirely of his own making. He will have to fill it with words – later. But what to say when your actions are inexplicable even to yourself?

'I wanted to talk about the party,' his mother says.

Chris waits.

'That's why I phoned, earlier. And you weren't …'

He feels in the wrong already, but she can't expect him to apologise for not being in when she called.

'... and now, I – It's very wet outside, isn't it?'

'Yeah.' Chris's reply is met with silence. 'The rain's not too heavy today,' he adds, 'but everywhere's soaked.'

Earlier, before he drove to town, Chris did a job in Ainsdale where he cleaned out some guttering and then climbed up on to an old flat roof. The roof was shaped like the footbaths they used to make you walk through at swimming pools, and full of similarly freezing water. A drain in one corner was blocked by leaves, sediment and shavings of blown brick from the gable end of the house next door. Chris cleared the drain and disconnected the pipe before climbing down and attaching the drain-cleaning kit to the pressure washer. It was a messy, smelly job, and even though he stood off to one side, in expect-ation of the silty blowback, it caught his boots and the calves of his trousers.

'I'm wet through,' he says and waits again, frustrated by her lack of response. Spit it out or hang up, he thinks.

'It would be nice if we had a nativity. At the party. Amos, Nathan and Elijah have got costumes. They're going to be Wise Men at, you know, at Rob's ...' His mother means Rob's church, but she can't bring herself to call it that. 'I found a hobby horse in the hospice shop. For the donkey. And Emma can put something together for your boys, costume-wise, can't she?'

'I don't think she'll have time, Mum.'

Chris waits out the silence; he lets it settle and stretch. When he was younger, he used to fill her gaps, throw words at her, casting around for a way to induce reciprocity. Nowadays, he is up for the stand-off. It's uncomfortable, but conversation is governed by uncomplicated formalities and it's not his turn to speak.

'I was listening to an end-times radio programme,' she says.

'On the internet?'

When his mother got Ruth's old computer, Chris thought it might change things. Of course, it didn't. Did the translation of the Bible into the vernacular simplify the religious landscape? Not at all. Has the internet provided his mother with a window to the wider world? Hardly. It has worked like a telescope, allowing her to fix and magnify her view.

'All over the world Christians are having dreams about the end times. It seems the Lord is warning us.'

His mother's favourite saying comes to mind: 'If you can't say anything nice, don't say anything at all.' Words she lives by, her whole life punctuated by silences.

'There was a guest on the show,' she continues. 'He dreamed of earthquakes. And he moved his family away from Mexico City. Just in time.'

'There are earthquakes all the time in Mexico, Mum.'

'I've dreamed of floods.'

'I expect lots of people have.'

'You have, too?'

'The wet gets in your bones when you spend all day outside.'

'*In the mouth of two or three witnesses shall every word be established.*'

'There'll probably be a new record this winter,' Chris says. 'Next winter, too. It's just the way things are going.' He stops, realising he has presented her with an opportunity to remind him that climate change denies God's supremacy and, as such, is a false prophecy.

'There's water on the floor,' she says in a small voice.

'Ah-ha,' he says, wishing she would learn to ask for help without going all round the houses first.

'I think it's coming through the wall,' she continues. 'I've wiped it away, but it keeps coming back.'

'I'll come right over.'

The instant he has spoken, it occurs to him that she may have plans, and if she does, she will only reveal them later, having allowed herself to be inconvenienced.

'As long as it's a good time?' he adds, but his mother has already hung up.


Chris takes the coast road. Frothy-tipped tongues of water lick the sea wall, but the body of the tide is veiled by a weeping bank of cloud, into which the end of the pier disappears. He feels an affinity with its long iron legs stuck fast in the sousing air and salt water, imagining it – when the mist finally dissipates – emerging like a piece of deep-sea debris; biofouled, wearing a crust of mussels and weed. That's how he will emerge from this winter, too.

One day, though it seems aeons away, it *will* be June again. The warm air will be gritty and glass-like, and Chris will walk down on to the mudflats beside the pier and harvest samphire, taking care to leave the roots behind for next year's crop. It's ridiculous that they sell it in the supermarket, a luxury item imported from Israel. Each summer, families from Birmingham and Leicester come to the beach. Described as Indians in the local media, though they are almost certainly British, the visiting samphire harvesters pose for photographs and allow themselves to be filmed while good-naturedly suggesting complementary curry and pakora recipes. Chris goes alone, though lately there have been others like him on the beach: solitary men, scissors and buckets at the ready. When the samphire is at its freshest, Emma rinses it under cold water to get rid of the mud and they eat it raw in salads. Later harvests are blanched, placed in sandwich bags and stored in the freezer to be used in fritters and soups.

Despite the 50-mph limit, Chris keeps below forty; any faster and he'd catch air between the ruts in the road. At the northmost part of the beach there is no sea wall; instead, an ever-expanding grassy marshland acts as a bulwark. Now, the road is a corridor through water; the vertiginous beach to the left and acres of flooded marsh to the right. Eventually, the coast road angles inland again and Chris passes the sign that lets him know he has left Merseyside. It features a drawing of flat fields, a canal and a red barge alongside the declaration: 'WE'VE GOT IT ALL IN WEST LANCASHIRE'. Dylan and James find it hilarious. 'They've got it *all*, here,' they yell whenever they pass it.

Stopped at a set of traffic lights, Chris lets go of the wheel, unbuttons his cuffs and rolls his sleeves past his elbows. There. He is not good at waiting. Preparations are, to an extent, a way of alleviating worry by filling the time until action is required. It was like that when Emma was pregnant and in labour, particularly with James. There were things to organise and arrange but he was horribly aware of his inability to influence proceedings and was much happier after each baby's arrival brought with it the necessity for action. And so it is today. He'll remove the caravan's interior wall board and check the timber framework and insulation for damage. He grips the steering wheel, ready for the green light, heartened by the possibility of making something better.

## BLIGHT CHRISTMAS

In previous Decembers, a variety of winter squash rested on boards in the shed like a fleet of retired fairy-tale carriages. This year, there is one lonely pumpkin. Emma places it in the canvas bag on top of the potatoes she dug out of the storage bin and the onions cut from their ceiling strings. Chris is late and the boys are waiting. When he returns, they will make baked, stuffed potatoes, an onion and potato tart, and biscuit dough. In the meantime, she'll let the boys loose on the pumpkin.

On her way back, she passes the rabbits. They seem miserable. She has angled the hutch's mesh front away from the rain, but the newspaper sheets she places under the sawdust and hay are forever damp, and neither rabbit is keen on spending time in their downstairs run which rests on the puddled patio. When Chris gets back, she'll ask him to have a look at them.

It's a tradition to prepare the Christmas Eve food together. They use the last of the fresh produce and then freeze or refrigerate their creations, ready for the party. Rob jokes that the party is essentially a harvest festival with carols. Two years ago, he suggested he and Ruth might host, but Dylan and James objected; it was their party, their food, their tradition. The boys have reached an age where they swat Emma away, reclassifying help as interference. She is learning their new rules and trying not to take them personally. Yet, if *she* attempts to remove any of the scaffolding structures of their childhood, they are indignant – how could she change something without asking?

When the boys were small Emma used to gnaw on their legs, lips screening her teeth: 'Nom, nom, nom,' she'd growl as they shrieked. It was a way to induce laughter while simultaneously expelling the steam of her affection. There are fewer acceptable ways to do that as children grow. Dylan will occasionally hug her hard, and James still rests a gentle hand on her arm in passing, but she tempers her responses, and the fierceness of her love – its devouring, expansile attributes must be expressed in other ways. This afternoon, like a fairy godmother, she will express it with a pumpkin.

Emma cuts the pumpkin in half and the boys scoop out its insides, discarding the stringy guts before washing the seeds and patting them dry with kitchen towel. Emma spreads the seeds on baking sheets and Dylan drizzles them with olive oil, rock salt, cayenne pepper and garlic powder. They roast them until they are dark and crispy. And they roast one half of the pumpkin, too, until its flesh is soft enough to make a puree for muffins. James cuts the other pumpkin half into chunks which Emma places in the slow cooker with red pepper, chopped ginger and coconut milk. Soon the kitchen smells of roasted seeds and allspice. Dylan, Emma notices, is not so fragrant.

'When did you last shower?'

'Thursday?'

'I can smell your armpits.'

'It's James's hockey kit, not me.'

'James's kit's in the lounge, and the door's closed. I can smell *you*.'

'Dad'll be back soon. I'll wait.'

'No, you reek.'

He bursts into feigned tears. 'You're a terrible parent; I need support, not body-shaming.'

Emma flicks him with a tea towel.

'Get. In. The. Shower.'

'All right. All right.'

She looks out of the window. Misty cloud looms low, already blotting the last of the afternoon light. She rubs her eyes, tired after a series of late nights spent finishing a craft bag and knitting-needle roll in time for the last post and sorting out family presents: the nephews' book bags, Rob's Santa apron and Ruth's water-bottle sling. It was a busy week at work, too. The infants were over-excited and cantankerous and while mopping up spilt drinks and tears or chopping sausages into bite-sized pieces

– 'You're big enough to do it yourself now' – she had to remind herself of the job's upsides: regular hours, a permanent contract and the same holidays as the boys.

There is still tidying up to be done, and she has never been so late with the decorations. The poor tree – she can see it through the window, flaccid and yellowing. She has been waiting on it, hoping to come down one morning and find it recovered: a Christmas miracle! She needs to wrap the socks, Lynx and chocolate coins for the boys' stockings. And their Christmas money must be sorted. It has plateaued at a hundred pounds each for the past few years, and James' snark about the Consumer Prices Index has resulted in her attempting to at least present it in interesting ways. Last year she bought him a packet of Sharpies and wrapped a note around each of the pens, while Dylan's money was rolled tightly and placed inside inflated balloons, accompanied by a ribbon-strung darning needle. This year, she will place Dylan's money in a tissue box, between novelty £50 napkins – 'Don't blow it all at once!' – and she will fold James's notes like flowers before attaching them to a broken branch: a money tree for Mr Consumer Prices Index.

She remembers her first Christmas with Chris, before they bought this house, before they had any traditions of their own. Already living together, they visited both sets of parents in the morning. Janet presented Emma with a three-pack of thermal vests. Emma's mother bought Chris a pair of neckties.

In the car, on the way home to cook their first Christmas dinner, Chris repeated a story he had heard during a carol service at one or other of the churches he'd attended as a boy: a man sold his pocket watch to buy some hair combs for his wife, who had sold her hair to buy a chain for the pocket watch. Other people found the story heart-warming. But Chris said the useless presents had made him sad. Sensing incipient gloom, Emma intervened. It was wrong to conflate the *useless* presents in the story with the *unwanted* ones their parents had bestowed: unwanted presents were not necessarily useless. And yes, it may be that the ties were a comment on Chris's job – not professional enough, in her parents' opinion. While the vests were probably a criticism of her attire – not modest enough, in his parents' opinion. But it really didn't matter. And, incidentally, the story was about love, not presents.

When they got home, she talked Chris into wearing the ties – both ties, and nothing but the ties. And she performed the dance of the three vests while mangling 'The Daughter of Herodias': '*She freed and floated on the air her arms above dim vests that hid her bosom's charms.*'

It was seven o'clock before Christmas dinner was ready.

Dylan dashes out of the bathroom and down the hall, a towel wrapped around his waist. His feet pound up the stairs, rattling the ceiling above as he hurries to get dressed before Chris returns.

A minute or two later and – *ker-thunk, ker-thunk, ker-thunk* – he descends, taking the stairs two or three at a time, and Emma hears the swoosh of his left hand palming the wall, evidenced by the greasy smear he insists he can't see.

'Hand. Wall. Dylan!'

'Where's Dad, then?' he asks, shaking his damp head like a dog.

'I don't know. Shall we start without him?'

The boys exchange glances.

'It won't be the same without Dad,' James says. 'Probably wouldn't be the same anyway,' he adds, leaving Emma to wonder whether he's referring to growing up or Chris's recent behaviour.

Dylan connects his phone to the digital radio. 'I've got a food-themed playlist, first. Chestnuts roasting on an open fire, mistletoe and wine, marshmallows for toasting, figgy pudding, loads more … Let's get started.'

Emma empties the potatoes into the sink and puts the onions on the worktop beside a chopping board. The potatoes are small. Washing them, Emma notices dark, rotten patches under their skins and, one by one, discards them. That's the stuffed potatoes and the tart off the menu.

'Shall we make some little hash browns, instead?'

'How do we do that?'

'You peel the potatoes, and James can cut out the rotten bits and grate whatever's left.'

The doorbell rings and Emma leaves the boys to it. A delivery driver hands her a padded envelope and a screen. As she writes her name with the tiny stylus, the driver returns to his van and collects a large box.

'Is heavy,' he calls, taking small steps, trying to keep his back straight while also hurrying in the rain. 'I put here for you?' He steps into the porch and lowers the box slowly, tattooed arms straining. 'You like, honey?'

Emma's face flushes as she returns the screen. She looks past him, saying nothing. He shrugs and heads back to his van. She watches him drive away, her expression stern and disapproving in case he glances in his mirror. When he is out of sight, she closes the front door.

The box is awkward. Emma angles it into the hall with her feet. Though she has broken their pact, she hopes it isn't a Christmas present from Chris. Irritated, she puts the padded envelope on the bottom stair and picks at a corner of the tape that seals the box until she has lifted enough to tear away the whole strip. The box is full of honey. *Honey* – oh, the man must have thought her so rude. Honey, in 15-kg tubs, like paint pots. She reseals the box and picks up the padded envelope, so light its weight barely registers. She opens it, too, and discovers several bottles of tablets. Fish antibiotics. There must be a mistake. Unless – oh God – there aren't fish you can farm from home, are there? She reseals the envelope, too, and as she places it on top of the box her phone pings. She expects a message from Chris, but it's Ruth, asking whether Chris is all right.

So, he wasn't shopping in town, then. Emma wonders who else has seen him standing by the memorial, and what they think. Dylan's friends would have surely said something by now. They are not kind. Oh, they are polite, to Emma at least: it's *Mrs Abram* this, *Mrs Abram* that. Thanks for the tea, *Mrs Abram*; thanks for the drinks, *Mrs Abram*. They make her feel old and invisible and she has no idea how to talk to them. When she tries, they stiffen and nod, as if she is a drill sergeant. She happens to bake cookies while they are around. Happens to make a little extra at teatime so they don't have to hurry home. Happens to keep a few cans of store-brand pop in the fridge in case they are thirsty, though they take the piss out of it and call it *jarg* when she leaves the room. Callum, Jonesy – whose first name she doesn't know, and Towhead, so named, she believed, because of his light hair, until Dylan corrected her, pointing out his friend's long face and flat features, hence: Toe-head. Emma is nice to them because, for some reason, Dylan likes them. James's friends, though real enough, prefer to interact in the virtual world, via headphones and instant messages, rarely making in-person appearances. Dylan's sometimes include James when they visit, having declared him to be *sound*, a pronouncement Dylan received with so much pleasure Emma felt obliged to consider the possibility that it may be a subtle insult. There have been times when, having walked down Moss Lane to the bakery, Emma has seen Dylan's friends riding their bikes, hands-free, backs straight, wilfully casual, avoiding any possibility of interaction by never quite looking her way. Perhaps Dylan does the same when he sees their mothers.

'Mum, can we have a muffin?' Dylan calls. 'Hello? *Emma-Jane?* Are you there?'

'They're for later,' Emma replies, feet firmly planted in the hall, resisting the urge to burst back into the kitchen and tell James, who has a knack for niggling, to pack it in. She can smell his hockey kit, which is sprawled behind the closed lounge door as the dehumidifier attempts to suck it dry: armour, deflectors, guards, protectors and wheelie kit bag. The stink is creeping under the door, wafting towards the kitchen where it will, for now at least, be overpowered by the various pumpkin smells. Ideally, the kit should be aired after every match. If it was dry outside today, she would have persuaded James to soak the pieces in the bath before attacking them with the scrubbing brush. The kit does not belong to him; it has been passed down by the club, from goalkeeper to goalkeeper, a receptacle for the blood, sweat and tears of a generation of young men. Later, when Emma opens the lounge door, the air will be bone dry and razor sharp, infused with the vinegary reek of feet and the stale milk and stilton stench of BO. She'll put all the pieces back in the wheelie kit bag, making sure to include a thermal top so James can create a layer between his flesh and the elbow pads in order to combat the eczema in the creases of his arms. And he will forget to wear it. Sometimes she thinks he does it on purpose.

Defeated, she sits on the bottom stair. She is tired, that's all. What she would give for an undisturbed night's sleep. Chris can't help his snoring. But, the thought whips back, he *can* help other things: his unrelenting gloom, his recent unreliability, the way he has started to present her with things she hasn't requested and doesn't want: a solar charger, a Swiss army knife key ring, a She Pee.

'I'm trying to do something nice for you and you won't let me,' he said when, having discovered how much the personal water filter cost, she insisted he return it.

The fish antibiotics! It comes to her, suddenly, a conversation they had months ago in which Chris asked what she would do if James had one of his chest infections and there weren't any antibiotics.

'But there *are* antibiotics,' she had replied. 'They're getting less effective, not running out.'

'Fish antibiotics are closest to the real thing,' he continued, as if she hadn't spoken. 'They haven't been tested on humans, but they're basically the same – amoxicillin, penicillin, cephalexin, and you can get them online.'

'They could send you *anything*. How would you know what was in them? *If* antibiotics stop working, there'll be something else. We've only been technically advanced for a hundred years. There's *so much* more we can do.'

'God, I'm so sick of techno-utopianism: ooooh, wait till you hear about geoengineering, it's going to save us all! You might as well believe in God. It's just as stupid and childish.'

Emma glances at the envelope. Here it is, at last: the line, the tether, the point of resistance; she will *never* let him give James this stuff – it could be anything. She'll leave the honey in the hall for Chris but, when she gets a moment, she'll slip the envelope into the top of the wardrobe with the Christmas presents; he has no reason to look there.

'The potatoes are peeled,' Dylan calls.

'And ruined,' James adds.

Emma gets to her feet and returns to the kitchen. Marred by spongy bruises and dark rotten veins, the potatoes aren't remotely salvageable. She piles the whole lot into a bowl to be taken outside and dumped in the compost.

'Who's doing the onions?' she says.

'Me,' James replies. 'I heard you don't cry if you put a spoon in your mouth, so I'm going to test the hypothesis.'

The experiment doesn't work, and when, having peeled each of the onions, James cuts them in half to discover brown, mushy centres, Emma too feels like crying.

The outer two layers of each onion are useable. She adds the soft, sticky hearts to the pile of rotten potato pieces, grateful Chris isn't there to see.

They make mini onion quiches and cheese and onion straws. Then gingerbread, using a grated root of the plant on the windowsill. She'll make mince pies on Christmas Eve morning; they're always better fresh.

'If I put the quiches in the fridge, and the cheese straws in a tin on the side, once they've cooled, do you promise not to pinch any before the party?'

Emma gives the boys a moment to reply.

'Freezer it is,' she says, catching a conspiratorial look between them.

Dylan makes a half-hearted protest before announcing a second playlist, titled 'Songs that Might Make Mum Cry'. It begins with 'Believe' from *The Polar Express*, the boys' favourite Christmas film when they were small and, as the music starts, he removes a roll of ribbon from his trouser pocket which he must have stolen from her sewing room, earlier.

'Remember this?' he says.

'Oh, Dylan. You know I don't like you messing with my … It's all unravelled, now.'

James laughs as Dylan whips the ribbon around his head. Emma rolls her eyes: she once cried as a shoal of ribbon-waving children twirled their way around the school hall during a reception class performance of *The Rainbow Fish*, and the boys have never let her forget it. This is familiar, comfortable ground. She knows the requisite response, the boys know theirs and, accompanied by the music of Christmases past, Emma lets them tease her.

The quiches and cheese straws are boxed and ready for the freezer, the gingerbread dough is covered in beeswax wrap, and the boys are nibbling toasted pumpkin seeds from a bowl on the kitchen table, when Chris's van finally pulls into the drive.

Emma marches down the hall and swings the front door open, ready with, 'Where have you been?' But the words dissolve as she beholds Janet, climbing out of the van, clutching a hobby horse, and Chris, unloading a portable gas heater.

The boys join her. James rests his chin on her head. Dylan props an elbow on her shoulder, and she can smell his salt-licked fingers.

'Come and help, lads,' Chris calls. 'There's Nan's keyboard and suitcase to bring in.'

There is a moment of resistance. Emma feels it in the sharp press of chin and elbow and then Dylan steps outside to help. James follows a moment later, glancing back to send a cheeky whisper whipping like ribbon over his shoulder. ''Twas the nightmare before Christmas.'

# THE GOOD NEWS

'You *must* have the bed,' Emma says.

'Oh *no*, I'll sleep on the sofa or the floor. Anywhere. I can sleep anywhere. Sitting down. Standing up.' This is an outright lie, but Janet can't stop herself. 'It really doesn't matter. Jesus only had a stable, didn't he? A manger filled with hay. And I'm sure he slept very well. I don't want to be any trouble. There's only one of me: it makes more sense for two people to sleep well than one. It doesn't matter if I'm tired. Chris needs his rest. He works so hard, doesn't he?'

'I've changed the bed,' Emma says stiffly. 'So it's best if you just sleep in it.'

'Oh, I will, then. Thank you. Thank you very much,' Janet replies as she follows Emma. 'I've never slept over before,' she adds, immediately regretting her words because they make her sound like a teenager, and yet she is thrilled to be ascending the stairs as a guest, while Emma carries her case like a bellboy.

Outside, it's already dusky. Emma presses the light switch and pulls the blind over the skylight.

'I'll leave you to unpack. I've cleared the drawers in the bedside table for you. When you've emptied the case, I'll take it out to the garage, so it won't be in your way. Would you like a cup of tea?'

Just a small one, Janet tells her. She doesn't want to be any trouble.

*

Janet Abram's suitcase contains several changes of clothes, a pillow and towel, a dozen pairs of knickers, a nightdress and dressing gown, slippers, a black gift edition of the King James Bible and her fate, in the form of the letter from the hospital. Janet's heart contains – barely contains – a surfeit of love and doubt.

There isn't enough room for all her clothes in the bedside drawers so Janet places some of them on the floor beside the bed before retrieving the letter from the suitcase.

The wardrobe stands at the apex of the room. It's old-fashioned, wide and tall, with heavy doors and panel mouldings. Inside, a rail holding Chris and Emma's clothes is flanked by shelves containing folded towels and bedding, and topped by a shelf of what looks to be Christmas presents wrapped in newspaper. Standing on tiptoe, she slides the letter in among the presents, alongside a padded envelope. After she has fastened the now empty suitcase, Janet sits on the edge of the freshly made bed. She strokes the crisp duvet cover and decides, when the moment is right, to recommend a nice fabric conditioner to Emma.

They don't say grace. No matter, Janet offers her thanks silently.

'This rain is never-ending,' Chris says, leaning over his soup, shoulders hunched.

'It'll stop,' Emma replies. 'It always does. Remember last winter? I went to the sand dunes at Ainsdale and the wooden walkway was under the water; deep pools on either side. Daft dogs were swimming in it. Kids were *soaked*, the water well past their wellies. Everyone was having a great time.'

How lovely it is to sit and listen to small talk. This is what they discuss when Janet isn't here: the weather and walking in the dunes. How fond she feels of Chris – and the boys who, occupied by their soup, are unusually quiet.

'You know Frog Lane, out at Hoscar?' Emma continues. 'The ditch beside the road was full of water last winter. Remember? It looked like a canal, and the road flooded, too. There are pictures, online. And the other winter, when it rained and rained, and the coast road was closed? There were floods in town, too, weren't there? Whole roads where drains were blocked, and water trickled on to the pavements. I was driving back from work and I pulled over because the water was nudging at garden gates. And there were *idiots* – sorry, Janet, but that's what they were – trying to drive on. Every time anyone passed, even at five miles per hour, it caused a wake, and the water crept closer to people's front doors. So, a few of us stood at the junctions to warn people. Most of them were great. "Oh, I didn't realise. I'm sorry, I'll turn around," they said.'

'There were others, though, weren't there?' Chris interjects. '"I've got every right to be here. You can't stop me! It's the public highway! Who cares if people's houses get flooded as long as I can drive my car wherever I like?"'

'Most people are decent,' Emma says.

Janet nods in agreement. It is such a pleasure to sit with her son and grandsons. And Emma, of course. She thinks of the letter, sitting in the wardrobe beside the presents, waiting to be opened: if all is well, she will suggest a similar pre-Christmas visit next year.

'Most people!' Chris scoffs.

'Yes, most people! People come together when bad things happen.'

'Oh, I'm sure Chris didn't mean …'

'On September the eleventh the US Coastguard asked for help, and half a million people were rescued from Lower Manhattan by boats,' Emma continues. 'That's more than Dunkirk. They worked for nine hours. In a dust cloud.'

'I've never heard that.'

'Well, it's true. And it's no wonder you don't know. You're always looking at horrible news. Never at anything that might make you feel good.'

'Lovely soup, Emma,' Janet says. She glances at the boys, so big, and in need of proper nourishment. 'You could add some meat next time. A nice bit of smoked bacon. Or some beef stock.'

'This isn't a *restaurant*,' Dylan says in a high voice. 'There isn't a *menu*.'

The boys laugh, and Janet attempts a smile, demonstrating, she hopes, her ability to take a joke.

'Emma-Jane thinks she's doing the right thing by *not* eating beef because cows create a lot of methane,' James explains. 'But we eat cows. Ergo, less methane.'

'Ooh, *ergo*,' Dylan says.

'She's Mum, to you,' Chris tells James, wearily.

So it was *Emma* they were poking fun at. Janet glances at her daughter-in-law who shows no sign of being offended by the boys' jokes about her faddy eating. The boys, she decides, might be less inclined to make fun of a mother who fed them properly.

'Do you think it's wrong to *make* your children be vegetarians?'

'We don't, and they're not,' Chris says.

'Oh, of course not, I was only—'

'I don't think parents should force *any* of their particular views on their children, Mum.'

Spoons scrape the bottoms of bowls and Emma refills everyone's cups with water from a jug.

'Are you looking forward to Christmas?' Janet asks the boys.

What a stupid question, she thinks. Of course they are. She looks at their faces. There is a lot of Chris in Dylan. James's features are softer, more like her own, she decides, losing track of the conversation. It's been a long day and her head aches. She sips her water and forces herself to concentrate on Chris, who seems cross.

'… the Seine's going to flood again and there's no water in Cape Town. And fog. There'll be fog in the south,' he says. 'So I expect flights will be grounded tomorrow, and Christmas Eve, just in time to ruin people's holidays.'

Emma puts the jug down on the table a little more firmly than is necessary.

'You must be worried about your kitchen, Janet,' she says.

Janet hesitates, wondering whether this would be a good time to request prayers for better weather. 'Well, I—'

'Global supply chains are going to be interrupted at some point,' Chris says.

'By the fog, dear?' Janet asks, confused. 'Why's that, then?'

'No, by the rising South China Sea and Pearl River network. By the continuing destruction of the wetlands and mangrove forests. By tidal surges and storms.' Chris checks each remark on a different finger: one, two, three. 'It won't be long before you can forget your smartphones. And your cheap T-shirts. And your biopharmaceuticals.'

'Well, I don't have a smartphone. But it all sounds very unfortunate, dear.'

'What biopharmaceuticals?' Emma asks.

'I don't know. Does it matter? One thing – that's all it'll take for everything else to topple. For the entire global supply chain to be interrupted.'

Emma stands and retrieves the cooling rack.

'Would anyone like a muffin?'

She distributes them, without plates, before anyone has a chance to reply. Dylan bites the top off his without removing the case. James peels away the paper and cuts his into segments with the wrong end of his soup spoon. The muffins are an odd colour, faintly green under their crusted tops.

'How unusual! What flavour are they?'

'Pumpkin,' Emma replies. 'And avocado.'

'Did you know you need two thousand litres of water to produce a kilo of avocados? In Chile, rivers are being drained to grow your avocados, Em. They bring in drinking water for local people. By truck. And it's got sh— faecal matter in it.'

'Oh, what a shame! I'm sure Emma didn't realise—'

'Chris doesn't care if I buy them. Not really. He's just trying to make me feel bad about it.'

'You could use banana, next time, couldn't you?' Janet suggests. When you've been married as long as she was, you learn a thing or two. The easiest way to defuse the situation would be for Emma to promise not to do it again. 'All this rain reminds me of Noah!' she says, brightly, directing the conversation back to its innocuous, weather-observing beginnings as she eases her muffin from its paper case.

'I read the story of Noah,' Emma replies.

'She found this book in Oxfam. A great big thing. This thick.' Chris gives an approximation with his thumb and index finger. '*The Book of Miracles*. Got her interested in the Flood.'

'It's beautiful, Janet. I'll show you later, if you like. It was originally put together around five hundred years ago and it's full of paintings of things people believed were signs from God: heavy snowfalls, red moons, thunderstorms, earthquakes. It starts out with Old Testament stories and goes all the way up to the fifteen hundreds. Then it does Revelation – I'm not so keen on that part – but I really like the painting of the Flood. The foreground is taken up by people trying to swim. Some are managing. Others are being swept off their feet. And one man is trying to escape on a horse! It's nothing like the cartoonish illustrations in children's books – you know, Noah and the animals cuddled up and smiling at each other. It made me think about the poor drowning people, and I realised I'd never read the proper story.'

'And what did you think?' Janet asks, delighted at the turn the conversation has taken.

'Did you work out what was wrong with Noah?' Chris says. 'Why he never questioned any of it? He cut down all those gopher trees without any argument. What if he'd said, "No, I'm not building an ark. Your move, God."'

'Oh, that reminds me of a story I heard at work,' Emma says quickly, frowning at Chris. 'It's probably an urban legend. Still, one of the teachers said there was a little boy who was supposed to play Joseph in the nativity, but he did something naughty in class, so they demoted him to Innkeeper One, meaning his only line was, "Sorry, there's no room." He was very cross about it, and when Mary and the new Joseph approached him on stage and asked whether they might stay, he said, "Yes, there's plenty of room, come in," changing the whole story.'

'It seems "I was just following orders" was the "Noah defence" before it was the Nuremberg defence.'

'Oh, now, Chris, I don't think—' Janet begins.

'You've got to admire Jonah more. At least he fought back. Ran away. Argued. Sulked. Whatever. At least he *did* something.'

'But did it do any good in the end? Did it achieve anything? You can't run away from God.'

'Can we leave?' Dylan asks.

Emma nods and the boys' chairs scrape the floor as they stand. They hurry out of the kitchen and Janet hears their galumphing feet on the stairs. Chris follows, muttering under his breath – something about the garage. And Janet can't help but feel they've run away from her.

*

Janet has decided she is too old to kneel. Noah is supposed to have fathered children when he was more than five hundred years old. The very thought makes her feel like laughing, though she mustn't, no matter how much she would like to: Sarah laughed when Abraham said they were to have a son, and look what the Lord did later.

Janet's prayers are always answered. When James was born just eleven months after his brother, and Emma was so ill, Janet spent every waking moment with a prayer in her heart: don't let Emma leave those boys behind, don't let her, don't let her. Boys need mothering – oh, girls do, too, but boys need an eye kept on them: a father to supply correction and chastisement, and a mother to soften the smart. Emma hadn't left the boys behind, and she'd been fine, eventually, hadn't she? And when Dylan went through that difficult patch where he wouldn't sit still and was always in trouble, Janet had prayed for him to calm down. 'What that boy wants is a good smack,' Frank used to say, but Janet held her peace as Chris and Emma struggled. She didn't even comment when Chris fastened a strap around Dylan's wrist and exercised him daily, as if he was a dog. She and Frank fasted and prayed, and Dylan mellowed, didn't he? Some of her prayers are works in progress. But here's something Janet knows to be true: God's time is not our time. And a lot of people forget that 'no' is an answer, too.

Prayers said, Janet is about to get into bed when there's a knock at the door and Chris appears, carrying the gas heater.

'I really don't think you need this, Mum.'

'I've got used to it at night. Just on low, for a few minutes, to warm things up.'

'Are you cold here?'

'Oh, dear, I don't mean to imply—'

'It's very mild.'

'I don't want to be any bother.'

'You're not.'

This is good to know as Janet has expended a lot of energy in the pursuit of being no bother.

'I'll tell you something, shall I?' she says.

'Go on, then.'

'Your children are lovely.'

'As opposed to yours?'

'Oh no, that's not what I was saying … I wouldn't dream of … Are you quite yourself, at the moment?'

'I'm fine.'

'You know, you'd feel better if you prayed.'

'I wouldn't.'

'It might surprise you to have your prayers answered.'

Chris places his palms together and stares at the ceiling. 'Dear Lord, please stop my mother from trying to reconvert me. Now, I'll be surprised if *that* prayer is answered.'

He smiles after he's said it, and she doesn't mind the joke – not much, anyway – because she said what needed to be said, and he heard her, even if he didn't take it to heart. It's a start.

'Don't worry about the fire, it won't cost you anything.'

'I know, but there'll be condensation, and things will get damp.'

'Oh, they won't! How could a fire make things wet?'

'If I open the window, just a crack …'

Janet lets him, watching the way he lifts the skylight's handle, so she can close it again after he leaves.


## HUNGRY CHILDREN


The sofa bed has the structural integrity of a hammock. There is no way to lie in it without touching Chris from shoulder to knee and Emma does not want to touch him. This evening, weary of her perpetual accessibility, she feels as she did when the boys were small and, overwhelmed by their demands on her body as canteen, conveyance and playground, she would retreat to the toilet for ten minutes while they set up camp outside, sliding scraps of paper under the door and knocking.

Chris pats the narrow space beside him, and she shakes her head, choosing instead to kneel on the floor beside the bed's metal frame. Earlier, while wrestling the spare duvet into its cover, she pulled something in her shoulder. Her cheeks ache from smiling at Janet and her head is humming with various iterations of the words she intends to say to Chris. He leans over and lazily palms her breast.

Emma stiffens. 'Not now,' she says, standing.

She heads back to the door and presses the light switch before shuffling to the sofa bed in the pitch dark, kneeling when her foot meets its metal frame.

'I couldn't leave Mum on her own, Em.'

'Of course not.'

'I suggested she go to Ruth's a bit early this year, but she said, "Oh, it'll only be a day or two," and asked to come here instead. It won't be a day or two. I reckon she'll be here 'til the new year. She'll have to call the insurance. I took the interior wall board off to check the insulation. It's wet. So's the timber framework. There's no point in me replacing them since I'm not sure where the water's coming in – I can't see any dents or cracks on the outside of the van.

'At least she noticed before season's end. Imagine the mess if she'd gone to Ruth's without noticing. The place would have been soaked through by the middle of February. I'm sorry if you're pissed off about her coming.'

'I'm – Look, she's your *mother*. And she's *so* pleased to be here. It's just the space situation.' Emma kneads her aching shoulder. 'I'm more pissed off that you let me think you were working this morning.'

'I did a job in Ainsdale—'

'Ruth messaged, to ask if you're all right,' she says flatly. 'I saw you, in town, the other week.'

'You never said.'

'I didn't know what to say. All the times you've talked about standing in the street with your father. How much you *hated* it. How stupid and embarrassed you felt. It made my heart *ache* to imagine you stuck beside him.'

'It's hardly the same. And you can't talk. You've done it – you had a *collection* of signs.'

'That was different. It was organised. There was a *point*. I wasn't standing around on my own, having promised the boys I'd—'

'What's more important?'

She thinks for a moment. Climate campaigners are often creative: they stage sit-ins and stick fake parking tickets on gas-guzzling vehicles; they congregate outside polluting companies wearing disposable coveralls and masks; they protest on beaches by digging buckets into the mud and kneeling over them with their heads in the sand – over the years Emma has seen all sorts. Chris has chosen to stand in the town centre, on his own, looking angry. And it occurs to her, unkindly, that it's less of a protest and more of a way for him to position himself so he can say, 'I told you so.'

'It's not a choice between the present and the future. You didn't *have* to be there today.'

'Don't you ever think about what's going to happen to the boys?'

'*Everyone* worries about their children.'

'What do you think will happen if there isn't enough food?'

'There are kids who are hungry, *right now*.'

In the time she has been working at the school it has become less remarkable to see a hungry child. Just as there is a difference between the dirt picked up during break times and a more ingrained grubbiness, there is a difference between children who declare themselves to be starving, and those whose ravenousness is eagle-eyed and furtive. Last week, when it was Christmas dinner day, Emma placed the largest squares of stuffing on the neediest plates. An unfamiliar child, signed up for Christmas dinner by his parents, declared he wouldn't eat anything but roast potatoes. Emma said she had to give him some stuffing or her boss would be cross. 'What's your boss's name?' he asked. 'Does she have actual hair, or just a blue hat, like you?' Emma explained her *actual hair* was under the blue hat which, though it wasn't required by law, was worn by every Welfare Assistant in the county. And, in return, the boy accepted his stuffing. She even managed to smile, later, as she served slices of festive ice-cream log. But once the children had left, and it was time to traipse back and forth across the hall in her steel toecap safety shoes, carrying freshly wiped tables and small stacks of chairs, Emma thought about the hungry children and wondered how they would fare during the school holidays.

The sofa bed creaks as Chris shifts.

'I can't go around feeling sorry for everyone, like you,' he says finally. 'It's a luxury. A form of self-indulgence.'

'And I can't go around feeling angry with everyone, like you,' she replies, stung by his codicil.

'You think it makes you better, but you're not above it; you're still in the denial stage.'

Emma rolls her aching shoulder. There was a time when she could air her worries and, having subjected them to the breeze of Chris's scrutiny, fold them up and put them safely away. How she misses it.

'The original stages-of-grief model wasn't for people who'd been bereaved,' she says. 'It was for people who were *dying*. It's been misapplied to—'

'Making it even more relevant! Every day there's terrible news about what's going to happen to us, to the boys. We're *all* living with a terminal diagnosis.'

'That's not necessarily—'

'What if there's civil unrest? Fighting? What'll happen to the boys?'

'They'll have the house.'

'It's mortgaged.'

'It'll be paid off one day.'

'And what use will it be?'

'It's a house.'

'Am I allowed to mention ice melt or water levels?'

'No.'

Emma shifts. Her feet are going to sleep and in the splintery, dehumidified air she smells the sour ghost of James's hockey kit.

'People are focusing on middle-of-the-road things,' Chris says. 'No one's giving any thought to high-end possibilities. They can't model the high-end stuff. It's not within their capacity. How can we be prepared for the worst when no one can even imagine it?'

'People should get in touch with you,' Emma says shortly. '*You* can imagine it for them.'

'For a while, I had a sort of failure of imagination. What I was reading didn't seem real to me. Now, I don't know how to see the world. Or what words to use when I talk about it. The idea that the boys might have a better life than us – it's gone. I hope they don't have children.'

'*Chris* …'

'If I imagine grandchildren, it's only to pity them. They'll be born into God knows what. There'll be a new Dark Age, and they'll live through it. If I could, I'd have the boys sterilised.'

How she longs to pull him out of this; to lower a rope and winch him to safety, but he doesn't want to be rescued or even reassured, he wants to pull her in after him.

'I don't want you standing in town any more.'

'That's all you've got to say?'

'And I want you to stop ordering stuff. You know we can't afford it.'

'Maybe we can't afford *not* to.'

'You promised you'd only use the credit card for essentials. We're *this close* to trouble as it is—'

'I've told you what kind of trouble we'll be in if we're unprepared.'

'When your dad decided to sell the house—'

'This is *nothing* like that.'

'—he made the decision unilaterally, and you, and Ruth, and *any* reasonable person could see the way he went about it was wrong.'

'This is *completely* different.'

'Your mother put up with it. I can't. One big expense – the washing machine, a new gearbox, James's bike – one broken, worn out, stolen thing could land us in trouble. Solar torches, honey, whatever you think of next won't save us if we get behind with the mortgage and I'm *not* asking my parents for help like we did when the clutch went.'

She swallows, angry now. It was low of her to mention the clutch – he'd *hated* asking her parents for help, but she has had enough.

'I won't sit down with my mum and dad while they draw up a payment plan and audit our bank statements

– can you imagine? "Was this wind-up radio an *essential purchase*, given your *present situation*?" Never mind, eh? If we default on the mortgage we can always go and live with your mother. You'd like that, wouldn't you? We can all wait for the end of the world together.'

His breath whooshes, and Emma experiences an uncomfortable mix of shame and pleasure; the former for delivering the blow, the latter for landing it.

'It's not just the boys,' he says quietly. 'I'm worried about you, too. This is going to disproportionately affect women, Em.'

'You've said, before.'

'Loads of women and girls can't swim—'

'I can.'

'—or climb trees, and they're less likely to run away from danger because they're looking after people.'

'All right, that's enough. I can't listen to any more of this.'

Emma stands and the blood prickles back into her feet.

'I mean, you *won't* run,' he persists. 'Ever. You won't even try.'

'I'm sure I could,' she says, reaching for her pillow. 'If I was really frightened and needed to get away.'

'Even when women make it to safety after disasters, emergency shelters aren't properly kitted out for them,' Chris continues. 'You *must* feel something about that.'

She would like to say no, though it would be untrue. Nevertheless, she has realised that to stay sane, most of her caring must be done right here, in this house, on this piece of land, on behalf of these particular people.

'I know the news makes you feel desperate,' she says gently now. 'But I have to get up in the morning and *not* feel like everything is hopeless. I can't start each day listening to you saying things like: "The ice is melting faster than we thought," or, "The giant African baobabs are dying, and it's like a parable of what's going to happen to us." It's morbid; it's like ... rubbernecking. I can't *do* anything about it. I'm not in charge and I can't make it better. It wouldn't be surprising if, given all the stuff you read, and the weather, and work, you're a bit depressed,' she tries tentatively.

'I'm *realistic*.'

'It's late. So, why don't we—'

'Did you know some mammals are becoming nocturnal, so they can avoid humans?'

Given Chris's relentless snoring and Janet's occupation of Emma's room, a modified, nocturnal existence sounds perfect. She says goodnight, leaves him alone in the lounge and tiptoes up the stairs to her sewing room, where she moves the chair – carefully, she piled her underwear and socks on it earlier when she made space for Janet's things – and positions herself on the floor, head under the table beside the machine's foot pedal, legs sticking out into the room.

She lies there for a while, staring up at the underside of the table, replaying the conversation. She thinks of the boys and the effect all this is having on them. According to Chris, Frank occasionally said, 'I wish I'd never had children.' Emma could imagine it: a wheedling, last resort to blackmail in order to persuade Chris and Ruth into behaving as he wished. Chris doesn't appear to realise he says something similar. Not in front of the boys, admittedly, and he usually says it somewhat more equivocally: 'Should we have even had children?' God said it before He destroyed the earth, too, didn't he? He regretted creating man. Emma hasn't got time for such regret. It's a kind of sulking, isn't it? Any mother would think as much. She remembers when the boys were small. Dylan was all fury, a little whirlwind, rage occasionally bursting out of him like vomit. But James was a sulker. There used to be a gas tower in High Park and James would spend ages creating his own versions of it with building blocks. When he made a mistake, or decided something wasn't quite right, he would kick the whole thing down. Not with abandon: he'd walk around his creation first, broodingly, arms folded, and then he'd demolish it with his feet in an Irish dance of deliberate, measured destruction. The impulse to annihilate an imperfect, inanimate project is forgivable when you're three years old. But when it comes to adults, when it comes to a human *life* … In a parent, the impulse to undo one's creation is regrettable. In a God, it's unforgivable.

Swathed in the blue velvet curtain she hasn't yet made into reusable gift bags, Emma sleeps in short bursts, repeatedly woken by the hard floor and the pain in her shoulder. She dreams the sea is eating the town, street by street. She dreams the Moss is a great maw preparing to swallow up the house. She dreams of expanding tidal zones; of liquid winters and arid summers; of envelopment and exposure; of the foundations of the house and the remains of the boys' plastic goalposts emerging from the water periodically, like the shipwrecks on Formby beach.

Emma waits until six thirty before she heads downstairs in her pyjamas, stiff and tired. She slips her arms into her coat and her feet into her waiting trainers, unlocks the back door and steps outside – *splash*. Flipping up her hood, she turns to gauge the step. It must be, oh, at least ten centimetres high, while the water underfoot is barely three. She sploshes across the patio, eyes adjusting to the dark, as the rabbits slope out of their sleeping quarters. They have become hers. In the way Janet will, in the coming days, also become hers. Emma doesn't know how to feed and water another living creature without also propagating an attendant sense of obligation and concern, which is why she has always refused the boys' requests for a dog. Later, in the daylight, she will feed the rabbits and change their paper and bedding. And she'll remind Chris to take a look at them, just to be sure.

Emma checks her coat pocket for her keys and torch, and steps through the water to the garage. She unlocks one of the steel doors and flicks the torch beam over the shelves and hooks that line the walls. *There*. Fumbling with the keys and torch, she wrestles the green stepladder out of the garage and then, having locked the door behind her, carries it into the kitchen where she leans it up against the worktop. She removes her coat and hangs it up. Before long, James will appear, waterproofed from head to toe, on his way to fetch his bike from the shed. Emma boils the kettle and spoons coffee into two mugs. Chris is usually awake by now, even at the weekends. She creeps down the hall, gently opens the lounge door and slips into the room. Light sneaks in behind her and she pushes the door to, so as not to disturb him if he is still sleeping. Chris yawns and Emma listens to the bristly scuff as he rubs his face. He pats the space beside him, and she lifts the duvet's soft, wash-worn cover and joins him under it.

Chris, still sleepy and warm, turns on his side to spoon her, the centre of the bed dipping to cradle their weight as he slings his arm over her hip. Drowsy and undressed, he's also stripped of worry.

'Em,' he begins.

She shushes him, and he acquiesces, slipping his hand under the waistband of her pyjamas. Though she can't retract the spill of spare skin, Emma automatically breathes in. She remembers standing in front of the bedroom mirror, naked, one evening, years ago. Chris came up behind her and instead of doing as she expected – placing his hands over her breasts – he positioned them on her hips and manoeuvred the baggy skin, smoothing it back, out of sight. She didn't know if his action was spontaneous or if he'd been wondering for some time whether it might be possible to excavate the old contours of her hips. They'd stood there, staring at her reflection; at the plane of her newly taut belly, the bones on either side of it jutting like a pair of kerb stones until, with a small harrumph, he'd let go, and her skin fell into its seasoned furrows.

Chris reaches past her stomach and slips his hand into her knickers. Emma closes her eyes. She can already feel his cock nudging her backside. There's still this, she thinks, last night's exasperation temporarily cordoned as she wills him to continue.

He does, tugging her pyjamas and underwear down before subjecting his boxers to swift rearrangement. She tilts her hips and he slips inside her, insistent, deft fingers resuming their work. And she can feel his breath on her neck, the brush of his beard, the bulk of him against her back, and she is nearly there, a few more seconds—

The door opens and light from the hall seeps into the room.

'The kettle's boiled,' James says.

'I know,' Emma replies, glancing down at the duvet, relieved that the outline of their bodies is conceivably innocent.

'Shall I pour water in the mugs before I go?'

'No, it's OK,' she says, Chris's breath escaping into her shoulder like a puncture. 'Are you getting a cold, James?'

'God, not now, Em,' Chris mutters.

'You sound a bit croaky. Have you got your scarf? Wear it round your face and it'll warm the air. Don't tut. And make sure you've got your inhaler.'

'All right, see you later, Emma-Jane.'

James leaves the lounge door open behind him – of course he does. They wait for the sound of the back door to mark his exit.

'Did he sound croaky to you?' Emma asks as Chris's fingers resume their work. 'If he's getting a cold, there's a good chance it'll settle on his chest on Christmas Night or Boxing Day, and I'll end up on the phone trying to persuade someone in a call centre that he needs—'

'Shush. Focus.'

But Emma can't find her way back; her orgasm lay at the end of a line of concentration – the rip cord to her engine, and she has lost it.

Eventually she murmurs, 'Just come.'

'You, too,' Chris replies.

'Go on,' she insists, 'Now. Do it now.'

And he does, thinking, Emma imagines, that she has retrieved the tail of her former excitement, when in fact she has heard the floor creak in the room above and knows it won't be long before Janet's slippered feet are visible through the still-open lounge door, as she shuffles down the stairs to empty her bladder.


## NOW AND NOW


Here's James Abram, pedalling down Moss Lane as the heavy sky drips like a saturated sponge. Hood up over his helmet, empty newspaper bag flapping at his side, James follows a trail of widely spaced streetlights illuminating the left-hand side of the narrow road; there is no pavement to his right, just a ditch, hardly visible in the present dark.

James used to cycle to the roundabout, turn left and continue for a mile or so before dismounting to collect the papers. But the newsagent went bust three months ago and his round was transferred. Now, he must cross the roundabout and head down Roe Lane and into town where the streets are strewn with chip wrappers and polystyrene burger boxes, the skies with screaming gulls.

Out on the Moss, a dank, tuna-ish smell occasionally perches on the breeze, but in town it permeates. Every breath is salt and vinegar and each morning, as James fastens his bike to the leg of a sign displaying the number of available parking spaces, he is reminded that he lives by the sea.

Across the street, the arcades and ice-cream shops hibernate. The shop beside the newsagent remains in darkness, 'EVERYTHING MUST GO' written on the glass. But in the sandwich bar and the pub that serves breakfast, the lights are on and staff are arriving.

In addition to papers and magazines, the newsagent sells buckets and spades, plastic windmills and over-bright images of the town printed on postcards, fridge magnets and boxes of fudge. In the pictures, the sand resembles caramel and the sea and sky are matching shades of turquoise; proof, James decided when he first saw them, that long before the invention of smartphones and Instagram, humans had the will and the means to lie about the world.

His new employers aren't unfriendly, but they never ask James whether he is tired, or if he has any exams coming up. They certainly don't appear to notice him enough to remark on his height or joke that he must be watering his feet with Miracle-Gro. He is the only paper *boy*; the other employees are adults. James doesn't speak to any of them beyond 'Hello', and occasional weather-related observations, though you can't help but learn things about people – they shed information like they shed skin and hair. Reg, who has been retired for ten years, wears spandex leggings and rides a wafer-thin racing bike. Zofia does her round in a clapped-out Fiesta after finishing a night shift at one of the care homes on the promenade. Liam lived at home while he went to university in Preston, keeping his round during his studies. When James first started here, the others would enquire about Liam's post-graduation job hunt. No one asks any more.

Standing beside the counter, James opens his waterproof bag so Terry can stuff it with papers. This is the moment when he should ask Terry a question about himself or remark on the weather. Dylan would think of something. Last time James had a hockey match in Carlisle, meaning an early-morning start, Dylan reluctantly covered for him and subsequently mentioned the recent death of Terry's mother and his inheritance, which amounted to an extensive Toby Jug collection and a grumpy cat called Keith.

The weekend papers are thick and heavy. James could deliver them on foot, accompanied by a trolley, but it would take ages, so he cycles, the chock-a-block bag looped across his body, banging his hip as he tries to counter-balance the weight. He wobbles past the amusements and several empty shops – his mother counted thirty last time she drove this way. He passes clusters of still-occupied sleeping bags and hurries on, past the war memorial and the remaining library, which is always closed when he passes. Fortunately, he isn't short of reading material. His Chemistry teacher Mrs Coe brings old copies of the *New Scientist* to school, and James is alternately thrilled and troubled by what he reads. Each morning as he performs his loop of the sleepy streets, he makes space in his mind for the quiet despoiling of the world's protected areas, or the decline of fresh water supplies, or the making of life from scratch, newly aware that what he knows about the world amounts to almost nothing. How insignificant he is. And how small the people around him suddenly seem, how ludicrous their aspirations and pressing concerns.

There is little point in discussing his reading with his family. His dad gets angry, his mother sad, and Dylan is indifferent. So James keeps things to himself. Recently, he has read that time is not linear. It doesn't flow; it just exists. All at once. Each part of it – past, present and future – equally real. James used to think the old versions of himself had vanished. Now he pictures them hanging in the air like mist. James imagines time as a collection of 'nows' which may be examined one by one, in any order, like the recipe cards his mother keeps in a red box in the kitchen. That sounds reasonable, until he attempts to mark a 'now' in his mind, and it is like catching a bubble: gone the moment it is grabbed.

Now, James circles the roundabout at the northern end of Lord Street.

Now, he notices the busted Christmas sign sitting in the roundabout's centre: 'WELCOME TO' it reads, the bottom half unlit.

Now, he pedals past Hesketh Park, centenarian trees looming like giants in the dark.

Now, he leans his bike against the wall of number 36.

Now, he sees something on the pavement.

Now, he bends to see better: a scattering of long twist nails with round, flat heads.

Now, he thinks of his poor tyres and kicks the nails into the gutter.

Now, he hurries down the dark path.

Now, he folds the paper, thick with its Sunday supplements.

Now, he scans the door for his tip – at some point during December most people put one in a Christmas card and affix it with Sellotape.

Now, he attempts to push the paper through the letterbox and into the mesh cage the owner has fitted to the back of the door, so they don't have to bend to pick things up.

Now, the paper is stuck behind another paper which remains in the box, and James remembers: the same thing happened yesterday and the day before.

He loses track of time, the nows no longer coming one after another, but all at once as he tuts and wiggles and pushes. Hurry, hurry, hurry.

Finally, he jams the paper behind its forerunners and then he zips down the path and jumps on his waiting bike, resuming his deliveries until, eventually, he heads for home, empty bag flapping at his side as he cycles past the terrace of nineteenth-century fisherman's cottages and the houses built on the plot of the demolished library where his mother used to work. Past the shops that circle the roundabout at the end of Moss Lane: the bakery, the pharmacy, the off-licence, and the barber shop – empty again but, before long, another young man, slick with optimism and moustache wax, will surely stand behind the latticed window, fretting about the lack of parking and clients.

James turns down Moss Lane. Past the golf club and the cul-de-sac of expensive houses. Past the bungalows and the orchard where rows of skinny trees quiver in the breeze. Past the allotments. And then the white lane-lines disappear. The road narrows, the vista widens, and in the feeble dawn of another wet morning, the flat fields emerge.

There is something about these early, all-weather outings that makes James dizzy. He imagines this part of his life as a hammer throw; around and around he goes until, eventually, he'll have built up enough momentum to fly far, far away. There are places he would like to see before they are irredeemably altered. He is decades too late for his own beach which, according to his mother, *did* once resemble the over-bright pictures on the newsagents' postcards, and was advertised as 'seven miles of golden sand'. When she said this, James and Dylan laughed like drains, though after she left the room, James said, 'Is there anything they haven't fucked up yet?' and Dylan muttered, 'Heavy!' – his go-to response when he wants to acknowledge a person's feelings without getting involved.

James read about the beach, hoping to discover why it now looks like a meadow in summer and a swamp in winter. There was speculation that spartina had spread along the sand because the chemicals formerly used to kill it had been outlawed. He read that fertilisers were washing off fields and into the rivers and the sea, feeding the unsightly grass. If it wasn't for the spartina, it was claimed, there would be wind-blown sand rather than vegetation resting against the sea wall.

'Not so,' his father insisted. 'They sold the sand. Twelve million tonnes of it. When the sand was there, it kept the silt from the Ribble at bay. Now? Well.'

'Was that the issue, though?' his mother wondered. 'I thought it was because there's no dredging in the estuary now. It's complicated, and I don't think you can blame—'

'I mostly blame the RSPB,' his father interrupted. 'They're the ones demanding the beach be abandoned to a *natural process*. And it's not just them. It's incredibly convenient for the council to suddenly embrace nature, isn't it? Doing nothing costs nothing – in the short term, anyway. It's all very well for the RSPB to encourage growth in migratory bird populations but they're doing it at the expense of *our* habitat. What do we get? A few marsh harriers and an invasion of mosquitoes.'

Who was right? James had no idea. They're hopeless: his mother, his father and the people arguing online – the whole lot of them. They can't agree about anything, including where to apportion blame: in his mother's mind it's no one's fault; in his father's it's everyone's. James sometimes wonders if his parents even like each other. He isn't sure whether he likes them: his father, stomping about, spewing news articles, his lit fuse burning towards some sort of explosion; and his mother, hiding upstairs in her sewing room, spinning gold out of old curtains like a princess in a tower. Boo-hoo, Emma-Jane, he thinks, newly aware of her as an actual person, faults and all; irritated by the way she measures her life via the library: BC and AC – before closure and after closure. Why didn't she *do* something, if she was so upset? She could have chained herself to the railings or superglued her hands to the counter.

James is currently staging his own protest by making himself disagreeable. In minor ways, but just enough, he hopes, to be irritating. He calls his mum Emma-Jane because he knows it makes her feel small. And she *is* small; she becomes less substantial all the time – he can already imagine a now when she is just a ghost. His annoyance with his father needs less nourishment – it's organic. James asks questions intended to annoy him. What reasonable parent can get angry with a teenager for showing an interest in the world around them?

James's mother has several aerial atlases. Hefty hardbacks with glossy full-colour pages. Coffee-table books, she calls them. They don't have a coffee table, so the books sit in a pile on the floor beside the sofa and when the boys were younger, Dylan browsed the Argos catalogue, biro at the ready, circling everything he fancied, while James studied the atlases and slid strips of paper between the pages of the places he most wanted to see. Then he'd show his mother who would say, 'That looks like quite an adventure!'

Now, when he talks about the future she says, 'You can live here for as long as you like,' anticipating the day when he, like everyone else his age, can't afford to leave home.

There are things James would like to see before they are forever altered, such as the Great Barrier Reef, Florida's prehistoric shell middens, and a 500,000-year-old geo-thermal pool in Nevada called Devil's Hole which is home to the world's rarest fish. James wants to stand on the viewing platform above Devil's Hole and imagine the cavern, so deep its bottom remains unmapped and so mysterious that its water occasionally sloshes about in a mini tsunami, signalling earthquakes in other parts of the world. The Devil's Hole pupfish has been living there for sixty thousand years. There are fewer than a hundred left now. No one knows why they are dying or whose fault it is. EVERYTHING MUST GO, he thinks.

James cycles on. Now, he approaches Three Pools Waterway. Formed from Fine Jane's Brook, Sandy Brook and Drummersdale Drain, Three Pools Waterway runs along the eastern boundary of the town. In previous nows, the water was everywhere. In this now, the water has a primed feeling as if its memory of old haunts hasn't faded, and while there is a politeness in its present occupation of this channel, it makes no promises. The arable fields and scrubland alongside Three Pools Waterway are at risk of surface-water flooding but, much to James's father's annoyance, the network of field drains and ditches located just outside the urban area has not been explicitly modelled for flood risk. There have been watery incursions. Not too far from here, and not so long ago, a tributary of the River Douglas burst its banks and tumbled into the sur-rounding fields. Crops were ruined, fifteen hundred newly planted trees submerged, and thirteen lucky chickens balanced on the roof of their floating coop until they were rescued by a dinghy.

Here is the spot where the sodden fields dip to cradle the waterway. Where, one August afternoon many summers ago, James and Dylan, slippery as eels, wriggled past the back gate and down the lane, and James, in his eagerness to both accompany his brother and draw their naughtiness to a speedy conclusion, accidentally slid down the bank and into the water. In a previous now, water pumps at the local pumping station failed, causing oxygen levels in the watercourse to fall, killing thousands of fish. But by the time James broke the glassy-dark skin of the waterway, it been restocked with tench, perch and pike from Skegness. James did not see any fish. He was – *is* – a terrible swimmer. At least when his bike has a tricky puncture, he can remove the inner tube, inflate it and hold it under water to clock the escaping bubbles; he has yet to discover the fault in him that leads the air to leak and his middle to sink.

Dylan slid in after him. Dylan dragged him out of the waterway and tugged him, stumbling and soaked, back down the lane and through the gate. Dylan concocted a story to explain their wetness. Dylan connected the hose to make the story true. And Dylan went to bed early after their mother caught him spraying a trembling, crying James in the face.

'You're not like your brother, are you?' adults frequently remark.

When said to James, it's a compliment. When said to Dylan, it isn't. Yes, Dylan is like a shaken bottle of pop, but under the fizz and the mess, he is inclined to kindness. Whereas James, like water, is disposed to accommodation and appeasement and favours the path of least resistance. This ease of compliance, he has noticed, is easily mistaken for goodness.

Here is the bridge over Three Pools Waterway and the spot where James's father used to take the boys on summer nights for bedtime re-enactments of 'The Three Billy Goats Gruff'. At the end of the story, one eye on the traffic and the other on his sons, he would stand on the town side of the bridge, gurning and growling as he counted to three. And James and Dylan, their howls equal parts fear and pleasure, would snatch their head start and sprint along the track, all the way home.

Here is the spot where James, initially enlisted as lookout, smoked weed with Dylan and his friends on a more recent summer afternoon, gradually becoming attuned to the way his T-shirt embraced his shoulders like a pair of cotton hands, and the aliveness of the grass, which he believed he might catch in the act of breathing, if he only focused hard enough. Emboldened by the new clarity of his thoughts and Dylan's friends' laughter, James expounded on the joy of August when, following his birthday, he catches up with Dylan and they are, for a few weeks, the same age. He also recounted the story of the group of young men who went diving in Devil's Hole one night in the 1960s, two of whom were never found. Dylan's friends pronounced the tale 'heavy' and haven't asked James to be lookout again.

Here is the water main that runs under the bridge. Here is the leak that started many weeks ago and was finally reported by an observant angler who was told it may take some time for United Utilities to apply to the council to close the road for the work to be carried out. Here is the escaping water, pouring down the bank and undermining the foundations of the bridge. Here is the crack in the concrete.

Here is James Abram, pedalling down Moss Lane as the heavy sky drips like a saturated sponge. Hood up over his helmet, empty bag flapping at his side, James travels down the lane and through time, never quite reaching the future which lies just beyond the now, now, and now.

## O, CHRISTMAS TREE

'I thought I'd get started on Chris's packed lunch,' Janet says as Emma steps into the kitchen. 'What do you usually make?'

'I'm not sure if he's got any work on this morning. Things are very quiet. And he makes his own lunch.'

'He's always liked a nice cheese sandwich. I'll do him one, shall I?' Janet opens the fridge and locates the cheese. 'And I'll tell him to move that ladder out of the way. He shouldn't have left it here. Men don't think, do they?'

'Oh, I brought it in. I'm going to …' Emma pauses as she notices steam rising from the bubble-filled sink. 'What are you …?'

'My washing. Just my underwear. Saves you using the machine.'

'I use it pretty much every day. There's a washing basket in the bathroom. Just put your things in it and—'

'Oh, I don't want to be any trouble,' Janet says as she slices lumps of cheese from the block and lines them on the bread where they zigzag like a corrugated roof.

'Janet, you are no trouble. I'm happy to do your washing in the machine with everyone else's. I'm going to make coffee. Would you like one?' Emma takes a third mug from the cupboard and spoons coffee into it. 'I boiled the kettle, earlier, but it looks like you've ...' Emma nods at the sink.

'Here, let me.' As Janet refills the kettle, its bottom dips in the steaming knicker-juice. 'There you are. Anything else I can help you with?'

'I don't think so.'

'What are you up to today?'

'I need to tidy up and—'

'You'll be buying a tree.'

'I tried to resurrect last year's, but it's a lost cause, and Chris hasn't had much work, so it's probably better if we just—'

'Oh dear, I'm sure it's not his fault—'

'—improvise this year—'

'—and it would be such a shame not to have a tree. It's an important part of Christmas, don't you think? And you *always* have one.' Janet wrings out her knickers and rests them on the dish rack. 'When Jesus was born it was winter and all the trees in the world shook off their snow and produced green shoots. It was a miracle. *That's* why we have Christmas trees.'

'Oh, I've never heard that before. I remember reading that trees were props in mystery plays during the Middle Ages. The twenty-fourth of December was Adam and Eve's feast day and they would pick a tree to represent the tree from the Garden of Eden, the one with the fruit, you know? They'd choose an evergreen and hang apples from it. But the plays were banned at some point, and people started putting trees in their houses, where they could enjoy them in private, instead.'

'Well, I don't know about that.'

'It's just something I read. I like your story too, with the snow and the green shoots—'

'Oh, it's not a *story*—'

'—it's a reminder, in the depths of winter, that spring is on its way.'

'Well, I suppose you *could* say that,' Janet replies, though it's clear *she* wouldn't.


The Christmas decorations live in a box under the stairs. Every year as Emma undresses the tree and carefully coils ropes of lights around empty wrapping-paper rolls, she wonders what life will be like when she next unravels them. Many months later, she opens the box, aware of all that has happened in the intervening time: the surprises and disappointments, and the pleasure of still being alive to contemplate them. Haunted by the slightly younger and less-informed self who packed away the decorations, Emma often wishes she could wind back time to offer reassurance or comfort; to say, 'Dylan will do so much better at school,' or 'I'm sorry, but they'll close the library, after all.' Today, in amongst the lights and decorations, she finds several DVDs, packed away for rediscovery. She examines them for a moment and then tucks them back in, burying them under a string of battery-operated snow-flake lights.

The stepladder waits in the kitchen. Now, with Chris and Janet at the caravan looking for the insurance documents and the boys upstairs watching something funny, judging by their distant hoots, Emma brings the ladder into the lounge where the sofa bed has been folded away and the bedding arranged neatly on the floor beside her stack of coffee-table books. She positions the ladder where she would usually place a tree, making sure the spreaders are locked so it is stable, smiling to herself as she adapts the words of the song: *O Christmas tree, O Christmas tree, How steadfast are your spreaders!* Then, having tested the lights, Emma wraps them around the ladder's metallic top and zigzags them between its long green legs. She hangs plastic candy canes between the bulbs and flicks the switch. It'll do, she thinks.

Emma hid the DVDs in the understairs cupboard on a Friday evening, eighteen months ago. She and Chris have tried to do something together on Friday nights since a game of snakes and ladders, played as they tidied up the boys' mess at the end of the day, resulted in a rematch the following week, and a game of snakes, ladders and shots, the week after. More recently, they have taken to banishing the boys to their room by ten o'clock and commandeering the television, taking it in turns to choose something to watch, often keeping their choices quiet until the night itself. Sometimes they pick for each other. Sometimes they choose something neither has seen – that's why they watched *The Exorcist* which, disappointingly, failed to scare either of them. Other times, they pick entirely for themselves, knowing the non-picker will suffer dutifully since revenge could be exacted later. Once, Emma made Chris watch the BBC adaptation of *Pride and Prejudice*, six hours spread over three weeks. Afterwards, he occasionally said: 'I must have my share in the conversation,' if, like Lady Catherine de Bourgh, he suspected he had missed out on something interesting. Once, on a lazy night when neither had thought of anything, they flicked through the TV menu and watched a documentary about polyamory.

'I think we should invite a third person into our relationship,' Emma joked afterwards, in bed.

'Oh, *great* idea.'

'But it'll have to be a man,' she added quickly.

Chris made an agreeing sound. 'I know just the person,' he said. 'Let's invite *Jesus* into our lives,' and they lay in the dark, sniggering, for ages.

Eighteen months ago, on the night in question, Emma was curled up on the sofa, one glass of wine down and another on the go, waiting to be entertained.

While Chris fiddled, first with the television, and then his phone, she told him about a tiny story she had read years ago called 'Jam', in which a woman had thanked her fiancé, firstly for agreeing to marry her, and secondly for being willing to accept her three ugly children. Her fiancé was shocked. He knew nothing about the children.

'To begin with,' Emma explained, 'it was a love story. But the addition of the ugly children, whose faces were sticky with jam – did I mention the jam? – turned it into something else.' Comedy, she asserted that night as she tipsily thanked Chris for marrying her.

Now, when she considers 'Jam', Emma isn't sure it's funny. It is, she suspects, more horror than love story. And perhaps there's a fine line between the two, finer than she had previously imagined.

Still, on the night in question, she was lounging on the sofa, thinking of the 'thank you so much for marrying me' part of the story, grateful that the young man in the tight T-shirt and chainsaw trousers was also the man with greying hair and capable hands who wanted to spend his Friday nights beside her.

Chris's selection that Friday evening was not a film. He'd chosen a mockumentary, which he streamed from YouTube, a dramatic, earnest production that cut between segments of interviews with 'experts' and enactments of a fictional global pandemic. For a time, Emma expected Chris to lampoon it. There had to be something – a rogue special effect, a particularly appalling section of dialogue, the American announcer's deep and humourless voice, a punch-line – Chris was waiting for her to appreciate and mock.

'In a long-term crisis, there will come a point when your city will be uninhabitable, and you'll be forced to move on,' the announcer declared.

'Really? Why?'

'Shush, Em.'

'But why will people have to move? I mean, all the infrastructure's right there, they've got shelter and—'

'Shush.'

There were tremendous traffic jams. The roads couldn't cope with the number of people trying to leave cities. People were dying in their cars, obstructing the routes out.

'Why are they dying in their cars? *Where* are they going? They're leaving their homes for total uncertainty. Why would anyone do that?'

'Shush.'

A group of men blocked a motorway. They had guns. The announcer revealed they were masquerading as police.

'Look – they're not even robbing people; they're just blocking the road and waving their guns around. What's the point of that? They're not getting anything out of it. Why aren't *they* leaving the city, too?'

'Are you even listening?'

'Yes, but—'

'In a pandemic, cities are most vulnerable because of population density – that's what he said.'

'What's the difference between a pandemic and an epidemic?'

'Are you making a *joke*?'

'No, I'm asking—'

But he shushed her again, this time pressing a finger to his lips.

'I'm absolutely convinced …' one of the experts began. He didn't cite any supporting evidence. It was all opinion. And though Emma was dying to interrupt the commentary, which was essentially a series of equivocations, Chris appeared to be watching seriously. So she sipped her wine and listened. She learned that in the event of a pandemic, hospitals would close, locking everyone out. Health-care providers would hide their skills and desert patients in order to protect their own families. Chaos would ensue. She glanced at Chris's face, which was solemn, set. The internet would fail and everything else would stop working – planes, trains, fuel deliveries and production lines. Shops wouldn't be able to restock. An average family has enough spare food for three days, someone said. Emma considered climbing off the sofa and stepping into the kitchen where she knew she'd be able to disprove it, or at least demon-strate they were far from average. The claims had the ring of received wisdom: you only use 10 per cent of your brain; 90 per cent of communication is non-verbal; there are seven different learning styles.

'*When* the lights go out,' someone began, and Emma zoned out. She was part way through her third glass of wine by then, cheeks humming like a pair of fan heaters.

She resumed concentration during a discussion of the problem of unburied bodies; thousands were rotting in the streets, leading to dysentery, cholera and famine. She was unclear as to how the presence of bodies led to famine; perhaps she had missed something. She paid more attention as a story emerged: a family – father, mother and teenage son – caught up in the terrible situation. Sewage plants were down and there was no longer any running water. The highly strung mother was elected to empty family-sized buckets of waste into a hole in the back garden. She was going to get hysterical. Emma could feel it coming. Here was a woman who was about to get slapped, hard. And all for her own good, of course.

'Do we know *any* women like that? Do you think they exist outside the imaginations of male writers?'

Chris ignored her.

Emma learned that sociopathic individuals would prey on other people. Prisons would empty as guards died and the remaining inmates revolted. Supermarkets would be stripped bare in a matter of days and marauding gangs would case the cities, grabbing food and medicine. It sounded more and more like a video game or a Stephen King novel.

After a failed shopping trip, the father of the family realised the key to survival was invisibility. He tried to make it look like the family home had already been looted by throwing bed linen on the front lawn. The mother reacted hysterically, sobbing because the scattered sheets were freshly laundered. She was slapped. Emma tutted. Chris stared straight ahead, refusing to look at her. She could see even the smallest aside about sexism would go down badly, so she emptied her third glass and considered a fourth.

It was Friday night, so they would have sex, though she suspected she might have had too much wine to enjoy it as much as she would like. Friday-night sex is a habit, not an obligation. Chris always knows when they last had sex. He doesn't mention it unless she enquires – it would be irritating if he announced it unprompted, like a pestering child. But if she ever asks, he knows. It's written in him, like a fossil record. And that's what Emma thought about as the mockumentary concluded. Sex. And whether they should head upstairs or just push a chair against the lounge door and do it right there, on the sofa. But when the music faded, Chris sat in silence, awaiting her response.

'What did you think?' he asked, finally.

She deliberated. For several months he had been making morose asides, but perhaps what she had categorised as misanthropy was fear. She wondered whether it was the moment to repeat some of the things she had been muttering to herself while washing the dishes or feeding fabric through the sewing machine, like an actor learning her lines: 'The thing is, we – humans, that is – survived the financial crash, the Japanese tsunami, Ebola' – the list varied, depending on what had featured on the news – 'and here we are. What if we survive more terrible things? Or is that too boring to contemplate? Are you longing for a life-changing disaster? Are you searching for a catalyst to get you out of this boring, everyday world?'

'I think ...' She responded, hesitatingly. 'I think as the world gets more complicated there are more ways things can fall apart. But I don't think it's going to be exciting. What if we get the apocalypse we deserve? What if it's a shit one, and it's just fake news, junk food and internet trolls? What if life goes on like that until it becomes unbearable? Basically, I thought it was fear-mongering bullshit. A survivalist's wet dream.'

He nodded, once, like a headbutt. Then he went upstairs and Emma, feeling as if she'd been left alone to think about what she had done, finished the wine. She took the empty bottle to the kitchen and dropped it in the plastic box with the other recycling before clumsily opening a cupboard and removing the mixing bowls and chopping boards to uncover the birthday presents she had been collecting for Chris: an emergency tyre-repair kit, a pair of waterproof deerskin gardening gloves and a small stack of reconditioned DVDs she'd bought from Poundland. Each DVD addressed a different meteorological phenomenon – hurricanes, blizzards, thunderstorms – and she had thought them ideal for her weather-watching husband. On reflection, she slipped the DVDs into the understairs cupboard where they'd sat behind the hoover and the picnic hamper that used to belong to her grandparents until months later when she swept them up with the lights and decorations in the post-Christmas clear-up, to be rediscovered in the future, when, she hoped, the world – *her* world in particular – might look different.

Eventually, she had followed Chris up to bed. When she got there, he was pretending to be asleep, but his tempered breathing gave him away and she knew he was stewing over her insufficient response. Maybe that was the start – no, not the start, but an irrefutable symptom of something that had been incubating for ages.

It would be nice, Emma decides, to see her improvised tree from outside. She collects her coat and trainers from the kitchen, walks back through the hall and out of the front door, into the dank, rain-clotted air.

The stepladder generates a triangle of light. It looks cosy and Christmassy. Incongruous, too, she thinks, in the absence of seasonal weather. She misses frigid air and silver skies, the crisp winter days when dawn mists ghost the wetland soil and the germs of myths and legends hang in the haze. When, walking the surrounding roads, breath like dragon smoke, it is possible to imagine how it might have been, years ago, for people living in these newly drained outskirts, fearful of the remaining marshland and on the lookout for boggarts hiding in the sluices and ditches, lurking under bridges and on the sharp, dangerous bends of dog-leg roads. Every sigh of wind, every rustle of leaves might be one, ready to jump on the shoulders of an unwary passer-by or take the form of an apparition: a headless woman, a white greyhound, a cow with eyes like saucers; each manifestation a harbinger of death.

And she misses other things, besides the weather. Camaraderie, friendship, the sense of being in this – marriage, parenthood, *life* – together. By hiding the DVDs, she, like Chris, created a stockpile for the future, only hers was meant for when things got better. But they're getting worse. Now, Chris spends Friday nights on his laptop, reading terrifying blogs. She spends them sewing, usually upstairs because to sit beside him is to invite apocalyptic commentary, and she won't listen.

Emma turns to face the road and there, on the lip of pavement that only runs for a few hundred yards along the nearside of the road, is the sandwich board, left out, she assumes, as a reproach to passing motorists. She strides out, grabs the sign and folds it flat. If she was as tall as Chris, she'd be able to slide it under one arm. Instead, she carries it, arms extended, as she would a soiled child. As she passes her car, she pauses for a moment to examine a line of green along the bottom of the passenger window. Moss. There is moss growing on her car.

The wind whips misty cloud into sticky wads, and the steady mizzle thickens to rain. The power is out again. Emma focuses on the novelty – cosiness, candlelight, Christmas Eve tomorrow! – hoping to divert Chris from dark inferences of unease and gloom.

Though it is far from cold, Janet sits at the table, arms crossed, cardigan buttoned up to her neck. Emma glances at Chris and their boys. When Dylan and James were small, she didn't want to carry or push them all the time. She wanted them to experience mud, crunchy leaves and puddles, so she bought some reins. But oh, it took ages to get anywhere. Giddy-up, giddy-up, she used to think, the reins slack in her hands. There were so many times when she wished things would happen faster. Nights when Chris lay on the landing, across the boys' doorway like a draught excluder, listening to James's croupy breathing or primed to pounce if Dylan attempted another breakout. Giddy-up, giddy-up: past spelling practice and times-table tests, past the muggy poolside wait of swimming lessons, past hurried drop-offs at breakfast club before dashing to work at the library. And now their entire childhood flashes past in a blur – was that *it*? How can it have passed so quickly? – and if there were still reins, Emma would be tugging on them: *Whoa, whoa!* This season's football and hockey leagues are already half completed; Dylan and James may only have one more season playing with these teammates, boys Emma has known since they were soft-skinned, with high, sweet voices. Exams are coming, the year after next. They'll be off to college before she knows it. There's no slowing this. Instead of *Whoa, whoa!* she will have to say *Goodbye, goodbye!* And here is Janet, cardigan crossed tight, staring at Chris in the candlelight. Is she wondering where the time went? Emma imagines a future in which she is sharing a table with her own boys, bearded, middle-aged, their faces lined and wea-thered. It is enough to make her eyes sting.

'I would like …' Janet begins.

Emma nods instantly. Having assumed Janet's sadness, she is keen to be accommodating.

'… to say grace at mealtimes.'

Emma's fork stops mid-air. Looking from Janet to Chris she tries, and fails, to think of a response that will please them both.

'I wouldn't tell you *not* to say grace in your home, Mum,' Chris says.

'Oh, I know, dear.'

'So I don't think you should expect to say it in ours.'

'Does it matter?' Emma asks, embarrassed.

'It's not important,' Janet says. 'I'd hate …'

No one asks what Janet would hate. No one starts their meal, either. The candle flame bends this way and that, and steam rises from five plates of vegetable chilli. Emma can smell the pears she blanched and bagged up in August, since defrosted and, thankfully, poached in the slow cooker before the power went off.

'You know Callum?' Dylan says.

'Yes,' Emma replies, grateful for the interjection.

'He supports Stockport. His dad supported them. And he's dead, Callum's dad.'

'Oh, that's awful. You never said.' Emma recasts Callum's sullen expression and nasty barking laugh as affectations, armour to cover his grief.

'So Callum supports Stockport, too. They're a bit crap. That's not an opinion; it's a fact. But no one would say that to Callum because they're important to him, with his dad and everything.'

Emma waits, but Dylan has finished, clearly feeling he has done his bit for soothing family relations by likening a belief in God to supporting a third-rate football team.

Chris shovels a forkful of chilli into his mouth and the boys follow. Emma waits for Janet to start before employing her fork.

'Well, it's edible,' Dylan says, mouth half full.

'Thank you. It's been my lifelong ambition to put a tremendous amount of work into feeding people, day after day after day, and then listen as they damn my efforts with faint praise. I hope it's something you all achieve in your lives too.'

James laughs, but Janet seems concerned.

'We don't do these things for praise though, do we, Emma?'

James's laugh segues into a cough.

'Oh, I think praise and gratitude are quite different,' Emma says, glancing at Chris: yes, he noticed the cough, too. 'Have you checked on the rabbits, yet?' she asks. She is concerned about them; they don't seem happy. But then, neither does Chris – perhaps she should ask him to check on himself, while he's at it.

'Remind me again when it's light,' he says.

'I was thinking we could move them into the garage where it's dry, but then they'd be in the dark. We could try them in the shed, I suppose ...'

'I'd have to put my bike in the garage,' James says.

'Not after you left it open that time. Anyone could have walked in and stolen my tools while you were delivering papers.'

'That was *months* ago. The only time anyone's ever stolen *anything* was when you took me to that hockey match in Manchester and someone crawled under the van and unstrapped the spare tyre.'

'Doesn't matter. You're not having a garage key again. Maybe you shouldn't be delivering papers at all.'

'Some people don't have the internet, Dad.'

'Getting a paper every day of the year is equivalent to taking a short-haul flight.'

'And? The internet's energy and carbon footprints exceed those of air travel, so—'

'It's really wet on the patio, Chris. And there's flies out there.'

'It'll be all the poo, Emma-Jane.'

'She's your *mum*.'

'I'm sure there used to be more flies, years ago.'

'At this time of year, Janet?'

'Just in general.'

'You know, I think you're right. When I was little, we'd drive down to Cornwall and the windscreen would be covered in insects. We'd stop for petrol and my grandad would have to wipe all the little corpses off the glass.'

'Last year in Biology we did an experiment on insect population and distribution,' Dylan says. 'Mr McDonald had this thing.'

James, mouth full, waves his fork, marking his place in the conversation before swallowing. 'A pooter,' he says.

'Yeah, that's right. And we went out on to the field and watched him do it, didn't we? The pooter had two tubes and Mr McDonald sucked on one and used the other to hoover up insects. The next lesson was Spanish, and Mr McDonald said we should tell Mrs Abanto that we'd been learning all about pooters. Because *puta* in Spanish is …' All at once it dawns on Dylan that he mustn't continue. 'Anyway …' He pauses, laughing. 'Mr McDonald is a *legend*. He's an absolute *lord*.'

'There's only one Lord, Dylan,' Janet says with a small smile.

Dylan glances at Emma. '*Lord* Voldemort,' he mimes.

Emma shakes her head at him. When Dylan was little and in trouble, he would wink or give her a double thumbs up in a calculated and often successful attempt to undermine her crossness. Emma looks down at her plate. Without an audience Dylan will stop, she thinks, but the moment she looks up, he begins again.

'The House of *Lords*,' he mouths. '*Lord* Sugar.' Or perhaps it was '*Lord* Vader.' Emma can't be sure.

'And when there are problems in the world, the Lord takes care of them,' Janet persists. She is usually circumspect, limiting sermonising to desultory asides. Perhaps Frank's absence has emboldened her.

'I'm not sure I like God's approach to problem-solving,' Chris says. 'It seems to involve a lot of smiting, and cursing, not to mention flooding. I don't think He can be relied upon to fix things. That's not how He works, is it?'

'Well,' Janet backpedals, 'it's also *our* responsibility to look after the world because the Lord has commanded it.'

'Some people might say it's our responsibility to look after the world because there's no God, and no *deus ex machina*,' Chris replies.

'Let's talk about something nice,' Emma says, topping up each cup with water.

'I read humans might evolve to survive in conditions that aren't currently suitable.'

'James, I meant something *light* and *cheerful*. That's not—'

'*Evolve?*' Janet says. 'Oh dear. If your grandad was here, he'd say, "*You* might be descended from monkeys, but I'm not." All this' – she taps the table with her fingernail – 'didn't just appear one day, out of nothing.'

'I hope you've got insurance for that claim – that's something Mr McDonald likes to say,' Dylan adds unhelpfully.

'Nothing is always *something*, though, isn't it?' James waves his hands in the air in front of him. 'I mean, you could call this nothing. Except it's oxygen, and nitrogen, and carbon dioxide—'

Dylan sniffs. 'And methane.'

'Not at the table!' Chris exclaims.

'*In the beginning,*' Janet begins, placing her knife and fork side by side on her plate, though she has barely touched her food, '*God created the heaven and the earth.*'

All right, Emma decides. In for a penny …

'I was thinking about Genesis and the creation story, not long ago,' she says, before Chris and the boys have a chance to interject. 'You know, the *darkness was on the face of the deep* part?' She begins to stack the plates, her movements nudging the air, making the candle flicker, and it is tempting to blow it out as an illustration. 'People assume it was dark because God hadn't created the light. But it'd be interesting if it was dark because something bad had happened. I know it starts with *In the beginning*. But what if, say, there had been a nuclear winter and the earth was covered in ice and a dark, smoky fog? And instead of *the* beginning, it was just *a* beginning? What if the story opened with: *In* this *beginning God created the heaven and the earth*? And what if,' Emma continues, warming to her theme, 'the division of the firmament was the separation of the ice and fog into water and cloud?'

'So, you think Genesis is about a global clean-up?' Chris asks.

'Not really, I … We need new stories, don't we? Stories that say something about the world now.'

'You don't like the old, made-up versions of the world so you're inventing your own?'

'No … I just think we could make the old stories more relevant. Anyway, it happened right here, didn't it? On the Moss. Once upon a time, our land had to be separated from the water.' Emma taps her feet on the kitchen floor. 'We're living on land that was created, especially for us.' She places the plates on the worktop beside the sink. 'And I'm not just talking about creation stories,' she adds. '"The Boy Who Cried Wolf", say. You could change it to "The President Who Cried Fake News".' She glances at Janet. Perhaps the example was unsuitable. Her mother-in-law's tendency to find her news from unconventional sources has resulted some strong and surprising opinions about American politics and politicians.

'I've got one,' James says. '"Snow White and the Seven Wharfs".'

'What's that about, then?' Dylan asks.

'Ice melt and rising seas.'

Emma lifts the slow-cooker lid and spoons quartered pears and warm, gingery juice into five bowls.

'"The Three Little Twigs",' Dylan says. 'That one's about green energy.'

This is better, Emma thinks as she carries the bowls to the table. It's harmless and silly, a game to see them through to the end of the meal without anyone's feelings getting hurt.

'"Aftershocks and the Free Bears",' James says. 'There's this earthquake near a zoo, and then: *RAWWW!*'

'Good one!'

'"The Ant and the Grasshopper",' Chris mutters. 'It's about an ant who prepares for winter. And he's married to a grasshopper who knits stuff and listens to audiobooks.'

Emma waits for him to look up. She meets his gaze and he returns immediately to studying the contents of his bowl. She will put up with – *is* putting up with a lot. But contempt is something else altogether.

'I was wondering why people don't think about these things. That's all,' she says.

'*Theirs not to reason why*,' Janet replies firmly.

Emma severs the softened neck of a pear with the edge of her spoon.

'*Theirs but to do and die*,' James adds.

'Tennyson,' Emma says wearily. 'The boys have been doing the poem at school—'

'*Cannon to right of them, Cannon to left of them, Cannon in front of them*,' Dylan quips, thumb and index finger mimicking a gun as, one by one, he shoots them all.

Emma sits on the sofa, the central panel of the landscape quilt resting on her lap as she examines spools of cotton, selecting colours for the echo lines within and without the appliquéd fields. The power is back on. In the first moments of its return, it always seems miraculous. Chris's laptop sits on the floor beside Emma's feet, a selection of houses in the Peak District on its screen. He has a type: unaffordable, isolated farmhouses surrounded by grassy hills. Emma doesn't like them. No matter the season in which the external photographs were taken, she imagines the houses in summer, ringed by parched, burning grass. Rather flood than fire, she thinks, though it's immaterial – they can't afford to move. Chris is angry about that, too. He says climate gentrification is the next big thing. Perhaps it won't be long before children sing 'The *Rich* Man Built His House Upon the Rock'.

Janet's elderly computer lies open on the sideboard, playing carols, accompanied by a slide show of religious art: haloed mothers, glowing babies and reverential, plump livestock. Sitting beside Emma, Janet examines *The Book of Miracles*, which Chris placed on her lap before leaving the room. Emma can't tell whether Janet is enjoying herself or merely turning the pages out of politeness.

'My favourite painting is of Milan in the eleven hundreds,' Emma says. 'It's somewhere round the middle; you'll get to it eventually. There's been a heavy snowfall, and you can just about see the roofs of the buildings. Everything's misty – blues and greys, with a soft, pink sky. In the text, underneath, it says the people fell into despair. Not because they were cold, or because they ran out of supplies. But because they couldn't visit one another. I think they got lonely.'

Janet turns a page. Emma has always struggled to know what to say to her when they are alone. For years, Janet used such moments to tell her about Chris's childhood. At first it seemed Janet was staking a claim. Later, that she genuinely believed Emma had missed out by not knowing the younger Chris. Earnest and pious in his mother's remembrances, Chris sounded like a child who, in the books of Emma's childhood, would have been de-scribed as a frightful prig.

Janet turns another page. Emma glances at the two paintings: one of an extraordinarily imprecise world map, the other of sheep standing on the banks of a canal.

'I've never understood the shepherd thing,' she says.

Janet looks up and nods encouragingly.

'I suppose lots of people kept livestock back then, so it made sense to tell stories about sheep. People could relate to it.'

'I think so, yes.'

'The Good Shepherd was searching for his sheep.'

'That's right.'

'The sheep was lost, and then he found it.'

'Yes!'

Emma thinks of the rabbits and of her and Chris's competing instincts: caring versus consumption. 'But …' she begins.

'Go on.'

'Isn't the shepherd just another kind of predator? Hasn't he saved the sheep so he can kill it later?'

It turns out that no, the Good Shepherd isn't that sort of shepherd. He's *looking after* the sheep. He doesn't *want* anything. Maybe just the wool. And the babies, when they come. But he would never *harm* his sheep. *Never*.

Emma nods, offering her agreement like an apology, and they sit quietly for a few moments, Emma thumbing the earthy colours and corrugations of the quilt panel and Janet turning the pages of the book.

'When a man's being difficult, it's best to ignore it,' Janet murmurs.

Emma suspects it is probably best to ignore your mother-in-law's marital advice too, though she can see Janet's counsel is meant kindly, woman to woman. Still, such familiarity has the potential to disrupt their present polite tolerance.

'They go through phases, men. They get big thoughts and silly ideas. We have to help them – we *want* to help them. *Thy desire shall be to thy husband*, that's what the Lord said to Eve. Do you know the Parable of the Talents?'

Emma nods. She remembers hearing it in RE and empathising with the poor fellow who chose to keep his talent safe. It had struck her as a story where intent is glossed, and outcome is all. It could be a parable about capitalism, she thinks: the rich get richer, and the poor are lazy for trying to protect what little they have.

'Frank used to say five talents go to men, and women are given two. Now, don't think he was being unfair. It has to be that way because at least half of a woman's time is going to be spent making sure the man uses *his* talents. And sometimes men get cross with us when we try to help them. But we don't take it personally, do we? We just get on with it.'

'I can see how it might have worked for you and Frank ...'

'Oh, I mean in general.'

'I'll just check on Chris.'

Emma places the quilt panel on the empty seat beside her and escapes to the kitchen where she finds him, standing in the frame of the open back door. Tiptoeing, she peers over his shoulder. The rain has stopped but the standing water hasn't dissipated. The world smells wet. She stares out into the night, understanding, yet resisting, the notion of threat.

'You were right about James,' he says gloomily.

'It's only a small cough. I shouldn't have said anything this morning – I didn't mean to worry you.'

He sighs, and she suspects he, too, is remembering winters when James's every cold developed into croup. It's possible Chris may find some reassurance in the arrival of the antibiotics, but she won't mention them – in the hierarchy of dishonesty, a lie of omission is surely less nefarious than one of commission.

'Things will be fine in a few weeks,' she says, squeezing Chris's arm. 'The rain will stop. We'll get the Charlotte potatoes planted, and the onion seeds started.' His shirt is soft with wear and washing. She presses her cheek to it. 'You know, we're full of food made in that soil. All our growing bits: hair, nails – they're almost as much a part of the land as the grass and the trees. Isn't that incredible?'

He makes a sound that is somewhere between a harrumph and agreement.

'Before long, ten per cent of people are going to have to move,' he mutters.

Emma tightens her grasp on his arm.

'Can you just *stop* it?'

He extricates himself and as he returns to the lounge, she kicks the back door shut. The slam provides a moment of satisfaction. In the quiet that follows, she hears Chris's indistinct murmuring and Janet's faint reply, her tone concerned and placatory.

She locks the door and turns out the light and then she pops into the lounge to retrieve her quilt panel and say goodnight, leaving Chris to covet unattainable houses, while Janet dutifully thumbs her way through centuries of miracles.

Having requisitioned the spare duvet and several bath towels to make a temporary mattress on the sewing-room floor, Emma lies under the velvet curtain and thinks of Janet's reference to Adam and Eve. It's hard to believe some people move through their lives lugging a six-thousand-year-old shame. Emma rolls on to her side and closes her eyes. Her shoulder objects to the density of the makeshift bed and she directs her thoughts away from the jaggy, catching pain to Chris. He grew up blighted by original sin, the consequence of Adam and Eve's curiosity and bodily appetites, resulting in the guilt of human nature. She thinks of her own boys and ex-periences a flash of smugness, before it occurs to her that they may be growing up impaired by something similar: industrial sin, caused by their ancestors' curiosity and economic appetites, resulting in the guilt of human de-nature. These moments before she drops off to sleep, when her brain logs and files the day's ideas, remind Emma of the sliding puzzles the boys used to bring home in party bags: everything is shuffled until it slots into the right place. And just as her surroundings dim and her breathing slows, Emma imagines a diptych, a side-by-side, then-and-now illustration in which Adam and Eve are tempted by fruit, high in the living branches of a tree, and, beside them, a pair of more recent ancestors are tempted by fuel, deep in the dead roots of the ground. One pair climb and reach, the other dig and retrieve. Perhaps the consequence of each sin is the same: cursed ground and children brought forth in sorrow.

# PART 3

# The End of the Road

# Christmas Eve

## THE BEST PREPARATION FOR
## THE FUTURE

James mentions the backlog of papers in the letterbox cage at number 36 as he zips up his coat, preparing to leave for his round. Chris is listening, though he's a sentence or two in arrears, his thoughts mostly occupied by the rising water. It's Emma, entering the room in her pyjamas, list clasped in her hand, who responds.

'Sorry, what did you say?'

'I was telling Dad about this house near Hesketh Park. They haven't bothered to pick up their papers for days. And they haven't left me a tip.'

'Have you told anyone?' Emma asks.

James coughs. Now he has Chris's full attention.

'I could mention it to Terry.'

'So you've been strolling up and stuffing papers into a logjam?' Emma replies.

'Yeah.'

'What were you *thinking*?'

Chris catches a flicker of something in James's eyebrows, a balk at Emma's disappointment, and almost feels sorry for him. Then it's gone and James is pushing his glasses up his nose and being facetious.

'I expect I was thinking about gum disease and Alzheimer's and whether we should all start using mouthwash. Or I might have been thinking of—'

'Why would anyone ignore their papers like that?' Emma persists. 'You'll take James, won't you, Chris? See what's going on.'

'You want me to drive into town and sit outside people's houses with the engine idling?'

'It's a one-off.'

'I'm about to fill some sandbags. We haven't got much sand, but there's compost in the shed.'

'There's not much compost, either. The water's been higher than this. Remember the storm in 2015? There's supposed to be a break in the rain soon.'

'Call the police if you're worried, Em. They'll drive round and have a look.'

'I'm sure they've got better things to do. They'd probably have to come from Crosby or Formby – when did you last see any police officers just hanging around town? James is full of cold, and it's pouring. Why don't you drive him? Isn't it too late for sandbags – can you put them down in water?'

'It's not ideal. But better late than never. We can use them indoors, as a last resort, if we have to.'

Emma glances at her list. She opens a cupboard and, lips pursed, removes bags of marshmallows, chocolate drops, orange Smarties and a box of Matchmakers.

'I thought we could make little snowmen, later, like the one from *Frozen*, and—' She stops mid-sentence. 'Are you all right, Janet?'

Chris turns to see his mother shuffling down the hall in her dressing gown. Half her hair is pressed flat to her head, the other half stands to attention and she is holding the hobby horse.

'You don't look well this morning,' Emma says. 'Sit down and I'll make you a coffee.'

'Oh, it's just a headache. Don't worry about me.'

Chris watches as Emma places a mug of coffee in front of his mother, who leans the horse against the table, as if it is joining them for breakfast.

'I'm sure your dad doesn't want you getting wet, James,' his mother says – she must have been listening on the stairs. 'You'll drive him, won't you, Chris?'

'You know, I think being decent in the present is the best preparation for the future,' Emma says, glancing over her shoulder as she empties a bag of miniature marshmallows into a Mason jar. 'If we co-operate now, we'll have people to depend on in the future. It's about building networks. Like trees and their Wood Wide Web.'

'Guess what percentage of land plants are in mutually beneficial relationships with fungi, Emma-Jane. Ninety per cent.'

'Well, there you are.' Emma opens a second bag of marshmallows. 'Even plants know it's better to work together.'

'This may shock you both, but I know a bit about plants, too. They *compete* for resources, and some of them release chemicals that *harm* their neighbours. I don't mind keeping James dry, but I'm not keen on poking my nose in—'

'Oh, but it's *Christmas*,' his mother says.

Chris feels himself yielding. Emma manages to be a good daughter by remembering birthdays, calling her parents weekly and taking the boys to Cornwall for ten days each summer holiday, usually while Chris is conveniently busy at work. For him, it has always been trickier. His mother doesn't want presents or phone calls; she wants conversion, something he is unable to offer. And so, when she asks for something that is easily accomplished, it is hard to refuse.

'Fine. Christmas taxi, neighbourhood watch, police patrol: coming up. I'll grab my coat and we'll get going.'

Chris waits outside the newsagent, wipers cutting peepholes through the rain. Each time the water clears, he is met by the words on the empty window of the shop next door: 'EVERYTHING MUST GO'.

When James returns, Chris heads for the park, eventually pulling up outside number 36. The wind is up, the temperature has dropped, and it finally feels more like winter. James leads them down the path in the thumping rain. This time, instead of ramming another paper through the letterbox, James stands under the door canopy and rings the bell while Chris, hood up, cups his hands around his eyes and presses his face to the front-room window. There's a streetlight behind them and it's too dark to see anything but its reflection.

'Did you hear it ring?'

'No.'

'Try again and listen carefully. It could be one of those quiet ones. Or maybe the batteries have died.'

'Still can't hear anything.'

Compared to its neighbours, the house looks tired. The wood-framed windows need sanding and painting, and the render is cracked and stained. Chris looks over his shoulder at the front garden. The borders are overgrown and a deep puddle in the corner opposite the gate indicates a problem with drainage. The house next door is covered in scaffolding. Looks like they've been working on the roof. Terrible weather for it.

Chris joins James on the doorstep. The end of a newspaper pokes out of the letterbox. He tugs on it. The tip is damp; at some point, the rain must have found the precise diagonal to undermine the canopy. Once he has retrieved the paper, he kneels and props the letterbox flap open with index finger and thumb. With his other hand buried up to the wrist and, fighting the draught-excluding brush, Chris pulls out another paper, and another, continuing until the opening is clear.

'Know what you looked like with your arm stuck in the letterbox? A vet! Like you were *delivering* the papers!' James's laugh catches and erupts into a motoring cough.

When the rattle has died, Chris takes his phone out of his pocket and selects the torch setting. Crouching, he props the flap open and attempts to hold back some of the bristles while checking the hall floor for a body.

'I can't see anything,' he says.

A noise from above startles them and Chris edges back on to the driveway. An elderly man leans out of an upstairs window.

'What *on earth* are you doing?' he hisses.

'Nothing! I'm not – My son, here, delivers your papers.'

James steps out from under the canopy and into the rain.

'He was worried about you,' Chris lies. 'We wanted to make sure you hadn't fallen.'

'Well, I haven't!'

'Are you unwell? Are you stuck up there? Can I call someone?'

'No, no, and no. Have you moved the papers?'

'They're on the doorstep. If you come down, I'll pass them to—'

'Put them back.'

'The cage was full; they were sticking out of the letterbox.'

'For goodness' sake, you're as bad as the neighbours.'

The rain spatters fatly on their coats. Chris shades his eyes from the drops as he studies the man, no idea what to say or do next.

'Do you want today's paper?' James asks.

'I've paid for it, haven't I?'

'So, you want me and my son to—'

'—put them *back*.'

'Jam them all …?'

'Yes! Put them back. I've got family coming later.'

'They'll be worried if they see everything hanging out of the letterbox …'

'Yes,' he agrees and closes the window.

Chris and James ram the papers back into the letterbox.

'Maybe his family don't visit very often,' James says as they head back to the van.

'I *can't imagine* why they wouldn't.'

As they climb in, James coughs again.

'Any phlegm?' Chris asks.

'Why, do you want some?'

'Is the cough in your chest, or your throat?'

'It's just a cold, Dad.'

'Your mum's going to be disappointed,' Chris says as he follows James's directions to the next house. 'She was hoping we'd save the day. Prove we're as connected as trees.'

'Poor Emma-Jane.'

'You mean Mum.' Chris indicates and pulls over. 'There's a plant that pretends to be ill. It mimics moth damage to trick larvae – they think the leaves' nutrients are already eaten and go elsewhere. We could say our friend at number thirty-six was like that. Faking it. Except, unlike the plant, he *wanted* attention.'

'Tell Mum about the faking plant and she'll say, "Oh, that's really interesting." She'll mean it, too.' James unfastens his belt, opens the door and jumps into a puddle. 'You'll have to try harder to annoy her,' he says as the door slams behind him.

Oh, to be fourteen years old again and think he'd got the measure of his parents. To see their relationship in simple, two-dimensional terms: a goodie and a baddie, a leader and a follower. Even as an adult, he'd had a fixed and, it turns out, inadequate understanding of his parents. His father, wandering a forty-year spiritual wilderness of his own making, and his mother, the sidekick on a journey that was not her own.

'This is, like, an actual flood,' James says as he climbs back in, shivering. 'Someone should be out here, unblocking the drains.'

Chris snorts. 'Where next?' he asks.

'Left at the end of the road. I'm not joking about the drains, Dad.'

'No one cares. Some local authorities collect information about drainage systems as part of their asset-management plans. Others don't hold *any* detailed information. They haven't got time to protect people's homes; they're too busy fixing speed cameras to traffic lights and handing out parking tickets.'

'Take the next right. Keep going. I read about this town in Australia – it was deliberately flooded by its local government. Stop by the next lamp post.'

'The Environment Agency did it in York a few years ago.' Chris pulls over again and glances at James, face partially lit by the light they're stopped under. 'What? You thought things like that didn't happen here? Only a tenth of floodplains are fit for purpose. It's a mess.'

'You think everything's a mess,' James says as he jumps out again, not giving Chris an opportunity to reply.

These quiet streets by the park are flanked by Victorian houses and developments for the over sixties. He watches as water steals down the road, crossing the drowned mouths of drains. But for the odd Christmas tree and occasional strings of outdoor lights, the houses remain in darkness. Chris thinks of the people, still sleeping, or sipping coffee in kitchens and dining rooms that face back gardens, unaware of what is happening around the front.

Unprepared, too, he suspects. Serves them right for not thinking about the future. Some of them may have walked past him in town, preoccupied by Christmas, when there are more important things to consider. He can't wait to get home and fill the sandbags. Get them stacked and shut everyone in, safe and sound.

Remembering what Emma said about not causing waves, Chris drives slowly once James returns. Still, his wheels part the water, sending it up dropped kerbs and over pavement edges where it licks walls and slinks under metal gates. He recalls the builder who dug a moat around his house several years ago. The photographs were everywhere. The house, a three-storey red-brick affair with detached garage, sat on a turf island in the middle of the flooded Somerset Levels. Might Chris have tried something similar? He could have hired a mini excavator and dug a circle around the house – double digging on a grand scale! But it rains on the just and unjust, and it rains on the inside and outside of moats; Chris can't see how a make-shift barricade would save them from standing water caused by further rain.

The steering seems off as Chris crawls along the middle of the road. Leaden, and tugging to the left. He pulls up, gets out, and walks round to the passenger wheel. The rain slaps his back as he bends, digging in his pocket for his phone. The torch reveals the problem: several roofing nails spear the tyre. There's no spare. He never replaced the one that was stolen. But Emma bought him a repair kit that he keeps in the van. The sealant should reinflate the tyre enough so he can drive home, though he may be better off staying put and seeing if someone will come out to him.

'Give me your bag,' he says to James. 'Tell me where to go, and I'll finish your round. You stay here in the dry.'

Rain hammering his hunched shoulders, Chris trudges down avenues and alleyways, along crescents and closes, until the fluorescent bag is empty of papers. Then he heads back to the van where he sits in the driver's seat, water streaming from his elbows, trousers suctioned to his calves and thighs, as he searches his phone for the number of an old customer.

'Sorry to call so early, it's Chris Abram, I used to cut your lawn … Yeah, fine thanks. I've driven over some roofing nails and I'm stuck, not far from Hesketh Park. Hang on a sec.' He presses the speaker icon so he can hold the phone away from his dripping face. 'I was wondering—'

'Get your spare on and bring the tyre over in, say, about an hour.'

'There's no spare.'

'What've you got, then?'

'Sealant foam.'

'Ah, we don't fix tyres if they've been inflated with that stuff. Use it, and you're looking at a new tyre.'

'Which will set me back …?'

'Still got the same van?'

'Yeah.'

'Somewhere in the region of a hundred quid.'

'How about a roadside repair?'

'No chance today, mate. It'll be after Christmas before we can get to you, now.'

'All right.' Chris sighs. 'But it might be repairable?'

'Might be, yeah. Depends how central the repairs are. Hopefully, you didn't pinch the sidewall between the rim and the road. Did you drive far?'

Chris thinks. The nails were probably in the gutter outside the old bloke's house – his neighbour had scaffolding up. 'Not too far,' he says.

'All right. I'll give you a call first thing on the twenty-seventh and we'll sort something out. I've been meaning to ask, by the way – you know those living walls? The missus has been going on about them. What would you grow on one?'

'Um, I'd probably go for wild strawberries, thyme, lambs lettuce, oregano …' Chris glances at the floor mat, where he is making a significant puddle. He and James will have to hang their clothes over the bath and run the dehumidifier when they get home. 'Or, if you don't want to grow food, you could try perennials: spotted deadnettle, fuchsia, evergold – probably best to think of a colour scheme and go from there.'

'Cheers. Oh, and borders – is there a particular trick to getting them looking nice all year round?'

'Tell you what, why don't I pop round and have a look?'

'Nah, I'm just asking.'

'Raising them can help in weather like this,' Chris says flatly. 'You want them multi-layered. Underplant each bed so when something dies off, the new stuff comes into season, taking its place. And think about it, logically. If you like tulips, pick a narrow-leafed kind. Then the leaves won't cover and smother whatever you've got coming up next.'

'Cheers, I'll tell the missus. Speak to you on the twenty-seventh.'

Chris puts the phone back in his pocket and stares at the rain teeming down the windscreen.

'You should have asked him a few things, Dad.'

'Like what?'

'Oh, I don't know. Like, "Where's the cheapest tyre place in town?" And, "Do you know someone who might come out before the twenty-seventh?"'

Chris smiles. 'Right,' he says. 'We're going to have to walk home. Your mother won't be happy with me ...'

'Grandad used to do that: "Oh, Nan won't be happy if you do this, or that," when it was really him who was unhappy. Maybe you don't want us to get wetter?'

'All right,' Chris says tetchily. 'I don't want us to get wetter. There. Now, let's go.'

Off they set in the sopping dark of Christmas Eve morning. Past the park and then all the way down Roe Lane, until they reach the roundabout and cross on to Moss Lane, shoulders hunched, feet plunging through puddles. As they walk, James breaks the hush with humming, occasionally allowing words to break through.

'Hum-hum, hum-hum, hum ... *beneath life's crushing load, whose forms are bending low.*'

'Oh, *cheerful*. Where's that from?'

'One of Dylan's playlists: "Miserable Christmas Songs".'

James smirks and Chris realises his mistake – having commented, he's as good as requested an accompaniment of dirges.

'Hum-hum, hum-hum, hum … *toil along the climbing way, with painful steps and slow.*'

A maintenance vehicle is parked up by the bridge, hazard lights flashing. Chris glances at the red and white water-filled traffic barriers waiting to be unloaded.

'Looks like they're finally going to have a go at the potholes,' he says.

'Really? Looks like a lot of barriers and not much else.'

'They'll only be able to do a throw-and-go job in this weather.'

'*If* that's what they're doing.'

'They'll chuck a few buckets of Ultra Crete at them. Total waste of time.'

'Oh, *cheerful*,' James says.

Chris can't remember when he was last this wet – in the bath, perhaps. They pass the vehicle and cross the bridge, almost home.

'Hum, hum-hum, hum … *Oh, rest beside the weary road.*'

'I wish you'd give it a rest.'

Dawn isn't far off. Emma will be busy in the kitchen by now. She slipped a piece of paper under one of the fridge magnets the other day: *Think of all the beauty still left around you and be happy – Anne Frank.* Chris's clothes are stuck to him, shiny, like scales. He thinks of the sea rocking along the western edge of town, of the water sneaking up on the sleeping houses by the park, of forgotten mornings walking back from the farm with his father as they talked about the end of the world. How can he be happy, knowing what he knows? No one ever said facts were bliss, did they? It's ignorance, ignorance that's bliss.


## THE IRON, THE HITCH AND
## THE WARDROBE


Janet's *family Christmas* starts here, in the Christmas Eve kitchen as she sips the dregs of her coffee.

'What are your plans for this morning?' Emma asks.

'Oh, don't worry about me. I'll think of something.'

'You could run the hoover round the lounge, if you like.'

'Hmm.'

'Or you could peel the vegetables for tomorrow and put them in some water.'

'Oh, I *could*,' Janet agrees, though she would prefer the *family Christmas* to unfurl around her as she looks on in her dressing gown.

Emma reaches into one of the bottom cupboards and retrieves a small chalkboard. 'Well, I've got lots to get ready for the party, so I'll just ...' She opens a drawer and rummages for a moment, before coming up with a stick of chalk.

'Oh yes, you mustn't let me interrupt you.'

Janet waits a while, giving Emma the opportunity to offer her a second cup of coffee or begin an interesting conversation. But Emma writes on the board, face stiff with concentration.

'I'll just …' Janet says as she stands. 'Oh, don't worry about me – I'll just.'

But Emma doesn't respond.

Upstairs, on the landing, Janet thinks of Dylan, sleeping through the overture to *family Christmas*. Her own children rarely slept in. Frank used a radio alarm – all his awakenings were communal.

The boys' bedroom door is pushed to, rather than shut. Janet knocks and waits. No answer. But since she has given fair warning, she pushes it open.

The air is dense with an oniony, teenage musk.

'Dylan?'

Though it's going on for eight o'clock, it remains dim outside. Dimmer still in the bedroom, where the blind is closed. Janet feels for the light switch. *There*. That's better.

The bed is positioned in the middle of the far wall; there's *just* enough space for it before the roof slopes on either side. She can see the hump of Dylan on the top bunk. He groans and his head disappears under the covers.

'It's Christmas Eve, Dylan.'

'I know,' he replies, voice pained and gravelly.

'There're a few things to sort out before the party,' she says importantly.

'Now?'

'Do you want to be Joseph or a shepherd?'

He groans again, and Janet waits.

'The little ones are being the Wise Men, and I'm going to ask Ruth to be Mary. So it's either Joseph or the shepherd for you and James. It would be a good idea if you wear your dressing gown. We can have a look for a matching tea towel and fasten it round your head with your dressing-gown belt.'

'I haven't got a dressing gown.'

'Why ever not?'

'Cos I'm not Sherlock Holmes,' he mutters. Finally, he moves, pushing the covers back, apparently resigned to getting up. 'Sorry – I dunno. James hasn't got one, either. Old people wear dressing gowns. No offence.'

'None taken,' she lies.

He yawns, a great sliding sound, the air rushing out of him like a puncture.

'Once you've had a shower,' Janet says optimistically, 'I'll sort you out with a costume. Joseph is the better part. And you're the oldest. Would you like it?'

'I don't have to learn any lines, do I?'

'Well,' she begins.

'I'm not good at remembering stuff. It takes me ages. Once I've done it, it sticks like sh— *glue*. Actually, I was Narrator One in the nativity when I was in Reception.'

'Oh *yes*. Grandad and I came to see you.'

'Hang on.' Dylan frowns. 'I think I can remember. *And it came to pass in those days, that there went out a decree from Caesar Augustus, that all the world should be taxed.*'

'Very good! We'll open proceedings with that, shall we?'

'If you like,' he says.

And here is some of Janet's spare love, neatly wrapped and ready to be presented to Dylan. She offers it to him in her heart, like a prayer, and immediately things she never would have accepted from her own children seem amusing. Like the time many years ago when she said, 'You're going to be seven, so you'll get seven candles.' And Dylan had replied, 'I'd rather have seven cakes, thank you.'

Janet returns to her room – Chris and Emma's room, she reminds herself. For the first time since her arrival, the weather outdoors is cool. The house feels colder, too. It doesn't help that they keep opening the skylight. She reaches up and shuts it and then she sits in the bed, legs under the covers, nice and warm.

How strange it is to be on this end of the Christmas party. In years gone by, she had no part of it until she glimpsed the tree lights shining through the window as Frank pulled on to the drive. When the front door opened, Emma said, 'Happy Christmas,' and presented them with non-alcoholic eggnog which they sipped while the grand-children circled their legs. There was singing: the carols Emma had requested, and a selection of better ones slipped in by Janet. At some point, the cousins would disappear upstairs, eventually re-emerging in an avalanche of silliness. Later, James would hand out his Christmas quiz, full of questions he'd found on the internet, and there was always a game. Last year, the game involved putting together gingerbread houses which Emma had made, flat-pack style, providing bowls of glacé icing in lieu of cement.

This year, it seems *such* a long wait until mid-afternoon and, for the first time in decades, Janet remembers listening as her mother read 'The Night Before Christmas'. How she'd ached for the moment when she would be allowed to settle down for a long winter's nap, finally waking to discover a satsuma, nuts and a new penny in the old sock at the end of her bed.

Janet lifts her Bible from the bedside table and rereads Luke's account of the Christmas story. How moved she is by the glad tidings of great joy to *all* people. It won't be long before her family is here, ready to experience the marvellous story for themselves. Which reminds her, she has costumes to organise. She puts the Bible down, climbs out of the bed and opens the wardrobe. She pulls out folded towels and sheets; her rummaging is for a good cause, and therefore permissible. Everything has been jammed in so tightly, the sheets are crushed like tissue paper. They could do with an iron, she thinks.

Janet sneaks into the sewing room. Emma hasn't forbidden her presence, it's just she's never been invited, hence it feels as though she is trespassing. On the other hand, Emma has said she must make herself at home, several times, and it's only right to take her at her word. Janet plugs in the iron and drapes the first sheet over the board. Oh, but it's fitted, and the gathered corners are all wrong for what she had in mind. Still, she'll iron it as a favour to Emma. The next sheet is also gathered at the corners and no good at all. She irons it, too, her head feeling a little better now she's up and about, and primed with coffee. A third and fourth sheet are, thankfully, flat and will make passable toga-style robes for James and Dylan. Janet irons the towels as well, just to freshen them up.

Ironing done, Janet inspects the room. She fingers a pile of folded net curtains. Emma buys them from charity shops to make into drawstring bags for fruit and vegetables.

'People don't have net curtains any more,' Emma told her. 'They're very old-fashioned.'

Janet has net curtains, but Emma must have forgotten and, not wanting to embarrass herself, as much as Emma, she decided not to mention it.

On the floor, a blue velvet curtain has been flung over a makeshift bed. Janet doesn't like to think of her son and his wife sleeping separately, especially if it's a result of her presence. Though she supposes it could be Chris's occasional crossness that has caused Emma to withdraw. Or maybe Emma's night-time absence is the *cause* of Chris's crossness; men do get terribly cross about these things.

Janet stoops to stroke the soft curtain. It would work for a Wise Man, but Janet's three Wise Men, like Jesus's, will arrive prepared. Mary, then, she thinks. Yes, she can see it draped over Ruth's shoulders. Complemented by a white towel, tied with something silvery. There are rolls of ribbon on the bookcase. Janet is certain Emma wouldn't mind if she just ... *There*: she selects a white ribbon with silver edging and lifts the velvet from the floor. Having been wrapped around Emma during the night, it is crumpled. She places it on the ironing board and heats the iron again. When Janet can hear the water spitting, she runs the iron over the velvet, a big steaming sweep, from one end of the board to the other. And, oh dear, she has somehow flattened the soft blue pile. She must have ironed in the wrong direction. Velvet is funny, isn't it? Stroke it one way and it stands up, stroke it the other and it lies down. Janet moves the iron back, this time from right to left, but fails to resurrect the pile. She puts the iron down and uses her hand; perhaps it takes fingers to right the tufts. But no, the tufts can't be righted. She has seared an arc into Emma's curtain.

Her instinct is to hide it. That would be wrong, though. She unplugs the iron, folds the velvet over her arm and heads downstairs.

'I was getting things ready for the nativity,' she tells Emma's back. 'Finding something for Ruth. To be Mary. Smoothing out some wrinkles. But there's been a small, um, hitch.'

Emma turns and approaches, arms raised, her hands crusted with flour and flecks of pastry.

'Ah yes, I see.' Emma swallows. 'You can't iron ... I'm sure you didn't mean ... You weren't to know.'

'Was it very expensive?'

'One of Chris's old ladies gave it to him.'

'Oh, thank goodness!'

It's a relief Emma isn't upset. Velvet, Janet decides, is probably as old-fashioned as net curtains. Now Emma will surely say, 'Sit down and I'll make you a drink,' or 'You must tell me about Christmases when Chris was a boy.' Janet stands, the material draped over her arm, anticipating Emma's orders like a waiter.

'Would you mind popping the curtain back in the sewing room?'

Of course Janet wouldn't mind. Not a bit. Not at all.

How hard it is to feel at home while away from home. And how hard it is to feel at home when home alone. In the first scenario, Janet must manage without comforts; in the second, without company. And up here, in the room that seemed welcoming earlier but has inexplicably grown plain and chilly, Janet is without either.

It's boredom that has her standing on tiptoe and feeling around the top shelf of the wardrobe for the letter from the hospital. A present falls out, unattractively wrapped in newspaper – no doubt one of Emma's environmental ideas. The paper rips as the present's corner hits the floor. Janet doesn't mean to look, but she can hardly help it – when she picks it up and attempts to smooth the paper, it only tears further. The present is a road atlas. Odd, she thinks, given everyone's dependence on computers. She'll have to find Emma's sticky tape and fix the paper. She reaches up again, feeling for the letter. She ought to have kept it in the bedside drawer. There hadn't been any need to place it so high when she was hiding it from no one but herself. Unable to find it, she is filled with an irrational fear that it is lost. Of course it isn't, but there is no one to tell her so, and the longer it takes to discover the sharp corner of the envelope and the wrinkled plastic of its see-through window, the more worried Janet feels, until she steps up into the wardrobe itself, in order to achieve a little more height and, as she tiptoes at her new elevation, everything wobbles. Janet grasps the top shelf and the wardrobe leans, as if offering itself up to her. Items slide out: presents, shoes, a tiny pair of filmy knickers. She staggers back on to the carpet and extends both hands to stop the wardrobe from falling forward, but she is not strong enough to right it, and it slumps on her, drunkenly, doors open like spread arms, spewing its insides all over the carpet.

Dylan saves her. She hears the thud as he jumps from his bunk, appearing in the doorway, unshowered but nonetheless welcome.

'Fuck, Nan!' he shouts, diving into the room, where he replaces Janet in front of the reeling wardrobe.

Janet sits heavily on the bed, too mortified to tell him off.

'Fetch Mum,' he says.

But before she can get to her feet, the front door opens and the rain suddenly sounds in stereo: above them on the bedroom skylight and below them on the wind that whips into the hall. It must be Chris and James, finally back from their early-morning excursion – whatever can have taken them so long?

'DAD!' Dylan calls.

Chris's feet trudge up the stairs, quickening once he sees Dylan propping up the wardrobe, torn between trying to balance it so nothing more falls out, and causing further damage by righting it.

Chris is *soaked*. Janet can hear the water dripping off him. His feet squelch as he relieves Dylan of the wardrobe, the responsibility of righting it, along with any further spillages and damage, now his.

Righted, the wardrobe leans. The joints between top and side, and bottom and side, no longer make right angles; the wardrobe has morphed from rectangle to parallelogram. One of the doors hangs off, and the beading along its bottom has come unstuck.

Janet offers Chris one of the towels she ironed earlier.

'I'll go and get the tools,' he says, ignoring her outstretched arm.

While Chris is gone, Dylan picks everything off the floor: the newspaper-wrapped presents, the cards, the filmy underwear – how he groans! – and places it all in a pile on the bed. Janet sees the hospital letter, stuck to the partially opened tab of a padded envelope. Once they've all gone, she'll retrieve it and place it in the drawer of the bedside table.

Dylan leaves as Chris returns with a large metal toolbox, a drill and some small off-cuts of wood. Emma follows, face flushed.

'God, look at the state of the wall,' she says.

Behind the wardrobe, a niche which must have once been home to an airing cupboard is speckled by black mould. Janet thinks of Chris's comments about the fire. It would make the room damp, he said. But she only has a few minutes of heat before bed each night. This damp must be historic. It's not surprising given the way they keep opening the window in this weather.

'I'll scrub it and slather it with bathroom paint next week,' Emma says.

'I'll clean it,' Janet volunteers. It's not how she had intended to spend the morning, but she can't help putting herself last, it's just the way she is.

'There's really no need,' Emma replies.

Janet's appetite for cleaning the wall increases. Plus, if she remains upstairs, she can talk to Chris while he fixes the wardrobe. She hurries out of the room and down the stairs to the kitchen, where she can smell mince pies browning in the oven, and one of the worktops has been taken over by something called a 'HOT CHOCOLATE STATION' according to the chalkboard. There aren't any disinfectant wipes in the cupboard below the sink, so she grabs the dishcloth and hurries back upstairs.

Chris is alone in the room when she returns, plugging his phone into a charger behind the bedside table.

Janet sits on the bed and watches as he places a small, square block of wood into the wardrobe's top left corner. He drills a hole though the side of the wardrobe and into the block.

'Can you get me a chair from the boys' room, Mum?'

Janet does as he asks and then, balancing on the chair in a hunching crouch because of the low ceiling, Chris drills another hole, this time through the wardrobe's roof and into the top of the wooden block.

Janet squeezes past with the cloth.

'Mum, you can't wipe the mould,' Chris says, manually twisting a screw into first one drilled hole and then the other. 'It needs scrubbing. With a brush. And we'll have to get the dehumidifier on.'

'No harm in trying.'

Janet wipes the wall to the accompaniment of Chris's laboured breath and the give of the wood as he twists the screwdriver.

'Got these little bits leftover from when I built a bird table,' he says.

'That's nice, dear.'

'Knew they'd come in handy.'

'Your father would have done the same.'

Chris makes an agreeing sound.

'You know, when your father nearly died, he saw the—'

'Oh, Mum. Not this again.'

Janet searches for the right words. She can tell Chris is getting impatient; he always does when she pauses for inspiration. 'What do you think happened to your father, then?'

'I don't know.' Chris lowers the screwdriver and hunkers on the chair. 'He fell off the roof, and while he was unconscious, he was fighting for the surface, like people do when they're drowning. The firing of synapses in his brain created a surge of energy – a bright light. That's the simplest explanation. Afterwards, when he tried to make sense of it, the experience was filtered via his rational brain and it became something else; a story he—'

'You think your father's brain made it all up to *fool* him?' Janet asks. Oh, she knows she should turn the other cheek, but it is *very* hard to do so.

'No, that's not what I said.' Chris exhales. 'Dad's not here any more, so you don't need to take his side.'

He scrambles off the chair and she can see the boy in him, braced for a telling-off.

'God hasn't finished with you, yet,' she says.

'Why does that sound like a threat?'

'Just because you've rejected Him, it doesn't mean He has rejected you.'

'OK, Mum.'

Chris glances at the pile of things Dylan placed on the bed. He picks up the padded envelope and removes her hospital letter from its sticky flap. Then he drops her letter back on the bed and looks inside the padded envelope, eyebrows raised.

'Should you be poking your nose in Emma's Christmas arrangements?'

He turns his attention to the newspaper-wrapped present with the torn corner and peels it back, revealing its contents. 'Emma promised not to buy me anything, but this is just the thing,' he says. 'We're far too dependent on phones.'

'You shouldn't be opening it!' Janet drops the cloth, shoos him out of the way and begins rearranging the pile. If she takes charge of it, she can reclaim her—

'There's a letter here for you, Mum.'

'Yes.' She holds out her hand.

'You haven't opened it.'

'No.'

His expression is fleetingly puzzled; then he places his foot on the chair and lifts the screwdriver.

'I don't want you worrying about me!'

He returns his foot to the floor. 'Is there a problem?'

'It's from the doctor.'

Janet sits on the edge of the bed and tells him about her morning headaches, the nausea, the dizziness and her problems with concentration. How it happened the previous winter, and is happening again now.

'Sunlight might help. Are you getting out and about? Some people just feel bad in the winter. It's a thing, isn't it?'

Poor Chris, he doesn't realise the gravity of the situation.

'I had a *brain scan*.'

She lets it sink in and waits for him to ask about the results. He must be anxious to know, but he holds back. And it seems cruel to leave the envelope unopened when it's in her power to reassure him. Full of love for her son, Janet tears the paper.

Her eyes search for alarming words: 'tumour', 'aneurism', 'dementia'. And they discover 'normal'. She reads the surrounding sentences – there are only three in all. *Normal*. There is nothing wrong with her.

The doctors have seen inside her head, and everything is in order. How strange that she must be told this; it's *her* head, after all – you'd think she might know what was in it.

It's a little like the final judgement, she realises. When it is her time – not now, thank goodness! – the Lord will look in her heart and see whether everything is in order.

And, oh, the news takes her breath away for a moment. Many years ago, the Lord welcomed Lazarus back to life, saying, 'Lazarus come forth!' Today, he has, in effect, welcomed her back to life, saying, 'Janet, come forth!' What a relief. What a blessing for the whole family.

'It's really good news, Mum,' Chris says.

How thankful he is! Men aren't good at expressing these things, but she could *always* tell with Frank, sensing the heartfelt words he *would* have said, if he'd been able. Nearly always. Mostly always, she thinks. And now, if she is not careful, those long-sunk thoughts will bob up like corks.

Chris moves the chair and starts drilling again. Janet resumes her wiping, experiencing a pang of regret at the loss of her licence to daydream. How she had enjoyed contemplating funerals. Did she want the mourners wearing black to reflect the solemnity of the occasion or in bright colours to reflect her warmth? There were pluses on both sides, of course. Would there be hot food afterwards or just sandwiches and nibbles? Should the gathering be held in a restaurant or in Ruth and Rob's newly converted living space? There had been so much to consider.

The mould isn't coming off as well as she had hoped. The wall is quite smeary – grey now, rather than speckled. And the sound of Chris's drill as he makes new holes is restoring her earlier headache.

Emma pokes her head around the door. 'Chris can finish off up here. I've got a special job for you, Janet, if you wouldn't mind?'

A request made in such a forthright manner is hard to refuse. So, no, Janet wouldn't mind at all. Not a bit. It would be her absolute pleasure.

She follows Emma down the stairs. The kitchen door is open, and she can see the boys, helping themselves to mince pies, juggling hot mouthfuls between puffs, greedily accepting pain alongside the pleasure.

'It'll be nice to have some live Christmas music while we get everything ready, won't it, boys?' Emma calls.

The boys step into the hall, nodding: Oh yes, it's just what they'd like.

'These two are off upstairs to tidy up before the cousins arrive. But I'm sure they'd love to listen for a moment.'

Knowing how much she will please everyone, Janet agrees. She plays a few bars of the 'Hallelujah Chorus', before pausing to tell them that it must be sung standing up, a tradition accidentally begun by George III, when the trumpets frightened him out of a nap and he jumped to his feet, followed by the deferential audience that believed his standing indicated pleasure. The boys like that, though they creep away when she starts playing again, first for more mince pies – she hears the noisy chomping – and then upstairs to their room where their efforts at tidying sound very much like wrestling, until James starts to cough and Chris shouts across the landing telling them to pack it in.

Not long after Chris has finished drilling, the power goes out and the keyboard is silenced. It's a terrible shame, but how fortunate that he was able to fix everything first.

It's important to be thankful, Janet tells Emma who is panicking about the food. There are nine food-related miracles in the Bible that Janet can think of, off the top of her head, and she begins to describe them, in some detail, until Emma interrupts to say Chris has a box of batteries in the garage.

What a blessing! Some of the food may not get cooked, and candlelight will have to suffice, but at least there will be music.

Chris appears with the batteries. They find the right ones and Janet plays for a while longer, wearing them in. But then, feeling removed from the heart of things and worried she is missing out, she abandons her post and, instead, wanders from room to room, offering advice and instruction, ensuring the day unfolds with herself at its heart.

## THE FIGHT BEFORE CHRISTMAS

'I'm not making any lunch. It isn't long 'til the party. I thought people could just help themselves to a little snack if they're hungry.'

'I see.'

'Would you like me to make you something?'

'Oh, you're busy.'

Emma places a big bar of chocolate and a knife and fork on the dining table. She pokes her head around the kitchen door and calls, 'Dylan! Come and get the stuff for the chocolate game.' Turning back to Janet she says, 'What would you like?'

'Oh no, it's all right.'

'Are you sure?'

'Are *you* having something?'

It occurs to Emma that this is a test; she is meant to guess what Janet wants, and her inability to do so confirms to Janet that she is unloved and misunderstood.

'No, I'm going to wait.'

'If you're not having anything, I won't either.'

'Well, I'm going to hoover the lounge, but please, help yourself to anything. Treat the kitchen like your own,' Emma says, regretting it as she remembers the knickers in the sink.


'You won't be able to cook the gingerbread,' Chris says.

Emma looks at the raw shapes on the baking trays. 'I thought a biscuit nativity would be just the thing. Your mum would have loved it. And the children could have iced their own characters.'

She consults her list, trying to work out what can be done without power and what must be abandoned.

'We'll stitch the trotters instead,' Chris says.

'No,' she snaps.

'I've put them on a plate on the side. They'll be defrosted by the time everyone gets here.'

'We are *not*—'

'The boys will *love* it.'

She glances at Chris, wondering whether she is missing something. He *can't* be pleased about the power outage.

'It's a *Christmas party*, not a survival course. And your mother won't love it. Anyway, the electric could come back on at any minute. That's why I've left the trays out – the instant it's back, I'll stick them in the oven with the quiches and the cheese straws. Will you go out and check the rabbits?'

When Chris doesn't reply, she turns. He is holding a padded envelope.

'It was on the bed, with everything that fell out of the wardrobe.' He places it on the worktop, beside the Mason jars of goodies that make up her HOT CHOCOLATE STATION. 'I assume you were keeping it safe?'

'I was keeping *James* safe.'

'Me too.'

Emma's instinct – and that is all she can rely on when dealing with this since she lacks know-how – is to offer placation; to validate his worries while emphasising James's good health, despite his present cold. But it is exhausting to constantly urge herself to reasonableness, prioritising Chris's feelings over her own, applying words like balm. She doesn't understand how legitimate worries about local closures and the increasing difficulty of se-curing doctors' appointments have led him to online forums where foreigners without health insurance write favourable reviews of unregulated antibiotics. He is a *gardener* – what does he know about spectrum, dose and side effects? She can't say that; any mention of his job will be perceived as a criticism of the business and only distract from the matter in hand.

'I think—' she begins.

'Did you know British children are more likely to die from asthma than children anywhere else in Europe?'

'Chris, you're catastrophising.' Emma's shoulders slump and she leans against the worktop, drained and frustrated. 'James has spent *three* nights in hospital since he was born. And one of those admissions was for croup. He has *never* come close to dying.'

What to say, now? Emma can't think; she is running on empty and, instead of soothing him, she points to the envelope.

'That is a *red line*,' she says, surprised at the fierceness in her voice.

'A red line?'

'It's completely unacceptable.'

'I know what *red line* means.'

'Is everything all right?' Janet asks, tiptoeing theatrically into the kitchen, still wearing her dressing gown. 'You want to get out of those wet clothes, Chris.'

'He'll get changed in a minute. We're just popping outside to check on the rabbits.'

Water seeps into Emma's trainers the moment she steps outside.

'What a day!' she says, fastening her coat and raising her hood. She waves her arms at everything: the flooded patio, the leaden weeping sky, the house without power, again. 'It's one thing after another!'

'Well, it's not like we can say, "Oh, we'll take a flood, as long as we don't have to endure any other inconveniences." Remember the film we watched? The pandemic one? It showed how normal stuff goes wrong *at the same time* as large-scale stuff.'

Ah, yes, the mockumentary with the ludicrous woman crying over her washing. Emma won't comment; she doesn't want to encourage further discussion of it.

'You can't imagine a flood, can you?' Chris says.

Emma would like to deny it, but he is right, she can't, not really. In theory, yes. But in practice, no. Even though the water in which she is standing is over the tips of her trainers and her socks are already wet, she can't imagine it seeping into the house, rolling across the kitchen floor and into the hall. The wind is blowing a ripple through it and the sky continues to lob rain at them, but she can't shake the thought that the threats are idle, and an in-the-nick-of-time adjournment will save them all.

'Weird, isn't it?' he says. 'You're the one who reads books, who's always going on about empathy. But you can't picture it.'

'It'll be spring soon, and then—'

'By February we'll have bees, hill fires and cherry blossom, if recent years are anything to go by. Fruit trees need a period of dormancy like we need sleep, or they flower at the wrong time and, bam – no fruit. It won't be long before we have a summer with an ice-free Arctic, and that'll increase the warming we're causing with our $CO_2$ emissions by fifty per cent. Game over.'

Emma places a hand on his shoulder. 'Remember your dad, always quoting Job? How did it go? *For there is* hope *of a tree …*'

Chris exhales. '… *if it be cut down, that it will sprout again, and that the tender branch thereof will not cease.*

*Though the root thereof wax old in the earth, and the stock thereof die in the ground; Yet through the scent of water it will bud—*'

'—*and bring forth boughs like a plant*,' she says, finishing it for him. 'You're abandoning hope.'

'I am.'

'All right.' She stuffs her hands in her coat pockets and glances at the spruce sitting on the patio, thoroughly killed, simultaneously dehydrated and drowned. She looks away, past the grass and the meadow, and fixes her gaze on the fruit trees at the boundary. 'The space where your hope was, can we fill it with something less concrete? How about wishes?'

He snorts, and she leaves it, following him to the hutch where he unfastens the latch of Boy Rabbit's first-floor living quarters and lifts him out. She watches as he soothes the rabbit and, for a moment, he is the old Chris, the man who could do things she couldn't imagine her dad doing: operate an excavator, build a fence, bleed a radiator. In the face of his practicality, her knowledge of the world seemed abstract and remote. Wanting to share some of the things she knew, Emma used to read to him in the car. Over a period of months she read *Tess of the d'Urbervilles*, and when he asked questions about the novel, she offered expansive, definitive answers, the lack of overlap in their skills giving her a false confidence. It occurs to her now, as she watches him examining Boy Rabbit, his expression one of growing alarm that, on occasion, he may have done the same.

'You hold him,' Chris says.

She is not good at holding the rabbits. She is too cautious; they sense her uncertainty and, feeling insecure, struggle. Indifferent to her hesitancy, Chris bundles Boy Rabbit into her arms.

Emma clasps his warm body. Her coat is wet; it can't be comfortable being pressed to it. She hunches forward to protect him from the rain, and then they are face to face and she is studying the deep Y of his nose, the trellised veins inside his ears and the wiry white whiskers on his cheeks and above his eyes.

Crouching in front of her, Chris examines Boy Rabbit's hindquarters.

'I think it's fly strike.'

'What's that?'

'Flies lay their eggs on dirty rabbits and when the maggots hatch, they eat through the tissues. I can see maggots on the surface of his skin. I think they're under it, too. There's a sort of ripple.'

Emma shudders and her grip loosens. Boy Rabbit struggles and his motoring hind legs tear at the backs of her hands.

Chris lifts him out of her arms and places him back in his first-storey living quarters. Sickened, Emma retreats to the back door where the house offers a smidgen of shelter from the rain. Hands stinging, she searches her phone briefly and then reads aloud.

'*It's vital rabbits are kept dry ... Many owners think fly strike doesn't happen in winter months; however, it can happen at any time ... Rabbits should be checked daily* – Well, I've been out here every day. *Soiled bedding should be removed daily* – Daily? I had *no* idea … *If you find a maggot on your rabbit you must take him to the vet immediately*—'

'Oh, that is *not* happening,' Chris interrupts, suddenly less sanguine about simultaneous large- and small-scale misfortunes. 'I'm not *paying* to have him put down.'

'*Fly strike is an emergency* …' Emma reads.

'We should have cleaned his bum.'

'He lives outdoors; I thought it was natural for him to be a bit dirty – I didn't know!'

'That's no excuse, though, is it?'

'Are you serious? You bought the rabbits, without asking—'

'So, now I have to ask you before I spend—'

'—and just expected me to look after them.'

'—my money, which *I* earn.'

'*Your* money?'

'Go and get your tweezers.'

'It is not *your* money,' Emma calls as she turns and splashes back to the house. She hurries through the kitchen and passes the lounge, catching a glimpse of Janet sitting on the sofa, keyboard resting on her lap. Emma takes the stairs two at a time, accompanied by the 'Hallelujah Chorus'.

This will be one of those stories, she thinks as she grapples with the make-up bag on the floor beside her makeshift bed. It will be told on subsequent Christmas Eves and everyone will sigh and think how the passage of time is a kind of alchemy, allowing past troubles to transmogrify into anecdotes. Didn't James tell her, not long ago, that humans, when narrating experiences, tend to discount their duration and instead remember only two things: a peak moment and an end moment, ultimately assessing experiences according to their average. Childbirth, James said, was a good example of this, and Emma had been touched by the odd combination of knowledge and absolute ignorance with which he spoke. Here was the baby whose birth caused her so much pain, having a conversation with her about the mechanism by which she had probably forgotten it. And he was right, to a large extent. The end product – James – and the subsequent love and care of her family had induced a kind of forget-fulness that can only be undone by painstaking recollection.

She finds the tweezers and simultaneously catches a glimpse of herself in the mirrored lid of the make-up bag: face grey, eyes like fried eggs.

Outside, she hands the tweezers to Chris.

'Get him out then,' he says.

She lifts Boy Rabbit and tries to cradle him. He doesn't like it and pedals his fore and hind legs, catching her hands again. The added sting brings tears to her eyes.

'Shouldn't he be sedated before we do this?' she says, struggling to keep hold of him. 'In the piece I was just reading it says—'

'Hold him still.'

'—a vet should—'

'Tighter. So he doesn't wriggle.'

'I'm trying.'

'Try harder.'

'I'm. *Trying*.'

'This is going nowhere.' Chris feels in his pocket for the key. 'I'll get a broom handle.'

At first, she thinks he plans to sweep Boy Rabbit. She can't think why but, painfully aware of her ignorance, the idea is fleetingly plausible until it hits her: he said broom *handle* – he is going to fetch one of the redundant handles from her dismantled signs. Then he is going to lay Boy Rabbit on the flooded patio and break his neck.

If the antibiotics were a red line, this is something else entirely, and all the discomfort Emma has swallowed over the past days and months – the strange ideas and incremental indignities, rise to the back of her throat like vomit. She presses Boy Rabbit to her body, refusing to give him up.

'I'll take him to the vet,' she says, turning her back on Chris, who surely can't think she'll stand by as he kills the creature. 'I won't let you. Not here. On Christmas Eve. You don't know what you're doing. He might be fine. There's a vet not far from where the library was. I'll take him there.'

'Don't be ridiculous,' he says, face set, not heading for the garage now, instead extending his arms to receive Boy Rabbit.

Emma has never smacked her sons. Once, on returning from a classmate's birthday party, tired and grumpy, she shouted at her dad because he wouldn't let her eat a napkin-wrapped slice of cake and, before she knew it, he'd braced his leg on the arm of the sofa and thrown her over his thigh. Her party dress tipped over her head and he battered her backside with the flat of his hand until her mother stopped him. It can't have been about cake, Emma realises now. But at the time, bent over her father's leg, head upside down, legs thrashing helplessly, she thought only of herself. Bewildered and inconsolable, she'd been put straight to bed. The memory is lurid and disturbing; she could never do that to someone.

So, when she shoulder-barges Chris, Emma is as surprised as he is. And though it's a futile, ineffectual assault, she is desperately aware of having stepped outside the conventions of their relationship. Here is the man she elected to love and cherish until the end of everything, recoiling in surprise. Here is the cusp of her already sore shoulder, bemoaning the contact with his ribs. Here is the unwelcome certainty of her hypocrisy – if he rammed her, she may not forgive him.

She isn't expecting Chris to retaliate. But he does. Hard. And, unable to extend her arms because they are full of rabbit, Emma topples backwards, elbows smacking the patio.

Feet scrambling, she propels herself back. Chris advances and she kicks out at him, stomach pitching with the bewildering upside-down fear she last felt decades ago. Her jumper blots the water seeping through her coat. The backs of her legs are saturated and fingers of wet meet around her ankles and knees like manacles.

'For fuck's sake, Em.' Chris extends a hand which she can't take without relinquishing her hold on the rabbit. 'Get up,' he snaps.

Finally scared of the man whose own fear has so disrupted her life, Emma drives herself farther with her feet.

Embarrassed by the depth and speed of her breath, she can feel her face making grotesque shapes as she wonders what to do next.

'If it doesn't stop raining, the house is going to flood,' he shouts. 'And you're lying in a puddle, crying about a rabbit.'

Chris turns and splashes through the water to the garage where he unlocks one of the doors and steps inside. Emma scrabbles to her feet and shuttles Boy Rabbit back to his living quarters. She stumbles across the patio and grabs the garage door. The key remains in the lock and, quick as she can, she pulls the door closed, turns the key, and pockets it.

Chris yells. And swears. She hears him thrashing about in the dark. There'll be a torch somewhere – he'll find it, eventually.

He shouts again.

Guts watery with fear, Emma lumbers into the recently cleared gap between the fence and the garage. Elbows aching, bleeding hands held over her mouth to catch the noise, she sobs. This can't be undone. She can't take it back unless she opens the garage right now and makes a joke of it, pretending everything is OK. But her legs won't take the steps; she knows Chris will kill Boy Rabbit if she lets him out.

And he pushed her. He pushed her *hard*.

Hot tears line her cheeks, dribbling over her hands where they mingle with mucus and cold splats of rain. The climate of her marriage has been changing, and she has been in denial about it for a long time. She has ignored the warning signs, preferring not to think about them, failing to act until this crisis moment.

Chris kicks the doors. Not too hard – he won't want to damage them, will he? It's not as if they can afford replacements. Can he unfasten the hinges? she wonders. And then she remembers his toolbox, up in the bedroom. He's not going anywhere for now.

Emma wipes her face with her sopping coat sleeves before splashing across the patio and into the house. The boxes in which the rabbits arrived are in the garage. She'll have to use something else. She steps into the bathroom, upends a washing basket and picks a towel from the jumble on the floor. Back in the kitchen, she covers the basket's bottom with the towel and rips a binbag from the roll as her breath erupts in a burst of the tremors that follow tears.

Outside, she removes Girl Rabbit from her side of the hutch and tries to examine her bottom.

Dylan interrupts her. 'All right, Mum?' he shouts, head poking out of the back door.

She wonders whether he saw anything, and if he did, how much. 'Yes!' she calls, her voice thin and wobbly.

'Good,' he replies.

Emma clears her throat and tries to sound normal. 'I just need to take Boy Rabbit to the vet.'

'Is he OK?'

'That's what I need to find out. Keep Nan busy, will you? I – *We* won't be long,' she says, hoping her belated correction will prevent him from enquiring as to Chris's whereabouts.

Dylan makes a grumbling sound and then checks himself. 'All right,' he says, and closes the door.

Girl Rabbit looks fine. Emma returns her to her living quarters and places Boy Rabbit in the washing basket. She carries him through the side gates to the front of the house where her car is parked on the drive. She wraps the passenger seatbelt around the washing basket, smooths the binbag over the driver's seat and sits down.

She has already positioned the car to turn right when she notices a 'ROAD CLOSED' sign and a line of red and white barriers blocking the bridge. There was talk, back in the autumn, of a leaking water main and a crack in the concrete; perhaps it was true. Emma sighs and reverses a little. She will turn left and make a diversion across the ditch-flanked tracks that dissect the sodden fields.

Before she pulls out, she stares into Boy Rabbit's unblinking eyes. He is an inconvenience she would prefer to ignore, but there's a big difference between disliking something and wishing it dead. Lately, she doesn't much like Chris.

The vet's waiting room smells of antiseptic and pelt. Ahead of Emma, a young bloke holds a wooden carry case with a silhouette of a ferret burned into its lid and a woman rocks a puppy like a hairy baby. Emma waits, holding the washing basket.

Paper chains have been taped to the reception desk and a tree decorated with cut-outs of animal paw prints stands in front of a pair of windows, rain streaming down the panes as George Michael sings about last Christmas.

Conversation in the waiting room is urgent and anxious, and focused on the weather.

'Grange Road's under water.'

'*Higher river levels and isolated areas of surface-water flooding are likely for the next day or two* – that's what it said in the paper. *Isolated areas.* Try not to worry.'

'It's up over the pavements on Balmoral Drive.'

'How's Preston New Road? It often gets bad there, by the playing fields.'

'It *is* bad. I couldn't see the kerb in places when I passed, earlier. Doesn't seem very *isolated* if you ask me.'

Still shaky from the altercation with Chris, and anxious to get home, Emma tries not to listen. She has become somewhat inured to Chris's catastrophic litanies, but the fears of these ordinary-looking people, sitting beside their poorly pets, are troubling.

The receptionist is an animal person. Emma can tell because her black trousers and cardigan are covered in tufts of fur. She probably has one of those 'IF YOU LOVE ANIMALS, DON'T EAT THEM' stickers in her car. Every so often, she angles her head at a microphone on the desk, presses a button and, with the air of a bingo caller, announces a name.

'Trixie Smith, that's Trixie Smith …

'Chester McLean – it's *your* turn – Chester …

'An-nd Minnie Sedgewick, yes that's Minnie Sedgewick.'

Emma is surprised at the camaraderie and lack of formality – it seems animal lovers don't bother with Mr and Mrs.

'Do you have an appointment?' the receptionist asks when it's Emma's turn.

'No, I – I think it's an emergency. I don't know if you've got time to squeeze us in—'

'Are you already registered?'

'No.'

'Surname?'

'Abram.'

'And your pet?'

'A rabbit,' she says, with a little lift of the basket.

'Aw, let's have a peek.'

Emma puts the basket on the counter and the receptionist stands.

'Lovely! Boy or girl?'

'Boy.'

'Name?'

The receptionist sits, hands poised over her keyboard. She hasn't been calling *people*, Emma realises, swallowing a snigger. She has been announcing the *animal*s and, like children, they have Christian and surnames.

'He doesn't have a—' Emma breaks off as the woman frowns. 'He's not a pet.'

'Well, what is he, then? Ha-ha-ha. You mean he's not *your* pet?'

'No, I—'

'You found him somewhere, did you? Is that what you're saying?'

'No … he's mine.' Emma *can't* say Boy Rabbit is for meat, so she says the first name that comes to mind. 'George Michael.'

'Sorry?'

'George. Michael.'

'Your rabbit is called *George Michael* Abram?'

'Yes.'

'Oh, really?'

Emma nods.

The woman jabs her keyboard with her fingertips, simultaneously typing and staring. 'Your trousers are soaked.'

Emma nods again.

'Looks like you've wet yourself,' she says.


The vet examines Boy Rabbit's mouth.

'We've got some malocclusion here. It often corrects itself by the time youngsters are ten weeks old. When it doesn't, the teeth don't meet and wear each other down. See? The incisors are overgrown. He'll have been reluctant to groom.

'And it looks like he's had a messy bottom. I suspect his bedding wasn't changed as often as it might have been?'

The vet is severe now, eyebrows raised, her expression one of chastisement.

'Have you kept rabbits before?'

'No.'

'You should have been better prepared.'

Emma remembers Chris's contemptuous reference to the Ant and the Grasshopper. In his mind, he is preparing while she wastes her time. It's all very well being consumed by the idea of everything falling apart, fixating on the moment in which one will be useful and vindicated, but who supplies the everyday needs of food, clothing, shelter, love? Not Chris. Perhaps he thinks those things are beneath him. Or maybe his fear is taking up so much space there's no room for anything else. Ultimately, it doesn't matter. She has been filling his gaps with respect to the boys; perhaps she should have realised she would also need to do it for the rabbits. It's bad enough that to be alive now is to feel a pang of guilt each time she turns the key in the ignition, plugs in the dehumidifier or opens the refrigerator – every action is multiplied; it's impossible to be one, she is always many. But here is something she could have prevented, all on her own. She holds the thought for a moment. And then resists. Chris did this.

'I'm afraid it's not good news, Mrs Abram. Rabbit skin is thin and tears easily. Rather than attempt to remove the maggots, I think the kindest thing would be to put him to sleep.'

Emma listens, face red with shame, as the vet explains what will happen. She accepts the invitation to be present – it's the least she can do. Trying to save money, she declines the offer of cremation. When it is time, she strokes Boy Rabbit's head, forcing herself to watch as the blue liquid seeps into his veins. How easy it is to think of oneself as a good person. How hard to acknowledge evidence to the contrary.

'You can say goodbye to George Michael now, if you like.'

Emma says nothing; any show of emotion could result in tears, nervous laughter or a dreadful combination of both. She waits, lips clamped, until Boy Rabbit is at peace.

'Have you cleaned the scratches on your hands?'

'I will.'

The vet holds Emma's hands and gently wipes them with antiseptic. This small act of compassion is all it takes to prise the lid off her upset. Eyes filling with tears, Emma experiences an unexpected longing for more kindness, which the vet offers, murmuring about sadness, and love, and the difficulty of saying goodbye, until it begins to feel as if she is talking about losing Chris and, weeping now, Emma concurs, half-formed sentences spilling out with her tears.

'Loved him very much …

'Certain he *was* happy …

'Think you're on top of things …

'Exhausting being responsible for …

'Tried so hard …

'Hasn't been enough, has it?'

When she has stopped crying, the vet says, 'Shall we wrap him in your towel?'

And Emma remembers Boy Rabbit, and the very-much-alive husband she has locked in the garage.

Emma pulls up outside a pair of semi-detached houses. Not content with closing the library, the council declared the building, which first opened as a reading room in December 1920, to be surplus to operational requirements and paid seventy thousand pounds to have it demolished. The plot sat empty for a while. Eventually, a fence was erected and a steel structure appeared behind it. For many months, Emma thought of gallows each time she passed. Now, the houses are finished, and fairy lights sparkle through downstairs windows. With the plot repurposed, she isn't sure where the library door used to be. She remembers arriving at work after the Christmas break to an enormous pile of books on the other side of the letterbox – it was as if they'd returned on their own like exhausted homing pigeons, and flopped, open-winged, to the floor. Perhaps a sofa or Christmas tree sits where the books once landed.

She thinks of all the objects that have vanished: the old-fashioned toilet with its overhead cistern, the temperamental oil-fuelled boiler, the kitchen's electric hot-water heater with the external overflow pipe that froze in the winters: one year a two-foot icicle dangled from it. She thinks of the people. The women who borrowed novels while on maternity leave and returned with their babies for Song and Rhyme Time, and Story Time. The children and teens researching homework and coursework. The university students and academics who ordered photocopies of obscure articles and requested inter-library loans. The book group members. The older people who popped in to read the paper, learn IT skills and chat. Those who, struggling to get out and about, said their goodbyes and switched to the Home Visits service.

When closure was mooted and arguments about the benefits of accessible local services were met with indifference, Emma naively imagined there might be some protection in facts and numbers. The library was one of the council's busiest, and she repeated the figures like a spell: eye of newt, toe of frog, 117,000 reservations, issues and renewals per year. But the library went the way of the maternity unit and children's A & E services, the

Magistrates' Court and the custody suite at the police station, 'valueless' direct trains to nearby cities and the Home Start office down the road that is now a sandwich shop. Order, access to health care, sustainable travel, compassion for those in need – all snatched away, notwithstanding increasingly despairing protests.

She glances at the towel-wrapped body in the washing basket beside her. She paid twenty pounds for the consultation and another twenty-four pounds to put Boy Rabbit to sleep. Chris will be angry about the cost. But Boy Rabbit met a peaceful, dignified end. To remove the trappings of civilisation and treat others badly is to lose one's humanity. And there is no excuse for that.

The light already dimming, Emma heads for home. Eventually, she approaches the house and pulls into the drive.

She turns off the engine and, in the quiet of the car, is struck by the absence of Christmas lights, and by the outlines of the boys' bodies, moving behind the lounge window like fish in a bowl.

Emma stands beside the car, passenger door open, staring down at the washing basket and its towel-wrapped quarry, wondering whether it's OK to leave it outside overnight.

The front door opens to reveal James.

'What happened to Boy Rabbit?' he calls.

'He had to be put down.'

'Oh no. Was it sad? Where's Dad?'

'Yes, it was sad.' Emma shuts the passenger door while she thinks. 'He went back to the van for something.'

'Really?'

'He ... There's a roadblock on the bridge,' she says, glancing at James's feet – he won't dash out to see for himself in his socks.

'Oh, right. There was a van there earlier. Dad thought they were doing the potholes. Wait – how did he get past?'

'He climbed over it,' she lies.

James laughs and Emma feels a stab of guilt, followed by resignation – Chris's recent behaviour is to blame for James's lack of surprise.

'What he's gone back for?'

'The LED beanie,' she says, stepping up to the house.

James turns on his heel, calling, 'Hey, Dylan, wait 'til you hear this!'

Emma stands in the doorway. The temperature is due to drop tonight. Boy Rabbit should be all right in the car – he'll have to be; she doesn't know what else to do with him. And she doesn't know what to do with Chris.

## CAST INTO THE DEEP

There's no power because he turned it off.

He turned it off to give Emma something to worry about.

He gave her something to worry about because he was irritated by her complacency.

He was irritated by her complacency because he found *his* envelope of antibiotics, opened, and hidden.

And now he is stuck in the dark.


If he can get some light, he can see about taking one of the doors off.

There are a couple of torches on one of the shelves at the back of the garage. Stored without batteries in case of leakage.

But the box of batteries is in the lounge beside his mother's keyboard.

The wind-up torch is on the windowsill in the kitchen.

The lantern torch is in the van, which is parked on a flooded street a couple of miles away.

His phone is upstairs, charging. With his toolbox.

The door hinges are on the outside, inaccessible.

The same multi-point locking system he chose to keep people out is going to keep him in.


Here he is, like Jonah. Swallowed up. Surrounded by water.

He waits, shivering. Wet clothes pasted to his skin. Eventually, the darkness thins to expose the ribs of roof battens, and tools, hanging from the walls like bones: strimmer, spade, shovel, axe. Obstacles reveal themselves: his mother's suitcase, hay bales, the builders' bag of wood, his wheelbarrow and lawn mower. He identifies the shelves at the back of the garage where he has been storing supplies. The hessian bags and the sand – he should make himself useful. But alongside the sugar, vanilla extract, salt and vinegar there's a bottle of vodka and one of brandy. Chris doesn't like spirits. He rarely drinks; it only leads to maudlinism. Still, he picks up the vodka, unscrews its top and takes a sip. The bitter liquid burns his nose and throat and leaves his mouth dry.

He fitted his own kitchen. He could have easily taken care of the rabbit. Two lessons he learned from his father: it's not hard to make something and it's not hard to kill something. He takes another sip and sits on a hay bale, holding the bottle.

Chris spent the early part of his childhood on a farm. It wasn't theirs; they lived in a tied cottage which was, in fact, a 1950s semi with no central heating and single glazed windows. Still, his mother insisted on calling it a cottage, and since she didn't insist on much, everyone joined in.

In his memory, it is always either the height of summer or the depths of winter on the farm. During the summer the air was thick with the warm, musky stench of manure and animal bedding, and he and Ruth played outside on a seesaw his father constructed by securing half an old tyre to a plank of wood. Fly papers hung from the kitchen ceiling, red canisters dangling from the sticky, poison-coated streamers like exploded fireworks. Trapped flies pedalled their legs and wagged their wings. Once, Chris stuck the tip of a used paper to Ruth's hair, and pretended it was an accident. In winter, it was freezing. His mother fixed curtains to the backs of doors and procured a series of draught-excluding animals: a snake, a sausage dog and a crocodile. 'Put a hat on,' she'd say in response to complaints about the cold. 'Put a scarf on.' 'Put your gloves on.' And finally, 'Put a blanket on.' And Chris and Ruth would stagger around, wrapped in coarse golden blankets like a pair of sausage rolls. In the mornings, ice formed on the insides of bedroom windows. In the evenings, baths had to be taken quickly: Ruth, his mother, then Chris and, finally, his father. If they were quick, the water was still just about warm when it was his father's turn to sit in the family gravy. No one retreated to their room until it was time to go to sleep because it was bitter upstairs. Each bed had a pile of extra blankets beside it and Chris and Ruth wore zippered sleepsuits with plastic-coated feet over their pyjamas.

His father arose at five o'clock every day to bring the cows in. He fetched them from the field in the summer and from the shed in the winter and then let them into the collecting yard, watching as they filtered into the milking parlour. Each cow's tail was wrapped in a different colour tape, indicating how much she should eat. The data was fed into a primitive computer system that controlled the length of time a trap door above each stall would open, allowing food to drop from the loft above and down a little chute into the trough. After the milking was completed his father washed out the pipes and took the cows back to the field. Then he hosed down the parlour and collecting yard. All before breakfast.

It was an Ayrshire herd, white and brown; you hardly see them nowadays. Each cow was named and numbered. Chris's favourite was 151, Silver Rose. He liked Dream, too. She was old and placid, and sometimes, if he'd been to the field to help, his father would lift him on to Dream's back and let him ride her to the yard.

Chris sought his father out after school. If he was in a good mood, Chris accompanied him to the milking parlour. There, Chris scampered up the wooden stairs to the loft and shovelled rolled barley into the hoppers, ready to drop down to the cows during milking. It was warm and dusty, and the air smelled slightly sweet, like flour. In the cubicle shed he'd watch the cows licking molasses from the five-gallon barrel which had a roller ball in it, like a deodorant. When the babies were born, they stayed in a pen with their mother for a day or two, after which they were removed and sent down to the yard, where they were reared with the other calves. If a calf wasn't doing well, his father would fetch a bucket of milk and tell Chris to cup his hand and place his fingers in its mouth; carefully, though – the calves had sharp front teeth. The calf would suck on Chris's fingers and, as it sucked, he would lower his hand into the bucket until it was sucking up the milk, too. Calf tongues were rough and long; scratchy, like a warm piece of sandpaper.

Chris knew where calves came from. For a while he imagined human babies arrived via different means. Prayer, perhaps. But, eventually, it dawned on him and, for a week or two, he went about in a state of disbelief, mortified at the thought of his mother on all fours, his father sniffing her backside and then climbing onto her as she stared straight ahead, trying not to mind.

*

His mother will surely miss him and come looking. And he will be blamed for his unavoidable absence. 'I thought you might have called while I was out,' she often says as a pretext for phoning. And the moment he says he didn't, he is guilty of neglect.

He remembers going through a growth spurt in infant school, leading his classmates to refer to his trousers as half-masters.

'Just wait 'til spring,' his mother said. 'I'll get you new ones, then.'

As he waited, the fabric bobbled and the threads covering his knees slowly parted, until, finally, it was spring and one Friday, after school, his mother took the trousers away. The following Monday morning she produced a pair of shorts.

'Nearly summer now,' she said.

Chris stepped into the shorts. They felt soft and worn around the waist, familiar in fact, and he realised he'd been had.

'These are just my trousers, only shorter,' he complained, twisting to view the bobbled fabric covering his backside.

'I never said they *weren't* your trousers.'

'I'm not wearing them.'

'It's them, or your underpants.'

Chris fumbled with the waistband.

'Oh, you can't do that,' his mother said. 'Mr Parry will be *very* angry if you go to school in your underpants. So will Miss Walling. And *I'll* get into trouble, too.'

He made it as far as the front door in his underpants before turning back to fetch his dismembered trousers. It was the thought of her being in trouble that made him surrender. *She* never required obedience – she was always petitioning on behalf of someone else, someone in authority who would be angry; it was better all round if he just did as he was told.

Chris takes another sip from the bottle. His parents stopped drinking after a brief flirtation with Methodism when he was a boy. But food was to be embraced. It was compulsory to clear your plate. Hot meals were served at midday, when his father was at his hungriest. To start school was to miss out, though there were consolations: ice-cream-scoop mashed potatoes and the option of chips and beans with everything. After school, his mother would place a stack of bread and butter on the table alongside a jar of jam, a block of cheddar, and a homemade cake or plate of scones. At the weekends and in the school holidays, Chris was home at midday and present for *proper* dinner: shepherd's pie, pasties, bubble and squeak or, when they'd bought a share in a pig, thick juicy sausages, the butcher's secret recipe. But sometimes there was liver, and then each of the familiar sounds of his father's midday return resonated like a tolling bell: the opening of the back porch door, the removal of each welly – thunk, thunk; the unfastening of his boiler suit – pop, pop, pop; the sound of the taps as he washed his big red hands in the little sink; and Chris traipsed to the table, where his plate awaited him like a punishment. He remembers a Saturday when, having eaten most of the mashed potatoes, his liver loomed like a stack of slugs.

His father liked to say: *Every moving thing that liveth shall be meat for you; even as the green herb have I given you all things.* In his mind, the verse equated to: *Everything upon your plate shall be eaten by you.*

In later years, Chris would respond with *Let not him that eateth despise him that eateth not.* But, as a boy, he was unaware of the suppleness of scripture.

'Eat up. It'll put hairs on your chest.'

'I don't want hairs on my chest.'

His father stabbed a lump of liver and held it near Chris's involuntarily pursed lips. Gravy dribbled off the end of the suspended meat. There was something jellyish about it. Chris imagined it might spring and squish between his teeth like the inner tube of a bicycle.

'We can't afford to waste food,' his father said, plate clean, as always. Ruth had finished hers, too. 'When I said grace, we thanked God for our dinner.'

Chris had not thanked God for anything. Certainly not liver, and he was annoyed that his thanks, which had not been proffered, had been stolen and offered up anyway.

'Fine. Fine. You sit there until you've eaten it.'

He couldn't. The more he looked at it, the worse it got. What would happen if he absolutely refused? Surely his mother would let him off when his father returned to work, he thought, not yet wary enough of her sporadic strictness, her tendency to arbitrarily act as his father's enforcer.

Chris sat at the table until eight o'clock, when it was time for bed. The gravy had separated. The liver looked like slices of suede.

Breakfast: liver.

'Do it for me,' his mother said. 'You don't want me to get into trouble with your dad, do you?'

Chris took a bite out of the cold meat. It squeaked between his molars. He fetched a large glass of water and swallowed each livery slug whole, until his insides were swollen and quivering.

'*I* got Chris to eat his dinner,' he heard her whisper to his father, afterwards.

In due course, he realised they were rivals in a competition to see who could win his father's approval. Chris, Ruth, his mother – they all vied for the honour, until he dropped out, then Ruth, and there was only his mother left.

Their time on the farm was mostly happy. Largely, Chris thinks, vodka bottle pressed to his lips, because his father was so busy. When you're busy, God fits into the gaps: in the moments of a field-observed sunrise, during a difficult calving, in the muffled silence of a snowy winter morning. Never home until six or seven o'clock most evenings, and as late as ten o'clock in the summer during haymaking, his father was utterly exhausted, spilling straight into sleep the moment he lay down. Outside all day, his father wore the weather; he bathed in it and was battered by it, forever soaking or sunburned, shivering or sweating. Life was an exercise in pitting and partaking: Frank Abram versus nature and Frank Abram nurses nature. And all the while his father was musing and meditating, pondering his purpose. *But ask now the beasts, and they shall teach thee; and the fowls of the air, and they shall tell thee: Or speak to the earth, and it shall teach thee: and the fishes of the sea shall declare unto thee.* Wasn't that what Erasmus had wanted – the farm labourer singing snatches of scripture at his plough? Or in his father's case, the herdsman humming hymns in the cubicle shed.

Back then, his father's inspirations were largely innocuous. The Lord spoke common sense, told him to seek after good things, grow vegetables, share his faith with others, and swap congregations when he fell out with people over interpretations of this or that scripture. Everything changed when Chris was ten. The Ayrshire herd's milk yield was low. A Friesian herd, then, his father suggested. But sheep were the way forward; less labour-intensive for most of the year, and Mr Atherton-Jones, who owned the farm, had a son who had just finished at Myerscough College and was ready to take charge of a flock, so there was no longer any need for a herdsman or stockman.

After Chris's family packed up and moved to town, after the cattle, and then the sheep, were sold, and after attempts at diversification failed, the farm was split into lots and auctioned off. Now, their old house is a holiday let. The area is advertised as well situated for fishing, birdwatching and horse riding, and within easy reach of Liverpool, Manchester and the Lake District. On occasions when Chris has had jobs out towards Parbold, he has driven into the old yard and turned the van around, pretending to be lost. The trees and the brambles that ran across the back of his childhood garden have been cut down. Manicured and transitory, it's a place of recreation, not work. Late on a Sunday afternoon a couple of years ago, he drove Emma and his parents out there. Emma stood in the yard, admiring everything, as if it had been placed there expressly for her pleasure.

'It's like a painting,' she said as the light changed.

'No, it's like a sunset,' his father replied.

Life was different at Victory Avenue. Chris's was the single bedroom at the front of the house, its window right above the door. There were times when he would spy his father, newly returned from work at the sweet factory, lingering in the front yard, savouring his last moments outdoors when, arms extended like branches to feel the rain or leaning into the wind like the figurehead on a boat, he briefly resembled the old, bigger version of Frank Abram, subject to and subject of nature.

Milk arrived in a glass bottle each morning, the super-market sausages tasted wrong, and the churches nearby seemed less tolerant of his father's inspirations. There was spare time after work and at the weekends. Time for his father to attend an Alpha course and time for the Jehovah's Witnesses, the Mormons and the local curate to pop round for discussions which tended to become heated. His father couldn't do religion like other people – they seemed able to turn their attention to goodness. But his father, inclined to periodic despondency and plagued by existential crises, couldn't divert his thoughts to more pleasant pastures and remained haunted by the fear that whatever path he was presently following might not, after all, be the right one.

The rest of Chris's childhood was dominated by his parents' epic spiritual journey, his father in the driver's seat, his mother beside him, and Chris and Ruth in the back, belted in and unable to get out. The journey was long, boring and cramped. There were no rest breaks. Heaven was the destination, but without a fixed route there were U-turns and diversions and sometimes the same roads were traversed year after year. There was no point in asking, 'Are we nearly there yet?' They were always nearly there.

His father never locked the car. What was the point of believing in God if he couldn't trust Him to look after it?

But, Chris said, wasn't the open car an invitation to thieves, and didn't it therefore contravene *Thou shalt not tempt the Lord thy God*?

He was big enough, by then, to defend himself. Which he did.

It was years before Chris could say, 'I don't believe.' He knew when he finally disappointed his parents it wouldn't be something that happened just the once; he'd have to stick with it. Such a small thing, he thinks now, years later, with almost-grown sons of his own. Yet, having spent his childhood listening to the way his father talked about people who didn't feel as he did: weak, worldly, sinful – it seemed momentous. So much of what his parents said and did had been about drawing a circle: 'We are this' and 'We are that'. Stepping outside the circle, Chris forfeited *we* and became *them*. 'We still love you,' his mother said once, voice quavering, as if she hoped to convince herself as much as Chris. But it was a provisional, last-resort kind of love. Their stories, songs and prayers condemned him. They had planted wheat and he had developed into a tare. What happens when you grow up to be the baddie you were warned about? Imagine how it feels to be the biggest disappointment of someone's life. Chris tried to explain it, once.

'I won't forsake my morality to make you feel better,' his father replied. 'Love the sinner, hate the sin.'

'Love your father, hate his God.'

'That is a *ridiculous* comparison.'

Oh, he is sorry for himself, now. Chris unscrews the lid and takes another drink, a longer one this time, his throat primed for the burn.

His father's inspirations increased. The end was approaching. Frank contacted friends to warn them. If their dismissals were lukewarm or polite, there was a chance they may be persuaded; if vociferous, they had felt threatened by the power of his words.

The year before Dylan was born, his father believed the tribulation would begin. He would sell the house and move to a caravan. A great and terrible day was coming – great for Frank and Janet, and terrible for almost everyone else. There were still several years left on the mortgage but, for a couple who lived frugally, the balance was a lot of money, even after the purchase of the caravan. And, having spent years pondering the meaning of *sell all thou hast and distribute it unto the poor*, his father set about giving his money away.

The world did not end, and his mother reinterpreted his father's pronouncements, making them less absolute and more plausible. What he had *really* meant was this, or that. It was her special skill to apply mastic to memories, attacking them with a little trowel, pointing and smoothing edges, filling in gaps and creating a watertight seal, all the while revealing the true shape of things as she saw them. As she wished them.

When Dylan and James were toddlers, the sweet factory closed, and production moved to Slovakia. So his father picked leeks and sprayed crops out at Rainford. He packed mushrooms in Ormskirk. Cut, harvested and planted salads in glasshouses in Preston. Worked until he was stiff and slow, and no one would have him.

'I'm fine,' his mother said when Chris asked about finances, after his father's death.

'Is there anything left?'

'It's not something you need to worry about.'

'I can't believe he— It was *your* money, too.'

'Your father felt it was a test.'

'Right. And did you pass?'

She didn't know or wouldn't say. All the lines of thought that should have made it from her brain to her mouth were diverted. The routes of any critical ideas and impressions were closed off, a series of dead ends, branching out like sidings.

Chris shuffles back on the bale and leans against the concrete wall. Rain thumps the roof and the wind whips down the passageway between the garage and boundary fence. The alcohol is warming him from the inside out. His own private radiator.

He thinks of his mother's ridiculous heater. Of her annoying habit of having it on before bed and her reluctance to allow ventilation. Of the quiet stubbornness that never progresses to outright disagreement yet leads to her closing the skylight as soon as his back is turned. He thinks of the letter from the hospital. Of her reported headaches and dizziness. And the meander of his thoughts sends him back to a spot where he can see them, looping, connected.

The heater; the headaches.

His *boys*, sleeping across the hall.

The alcohol works like loppers, blunting his emotions: chop, chop; it cuts the top off his anxiety, but when he gets out, he'll go straight upstairs, fetch the heater and bring it here. The temperature is due to drop in the coming weeks. He can switch the boiler back on, if necessary.

Connection made, plan devised, Chris lifts the bottle to his lips again and, staring through the shadows at the locked doors, waits. Emma will surely appear before long. It's hard to offend her. On their wedding day, his mother asked her to step to one side so she could have a 'family only' photo. Emma laughed and complied. She finds it amusing that his mother has that photo up in the caravan: a wedding with no bride.

But Emma shoved him on the patio.

Refused to give up the rabbit.

Locked him in the garage.

He reruns the moments before he was locked in.

Emma's face as she hit the ground.

Her scrambling legs as she tried to get away.

Her bleeding hands wrapped tight around a creature she doesn't even like.

On one level, he is appalled. He has behaved badly. He sees it. But he is pursuing the common good. Emma *must* understand that. She will, he decides. Soon the door will open and reveal her, standing in the light like an angel, come to impart a message of deliverance.

He screws the lid on the bottle and places it on the floor beside him. What if the factors of one's life, when multiplied, do not combine to make a whole number, but rather a series of fractions with no common denominator? What if the father who demanded perfection is the father who fashioned a bow and arrow out of a sycamore branch for your seventh birthday? If the father who made everyone kneel while he delivered imploring prayers is the father who patiently taught you to build a fire, tie a knot and jump-start a car. If the father to whom you were a perpetual disappointment is the father who returned at eight o'clock each morning for his breakfast break, carrying a four-pint churn of milk taken straight from the top of the refrigerated bulk tank because you liked the cream. In the days of Noah, there were giants in the land. It was easy to believe in giants when Frank Abram was your father; though, in the end, his father had been a big man grown small, gradually rubbed down, like a bar of soap.

How will his own boys remember him? Chris hasn't given it much consideration. Beginning to feel drowsy, he closes his eyes. He has tried to be a good parent. What's his number-one tip for fatherhood? Don't take parenting advice from a God who drowned his own children.


## THREE WISE MEN


Ruth holds the phone to one ear, her hand over the other, as Elijah pursues his older brothers with a fishing rod, a golden star dangling from its tip. The fishing rod was Rob's idea. A terrible one, given Elijah's talent for converting everyday objects into weapons. The boys are dressed to please Ruth's mother in costumes originally bought for the Sunday School nativity: polyester robes festooned with plastic 'jewels', each sweaty head topped by a magnificent crown.

'I can't quite – shush! Boys! That's enough! Sorry, Emma. I might as well be talking to myself ... and now I sound like my mother. Is she all right?'

Since the builders left last month, the boys have made it their mission to expose flaws in the design of the open-plan living space. Yesterday, they discovered the Velcro seams in the newly visible back of the leather sofa and attempted to climb inside. This afternoon, the kitchen island is a speedway. Amos, the oldest and usually most sensible of her boys – it doesn't necessarily follow that he be both; Ruth remembers her nephew Dylan as a child – skids around the top end of the island, uncharacteristically giddy. Thank goodness Rob chose worktops with rounded edges.

'Hang on, let me just …' Ruth steps into the washroom, now the only private downstairs space, and locks the door. 'There! I can hear you now.'

The day started well enough. Ruth's alarm went off at six o'clock and she rolled straight out of bed. As soon as her feet landed on the carpet, she touched the base of the bedside light with her index finger and retrieved the sports bra, T-shirt and leggings from the floor beside the bed. Ignoring her reflection in the mirrored wardrobes, she dressed quickly. There was no need to worry about waking Rob. More often than not, he occupies the spare room, where he remains at the boys' beck and call like a night receptionist. Their preference for his ministrations is such that when they shuffle into her room with their stomach aches and nightmares and ambiance-related complaints, alongside any irritation or exhaustion, she also experiences a spike of pleasure at having been chosen.

Ruth slipped into the en suite where she peed, cleaned her teeth and fastened her hair in a clip. Then she tiptoed down the stairs, filled her water bottle and unlocked the front door.

It was raining again. She didn't bother with a coat; shivering in the car is part of her routine, like taking an ice bath, and she's always hot on the way home anyway. She was indicating, ready to pull out of the drive, when she remembered the bloody elf. Having reported back to

Santa overnight, it needed to reappear somewhere so it could continue spying on the boys. It was the last day, too, which meant she was supposed to do something fancy: leave glitter footprints, presents, or a letter promising its return next year. She dashed back into the house and retrieved the thing. Where to put it? She'd looked up *easy* ideas online when she gave in and agreed to the whole performance; they included making clothes for it, staging various culinary 'accidents' – something she couldn't countenance in the new kitchen – and fashioning amusing props, such as a set of 'dumb-bells' made from drinking straws and marshmallows. Oh, there was nothing *easy* about it, which was why Rob, she later realised, had refused to have any part in it. Guilt at working late rendered her helpless in the face of the boys' pleas, and she clicked Buy It Now to a chorus of cheers.

Ruth opened the fridge, hoping for some inspiration. The bottle of wine she hadn't quite finished the previous evening sat in the door beside an unopened four-pint carton of milk. She grabbed the elf and wrapped it in a tea towel, leaving only its face showing, as if nestled in a sleeping bag. Then she stuffed it between the wine and the milk and shut it in. Good. She does not like the idea of a magical person spying on her children. It reminds her of the way God was employed during her childhood: a voyeuristic, sneaky fellow, intent on catching people out. But Rob, unaffected by the faff, thinks it's all harmless fun, and the boys seem to enjoy it – they certainly aren't cowed; their behaviour hasn't exactly improved during the lead-up to Christmas.

Ruth drove to town, reversed into 'her' spot in the multi-storey car park, and hurried down the concrete staircase, skipping over the desiccated splat of vomit on the first-floor landing. Throughout December, the gym has remained a Christmas-free environment. Not a decoration in sight, which pleases Ruth. It's supposed to be the most wonderful time of the year but her wonderful time has been hijacked by ephemera: finding a suitable Secret Santa gift for the new paralegal, wondering whether it would be possible to work from home on Christmas jumper day (it wasn't), trying to decide if avoiding the work Christmas party would affect her status as a 'team player' (it would), remembering the stupid elf, and listening to Rob's stay-at-home-parent complaints: the class Christmas parties for which he'd been required to send in fruit platters and antipasti (what was wrong with sausage rolls, and cheese and pineapple on sticks?), his search for matching pyjamas, and the rector's request for homemade hats at the Sunday School Christmas parade – as *if* the boys, excitement peaking, would sit and make hats with their daddy.

The treadmill in front of the television was free. The BBC news played, volume muted, and Ruth began her usual game of looking for mistakes in the subtitles, trying to work out what the interviewees had really said, before the corrections appeared. She likes it when there are lots of mistakes; it feels as if there is someone hiding in the screen, gently pulling her leg. When there's an especially fitting error, Ruth decelerates and types the incorrect word(s), and subsequent clarifications, into her phone: fierce stories (fear stories), migrate grandfather (my

great-grandfather), double mistake to me (double mastec-
tomy), wrecks it (Brexit).

Ruth loves the morning quiet. Initially, she worried
about looking silly while exercising, but no one pays any
attention to her. She has wondered whether Emma might
also enjoy it. It's hard to know what to buy for Emma,
who sends such thoughtful presents. Last year she made
gloves for the boys and, in an amusing nod to knuckle
tattoos, embroidered the fingers with 'Time Lord', 'Stay
Cool' and 'Born Wild' respectively. Emma probably
wouldn't want to drive into town each morning, though.
And there'd be no point in her walking; it's nearly three
miles from Moss Lane to the gym – Ruth checked. Unless
she cycled, like James with his papers. But Ruth isn't sure
whether Emma's old bike is still in use, and she doesn't
like to ask in case Chris thinks she is being nosy about
their finances, which, she suspects, are dire. The gym is
the cheapest in town. The monthly fee wouldn't cover two
coffee-shop lattes. But how do you present someone with
a gym membership without implying they are fat? Worried
about getting it wrong, Ruth has chickened out and bought
vouchers for everyone, again.

Having jogged for thirty minutes, she stepped off the
treadmill. As she left, she noticed a couple of mums from
the boys' school arriving for a spin class, sporting co-
ordinated leisure wear and carefully applied make-up.
Nice women who had invited her for coffee one Saturday
morning, though she didn't pass muster, or perhaps she
missed the cue for what should happen next, and now,
when she sees them, she gives a little wave from across

the room, and they wave back, smiling, but distant, as if from the opposite bank of a river.

When she arrived home, Ruth discovered a dog walker had left a bag of poo hanging from the magnolia tree beside the gatepost, like an awful Christmas decoration. Carrying the poo, she stepped through the front door to the sound of Rob singing a silly version of 'We Three Kings', which the boys would almost certainly repeat later, in front of her mother. The *Famous Five* book Rob had been reading to the boys at bedtimes lay open-winged on the hall rug. She stepped over it and into the newly knocked-through living space, where she stumbled into an abandoned bowl of cereal. Just before it tipped, she saw the elf sitting in the milk, arms wide across the bowl's rim as if relaxing in a hot tub.

Having put the poo in the outside bin and sent the boys to tidy their rooms, in case Father Christmas was offended by the mess, Ruth set about cleaning the floor while Rob sat at the island, holding the Christmas crackers like telescopes, trying to see if one of them contained a fortune-telling fish.

'Remember them? They were my favourite.'

Ruth shook her head. As *if* her peppery, red-faced father would have allowed fortune telling during Christmas dinner. Crouched on the floor with a cloth, she started telling Rob about the new boy who'd been at Amos's Kumon class, the previous Saturday morning.

'Imagine moving to a foreign country at eight years old, bless him. Everything would be strange. Even little things, like going to the supermarket.'

'I'm sure they've got food in …'

'Pakistan. Yes, I know, but he might not recognise things. I mean brands. Like us in the Polish aisle, except the whole shop will be different.'

'They've got normal stuff in the Polish aisle. They've got juice. I've bought it, before.'

'But there's loads of unfamiliar stuff, too. I wouldn't know what to do with half of it.'

'I would.'

'Anyway, *I* think it must be hard for him, for Babar—'

'For *who*?'

'Babar.'

'Sounds like a sheep. Baaaaa-baaaaa – ha-ha!'

Ruth had intended to conclude her anecdote with the news that while chatting to Babar's mother, she'd discovered he was a Liverpool fan, meaning he and Amos had something in common. Instead, she sighed. 'I don't know why you have to—'

'It was a joke.'

'I was trying to say something, and you interrupted me to take the mickey.'

'No, I was making a *joke*.'

'It wasn't funny.'

'Oh, stop telling me off.'

'I'm not.' Ruth got to her feet. 'I'm trying to talk to you and … I don't like it when you interrupt me with stupid, flippant … It's like being heckled.'

'It was a *joke*.'

Ruth thought of Elijah's maternity leave – the tiredest time of her life, when nocturnal cluster feeds left her with blurred vision and jelly legs. Given the boys' recent sleep patterns, Rob must be similarly knackered, yet each morning he managed to pour himself into jolly dad mould, all set for japes and hilarity. She suddenly felt petty for complaining, though she couldn't resist a further attempt at mitigation.

'I was just trying to tell you something about Amos and his new friend and—'

'I'm allowed to make jokes.'

'When I talk, it sometimes seems, instead of listening, you're thinking of silly things to say. You know I won't find them funny, but you do it, anyway. And if I ignore what you've said, or I get annoyed at being interrupted, you don't like it. What do you want me to do?'

'Laugh,' he said. 'You're not at work now. No one's going to complain to HR if you enjoy a joke.'

Ruth turned and squeezed the milk-soaked dishcloth into the sink. Shoulders hunched, feelings hurt, she felt like a clone of her mother. If only someone else had given birth to her. Someone fulsome and fearless. Someone with female friends and snappy repartee. Ruth's preparations for adult life had centred on achieving financial independence and avoiding the kind of man who might consider it his right to make unilateral decisions. But there are other traps. Other ways of partitioning families.

She busied herself with rinsing the cloth before trying again.

'Interrupting me, to say something you know I won't find funny – and you *know* because you've known me for more than a decade – feels rude.'

'Telling me off when I make a joke, like I'm a child –
what's that?'

Afraid there was something deeply unpleasant under
the surface words of their conversation, Ruth left it. They
were tired. It was Christmas Eve. There was the party to
look forward to.

And now she leans against the washing machine, listening as Emma apologetically cancels the party.

The boys are all dressed up with nowhere to go. There
will be tears; they've been looking forward to haranguing
their big cousins. Ruth is disappointed, too. She enjoys
Emma's peculiar party: the eclectic food, the nostalgic music
and the way the boys disappear upstairs to play games
with Dylan and James, eventually reappearing in a state
of ecstatic exhaustion. Last year they fell asleep in the car
on the way home, heads back, mouths slack and wide, like
three little chimneys puffing chocolate-scented smoke.


'Let's go, anyway,' Rob says, unperturbed by the blocked
bridge and the power cut. 'What do you think, guys? Shall
we go to Uncle Chris and Aunty Emma's house? Shall we
surprise them?'

The boys cheer.

'Don't you think it would be a bit rude—'

'Not if we come bearing gifts. We'll stop on the way
and buy a couple of rotisserie chickens.'

'Oh, not on Christmas Eve, Rob. It'll be—'

'Come on, they've got no power. We can't leave them
to *starve*.'

'I'm sure Emma—'

'We can't go without provisions.'

'Like the Famous Five, visiting Kirrin Island!' Amos says.

'Exactly.' Rob grins. 'Come on,' he says, nudging Ruth as they pile out of the house. 'It'll be fun.'

There are no baskets, so Ruth squeezes back through the supermarket doors in search of a trolley. At least it has finally stopped raining.

She can barely move in the shop. But the boys, in their robes and crowns, whip between people, singing.

'*One in a taxi!*'

'*One in a car!*'

'*One on a scooter, blowing his hoo-ooter …!*'

Having snagged the chickens, Rob pushes through the mêlée, ahead of Ruth, calling, 'Would Emma like a cheese-board? Do Chris and the boys eat salmon now he's gone all environmental?'

'Well,' Ruth replies, not certain whether she'd describe Chris in those terms. Incensed by problems he did not cause and cannot fix, Chris reminds her of their father who, right up until his death, remained attached to a notion most people shake off when they reach adulthood: any important happenings were somehow related to him – the weather, politics, Elijah's inability to sit still. If you believe in an authoritarian God, proffering punishments and rewards, perhaps you have no choice but to take everything personally. But Chris doesn't believe, making his behaviour less comprehensible to Ruth.

As usual, she can't keep up with Elijah and it's not long before he is out of sight.

'Amos, Nathan, will you go and find him, please?'

'We'll be by the bakery, guys,' Rob says. 'Come and meet us once you've got him. Keep up, Ruth! We might as well get some bread in.'

'You said there was bread in the freezer. Do we have to faff about with this now?'

'*Do we have to faff about with this now?*' Rob echoes in a silly falsetto. 'Come on, it's Christmas!'

Ruth follows in his wake, wondering whether the whiny, shrill voice is an imitation of her own, or an intimation of how he feels, under his coat of jokes.

She pays while Rob gets a head start to the car with the boys. She returns the trolley and removes the canvas shopping bags, slinging one over each shoulder.

As she approaches the car, Rob reverses out of the parking space. When she is within reaching distance of the passenger door, he edges the car forward. She takes a few steps, goes for the door again, and Rob nudges the accelerator. She can see the boys, unbuckling themselves, scrabbling to enjoy the view. Ruth won't run; she only runs at the gym, where no one is watching. She approaches the car again, attempting to maintain some dignity by not hurrying. Each time she steps up and tries to open the door, Rob moves away. And as she follows yonder car, three Wise Men watch though the back window, their faces contorted with laughter.

*

The last thing Ruth wanted was a life spent second-guessing a flinty, complicated husband. Rob is neither of those things. He is soft-hearted and straightforward. And he used to be funny. How would he reply, if she said that to him? 'You used to be fun,' perhaps.

In the summer, they visited the Lake District. On their way up to Easedale Tarn, the boys stopped and removed their shoes and socks so they could explore the freezing pool beneath a waterfall. Ruth watched from the water's edge, enjoying their delight, until she heard Rob greeting someone. She turned to see one of her work colleagues, Andy, and his wife, Liz; child-free and bronzed, both dwarfed by enormous backpacks.

'Ho! You're just in time. Ruth's about to take all her clothes off and jump in the pool with the boys.'

'I am *not*.'

'Oh, she is! We're in for a treat!'

Andy and Liz laughed politely, and Ruth turned to keep an eye on the boys, thereby excusing herself from further conversation.

'I can't believe you,' she said as the couple disappeared up the track.

'What?'

'Oh, ha-ha, look at Ruth. She's out of shape, isn't she? Wouldn't it be funny if we all saw her naked?'

'I didn't say that.'

'Oh, you did. And you *laughed*. You wouldn't have laughed if the idea of me, naked, in front of them, wasn't funny.'

'It was a joke!'

'A joke is when the *other* person laughs.'

'I was just being friendly. It's not my fault if you can't—'

'I am *not* your straight man.'

'It was a harmless—'

'You belittled me in front of them.'

There had been other jokes.

'Look at you two, lounging around, gossiping!' Rob said when Emma popped in to see the new kitchen. 'Where's the Prosecco, heh? Where are you hiding it?'

Ruth tried to ignore him. The ground floor of the house was now three times the size of Chris and Emma's, and she felt awkward about showing it off. They resumed their conversation, but Rob persisted.

'This is the life, eh? Ladies of leisure.'

'Why did you say that?' Ruth asked, later, when Emma had left.

'It was a joke,' he replied flatly. 'It was funny because I didn't mean it.'

'I work *extremely* hard.'

'So do I,' he replied. 'Who project-managed the extension? Who made hundreds of cups of tea and coffee? Who ensured you and the boys weren't inconvenienced while we didn't have a kitchen?'

The canvas bags slide off Ruth's shoulders and she tugs them back into place. This is a joke, she tells herself; it's funny because Rob doesn't mean it. But it doesn't feel like a joke; it feels like something else entirely.

She won't move again. She waits, feet planted on the tarmac.

A car pulls up behind Rob and, unable to remain stopped, he must follow the loop of the busy car park, forced at regular intervals to brake and let other drivers out of their spaces. By the time he returns, the boys are back in their seats, and no one is laughing.

They head east, out of town, before turning off on to a narrow road that cuts through fields and past occasional clusters of houses. Before long, the houses peter out and the dog-leg road is flanked by brimming ditches and sludgy fields.

At the approach to a half-barrier level crossing, the road is momentarily divided in two and then it narrows again, this time to a single track with intermittent passing places, its surface smeared by soggy clods of soil where tractors have been in and out of the fields.

Eventually, they reach Chris and Emma's house. Rob continues past it, nosing the car up to the bridge so the boys can examine the barriers.

The day is waning, though it's barely three thirty. It won't be long before the dark creeps across the fields and settles in the ditch that runs opposite Chris and Emma's house. On the other side of the bridge, Ruth notes the lazy glow of a newly awakened streetlight. In the distance, another streetlight stirs, sluggish and pale.

'Maybe the power's back on,' she says, pointing.

'I'm pretty sure streetlights can come on when domestic power's off. Something to do with the way power leaves substations.'

'The bungalows down past the allotments have power, don't they? Stand here. Look. Can you see Christmas lights in the distance?'

'I think power's sometimes split across two or three circuits before it's delivered to homes. If that's true, and the fault's in one circuit, you could have a street where there's some on and some off.'

Rob takes one of the shopping bags from Ruth and passes it to Elijah; it's a good idea to give him a task, the busier the better, but he struggles with it, adopting a slow shuffle, Rob's fishing rod dangling from his other hand, the star waving to and fro, catching anyone who comes close. In the end, Ruth takes the bag back, leaving Elijah to wave his star from side to side as Rob sings, '*Bearing chickens we traverse afar. Field and fountain, ditch and mountain, following yonder star. O-o, star of wonder, star of night, sit on a pack of dynamite!*'

'Why don't you practise your nativity words?' Ruth suggests, thinking to calm the boys as they reach the drive.

Amos delivers his line in a monotone, as if each word has been partitioned from its neighbour and bears no relation to the next.

'And. The. Star. They. Had. Seen. When. It. Rose. Went. Ahead. Of. Them. Until. It. Stopped. Over. The. Place. Where. The. Child. Was.'

Nathan follows with: 'When they saw the star, they were overjoyed.'

'They bowed down and worshipped him,' Elijah concludes, waving the star madly.

The boys have learned the modern words. As a result, the whole story sounds off to Ruth. Her mother will notice, too, and hanker after the old words: 'When they saw the star, they rejoiced with *exceeding great joy*.'

Oh, her mother won't say anything, but she'll wince or raise an eyebrow and Ruth, attuned to the nuances of her mood, will feel compelled to make a compensatory gesture. If her father were still around, he would comment – What a shame the Lord's *original words* had been altered! And then Emma, feeling obliged to intercede, might gently agree that the King James *translation* sounded more poetic. She might mention the original, fourth-century manuscript of the Book of Matthew, saying she believed it was in Greek. Then Chris would likely make a snarky comment, causing Rob to laugh because, no matter how many times Ruth tells him otherwise, he can't shake the idea that disagreements about religion are inconsequential.

'It's so quiet,' Rob says.

Ruth turns. There is something spooky about the inert fields in the dimming light. Not a car in sight; a drained, after-rain hush stilling the air.

'Well, it's access only, isn't it?' she says. 'Anyone nipping across from Holmeswood or Rufford will need to take the main roads.'

And then the quiet is broken as someone elbows Elijah: not Amos, and not Nathan, someone else. The invisible man, Rob suggests. But Elijah won't be placated. The culprit must be told off and no one will admit responsibility.

'Shall we get some of the silliness out of them before we go in? How about we race up to the road sign, guys?

See the white circle with the black line through it? Who can run that far? Tuck your robes into your trousers.'

The road is damp and muddy, dappled by rain-filled potholes.

'Oh, I'm not sure that's a—'

Too late, the boys are engaged, rolling their robes and aligning their toes with an imaginary start line.

'Elijah, give the star to Mummy.'

Ruth takes the fishing rod. 'Try not to get too wet,' she says ineffectually.

'Ready? Hold on to your hats. Go!' Rob shouts. The boys dash off and he trails after, deliberately slow, huffing and puffing like the Big, Bad Wolf.

Last to reach the sign, the resounding loser, Rob allows himself to be mocked and taunted.

'Let's wave to Mummy, guys,' he says.

They wave, and Ruth feels entirely separate from them, as if they have absolutely nothing to do with her and she has been tricked into a life with this man and the three sons he has brought into being by some strange parthenogenesis.

'Stand together nicely,' Rob says, moving along the road a little. 'Hold hands. Now, smile! Don't move, Elijah – Father Christmas is watching.'

Ruth watches too as the boys stand like a cut-out paper-chain family and Rob, who does not require a fortifying crack-of-dawn hour to himself, holds up his phone.

When the four of them are nestled together on the sofa as Rob tells a story, or rolling round the garden in a jumble of arms and legs, delighted shrieks of 'Daddy,

Daddy!' escaping the fray, she sometimes thinks, You should thank *me*, I picked him for you.

On the way back, Rob gives Amos a run for his money, leaving a sulking Elijah to bring up the rear. Ruth watches as Elijah stops running and scuffs his way to the cusp of the road.

'Come away from the ditch,' she calls, foolishly, because once he has her attention, Elijah embarks on a clownish procession along the road's edge.

From where she is standing, Ruth can't see the ditch. Repeated resurfacing means the roads have grown higher over time, while soil shrinkage has resulted in the fields dropping. But she knows it is there, lying in wait for her youngest, naughtiest son.

Elijah teeters and wobbles. He windmills his arms, calling, 'Whoa, whoa, whoa.'

Ruth abandons the canvas bags and fishing rod in the road and, galvanised by the thought of the little body she once breathed for being without air, even for a moment, she runs.

Delighted by her approach, Elijah intensifies his performance, losing his crown in the process. Ruth sees it disappear into the gap between the road and the field and, expecting Elijah to follow, runs at full pelt, newly aware of the molten mess of her insides – the pouches and sockets, the basin of waste in her middle.

When she realises Elijah isn't going over, it's too late to stop. Ruth has no choice but to follow through and leaps, arms wide like wings, over the ditch and down into the field. She skids and staggers but remains on her feet.

Heart pounding, she bends, hands resting on her thighs as she tries to catch her breath. She hears Rob approaching at a run, feet whacking the tarmac.

'That was *amazing*!' he yells, applauding. 'Can you jump back up?'

On the wrong side of the ditch, ankle deep in mud, she can't.

'I saw a car in a field off Jacksmere Lane the other winter,' Rob says to the boys, now standing in a line above her. 'It was a few days before it could be recovered. They had to wait for the ground to harden up before they could use a crane. Do you think we can recover Mummy?'

Ruth rescues the crown, which is floating on the water, and throws it up to Amos, who catches it, one-handed, and passes it to a subdued Elijah. Then she reaches for Rob, hoping their hands will meet across the ditch and, with his support, she'll be able to leap over and up.

'Lean a bit further,' he says.

'I can't. If I do, I think I'll ...'

'Come on, there's nothing to be afraid of.'

'Why would you say that?' Ruth asks, immediately afraid.

She retreats. The water between them is dark, and she has no idea of its depth.

She tries again, edging to the lip of the ditch, extending her hand to Rob so he can steady and raise her as she leaps. Their fingers touch for a moment, but Rob moves his hand away in a pantomime dodge and thumbs his nose at her.

The boys giggle delightedly, and for a moment it seems Ruth, already committed to movement, can propel herself on to the bank without him. But she doesn't trust herself and hesitates. Rob realises his mistake and reaches again, hand wide, fingers rigid, but it's too late; she loses her balance and tips into the black water.

# PART 4

# The End of the World

*Then the Lord said to me, 'Out of the north, disaster shall be let loose upon all the inhabitants of the land.'*

Jeremiah 1:14

# Christmas Eve

## A LONG WINTER'S NAP

Dylan and James carry the heater down the stairs. 'To me … To you,' they call, having caught some of their younger cousins' silliness.

Emma grabs Janet's dressing gown, a clean pair of her own knickers, and a T-shirt that's long on her but should be just about right for Ruth. She follows behind the boys and, as they transport the heater along the hall and into the lounge, she passes the dry clothes to Ruth who is shivering on the doorstep, refusing to set foot inside in case she makes a mess.

'Come in, it doesn't matter – I'm not bothered.'

'I'll just change here,' Ruth says. 'It's not as if there's anyone about. We've turned up without asking and I don't want to make any extra work for you. If you could get a bin bag, I'll stick my clothes in it.'

Ruth's teeth chatter as she speaks; she is drenched from the waist down and from her elbows to her wrists. Emma hurries to the kitchen where flickering tea lights line the windowsill behind the sink, and she can see the outline of the garage against the darkening sky. In the candlelight, the furnishings seem softer and the room holds her in its familiar embrace. The smell of chicken leaks from the canvas bags Rob dumped on the table and she can hear the boys laughing in the lounge. Once Ruth is settled beside Janet's heater, Emma will let Chris out. Who knows what will happen then? It is as hard for her to envisage his reaction as it is for her to picture the flood on the patio trickling into the house. Her imagination is failing her; she sees herself turning the key in the lock, and then – nothing.

Bin bag in hand, Emma watches Ruth's outline through the frosted pane of the front door, and once Ruth is wrapped in the purple dressing gown, Emma edges past the door and holds out the bin bag. 'I'd wash everything for you, but the power …'

'Oh, don't worry.'

Ruth lifts her jacket from the pile of clothes and stuffs her hand in a pocket to remove a bundle of soggy envelopes. 'Your presents,' she says. 'Good job gift cards are plastic now.' She opens a button-up pocket in the chest of the coat and retrieves her phone. 'Thank God for that.'

'How exactly did you …?' Emma asks as Ruth drops sopping clothes into the bag.

'Rob. He's such a …'

Emma waits, curious. But Ruth is not forthcoming, so she makes a sympathetic noise and ties the bag.

'We shouldn't have just turned up like this.'

'No, I'm glad you did,' Emma replies automatically, before realising it's true.


Flames dance behind the grille of the fire as Janet wraps James and Dylan in sheets, tying each grandson round his middle, like a parcel. A pair of lit candles sit on the side, barely penetrating the incoming dark, but with the children dashing about in flapping robes Emma won't light any more in the lounge in case of accidents.

'Sit down,' Emma says to Ruth, and she sits heavily beside the fire.

'Oh, *I* was … never mind,' Janet says, and Ruth shuffles to the middle of the sofa.

The stepladder tree which had seemed smart and amusing when Emma first thought of it is now so under-whelming, she feels stupid. She glances at the box of batteries on the floor beside Janet's keyboard and remem-bers the snowflake lights in the cupboard under the stairs.

'Back in a moment,' she says.

She crouches in the cupboard, delving one hand into the box of decorations while directing the torch beam with the other. Lights found, she straightens as much as she can and, as she backs out of the cupboard, her sore shoulder clips the consumer unit. She swears under her breath and then, in response to a sudden stab of suspicion, flips the consumer unit's lid.

The individual breaker switches point up, a line of raised hands in answer to her question. But the main switch, red, and twice as wide as its neighbours, points down. Emma's mouth drops, too. The power cuts. Every time she has been interrupted, inconvenienced, upset, Chris has watched from on high, toying with her like a god.

She pushes the switch up and is greeted by the sound of the microwave pinging back to life and exclamations from the lounge. She returns the snowflake lights to the box and remains crouched on the floor for a moment, hurt and furious.

'Well, *there's* an answer to prayer!' Janet's exclamation flies from the lounge and into the cupboard where it adds to Emma's anger.

She once read a translated novel in which home was described as a *third skin*. The description interrupted her reading and she paused to look it up, discovering a reference to epidermis, clothes and house: one, two, three. The house has been cool all winter thanks to the shut-off boiler. She has put up with it – wearing an extra layer, knitting herself a poncho, leaving the oven door open after baking – all the while joking with the boys about hardiness and their northern roots. She has done her best to understand and accommodate Chris's fear, and for him to inflict it on her in this particular way, ruining her Christmas hospitality for *his* family, literally *keeping her in the dark*, feels like a personal attack. A piercing of her third skin.

She'd intended to fetch Chris. He can wait, she decides, stepping back into the hall and heading to the kitchen where she turns on the oven. He can wait until she can be bothered to shrug on her coat and splash across the flooded patio. It's her turn to play God. Maybe she'll leave him there for a while. How about three days and three nights? They liked threes in Biblical times, didn't they? Does she like them, too? She entertains the thought for a moment and then dismisses it. Of course she can't: he'll get thirsty, he'll need to use the toilet, and it's Christmas Day tomorrow. But she could, she thinks; she *could*.

In the lounge, Ruth's boys lie on the floor, side by side, eyes closed, as Dylan stands over them. 'Right, sleeping lions, you need to—'

'Isn't it dead lions?' Rob asks.

'Sleeping lions,' Dylan replies.

'Oh, I'm sure we used to—'

'No laughing, from now,' Dylan says. 'First to laugh is out.'

Elijah laughs.

Emma edges around the boys and presses the switch on the plug beside the stepladder tree. The Christmas lights come to life and instantly the room looks better.

'Any word from Chris?' Janet asks.

'He left his phone charging upstairs,' Emma replies carefully.

'You're definitely out now,' Dylan says to Elijah. 'Come on. You're a big boy; no whining.'

'You took the words right out of my mouth, Dylan,' Rob says.

'You can have them back; they're covered in spit.'

Rob laughs.

'It's not so bad, Elijah,' Dylan cajoles. 'You get to help me judge.'

'How long do you think Chris will be?' Janet asks.

Having already lied to Janet and the boys, it should be easy to re-enact the deceit, but Emma hesitates; it's harder in front of Ruth and Rob.

'Well, he's on foot,' she says. 'It's a couple of miles each way, and there's water everywhere. He's probably stopped to help someone.'

'Oh yes, of course!' Janet likes this idea. Emma antici-pates her development of it and, sure enough: 'He'll be an answer to someone's prayers. I expect he's providing a family with their very own Christmas miracle as we speak.'

'He wasn't very keen on doing that this morning,' James remarks.

'So it's more likely he's doing it now, to make up for it.'

No one disagrees with Janet in the lull that follows.

'He won't want to miss the nativity,' she continues. 'Let's hold off and wait for him.'

They will wait, then. It will give Emma time to cook and, with the lights on, the gingerbread cooling, and the frozen party food in the oven, Chris will re-enter the house knowing he's been found out.

'Come on, then,' Dylan says to the cousins. 'We've got the games ready and we're going to absolutely thrash you.'

Ruth's boys scramble to their feet. Emma gently removes Janet's hobby horse from Elijah as he passes; no good can come of him taking it upstairs. He opens his mouth to complain but changes his mind and turns on his heel as the others push through the door and thunder up the stairs. Emma follows them out and slips into the kitchen where she fills the oven with gingerbread, removes the quiches and cheese straws from the freezer to go in next, and places several mince pies on a Christmas plate.

'She goes to the gym every morning, don't you?' Rob is saying when Emma returns, carrying the plate. 'Come on, show us your muscles, Ruth.'

Ruth ignores him, blatantly, making no pretence of preoccupation or mishearing. Emma closes the door behind her and sits on the carpet beside the mince pies. Rob starts to stand but Emma waves him away.

'Sit down. I'll be getting up in a bit. For the gingerbread,' she says.

'You don't do yoga, do you?' Janet asks Ruth.

'She runs,' Rob says. 'What's the problem with yoga?'

'It's dabbling.'

'Dabbling?'

'In *you know what*.'

'Shall we have some music?' Emma suggests.

'Opening the door to deceptive spiritual influences.'

'Mum,' Ruth says.

'Magic and witchcraft.'

Rob laughs. 'Janet, you are *priceless*.'

'Oh, it's no laughing matter.'

'Did you practise the "Calypso Carol"?' Emma asks. She kneels and picks up the keyboard. 'Would you play it for me?'

She passes the keyboard to Ruth who places it on Janet's lap. Then Emma sits again, back against the wall, knees up.

Janet presses a button. A bossa nova drumbeat sways into the room and she sings, mouth wide, forehead creased in concentration, her tuneful voice increasingly reedy with age.

'*Oh, now carry me to Bethlehem …*'

For years it seemed to Emma that there had been a misunderstanding between Chris and his parents, and if she just tried hard enough, she might fix everything. But she is coming to believe that the misunderstanding was all hers, and Chris and his parents understood each other perfectly, choosing to occupy trenches of their own making, while she bounced between them, like an idiot stretcher-bearer. He's on his own now, she thinks. The rescue effort, such as it was, has ended.

Janet stops playing, leans her head back and closes her eyes for a moment. It's warm and cosy in the lounge. Emma is drowsy, too; her head aches, and she feels a little feverish, as if she is coming down with something.

'You know what you'd enjoy, Mum? The carol service on the radio.' Ruth fiddles with her phone. 'I think I …'

'I can bring the radio in from the kitchen,' Emma offers.

'It's all right, I've got an app,' Ruth says as a male voice emerges, reading scripture.

'Oh, lovely. Can you turn it up a bit?' Janet asks.

Emma thinks of Chris, outside in the cold and dark. She thinks of the dead rabbit lying in the washing basket on the passenger seat of her car. She closes her eyes and opens them later – moments or minutes, she can't tell – to discover Janet, fast asleep, face pinkened by the heat from the fire. '*Still, still, still,*' a choir sings from Ruth's phone. '*Sleep, sleep, sleep.*' And despite the sounds from above – heavy feet and the boys' hooting laughter, the adults are all following the choir's command. Emma wants to comment on their tiredness, a little joke about their age might excuse her, as she too surrenders to the feeling. But the words are stuck in the back of her throat and she can't quite angle them out.

There is something she should do. The gingerbread. She must check on it. But her legs are like logs, and when she tries to stand, her co-ordination is off, and her arms lack the strength to push her body up from the floor. She decides to leave it for the moment. She is so snug, and warm. And there is music, beautiful Christmas music: boys' voices soaring and swooping as her eyelids droop and everything turns dark.

## SPORTS LEADER

When you're born first, you're the yardstick, and if you're unlucky enough to be followed by someone who is a tiny bit cleverer, politer, and less primed for trouble, you're going to look bad. Dylan looked bad for years but, recently, the adults in his life have started to comment on his newfound maturity. Kids, though, can see some of the old mischief. There's something in Dylan's expression and stance that reveals itself at opportune moments: as a kid braces themself in the face of a bollocking, or is shushed while they're trying to say something important, Dylan glances their way and some fellow feeling passes between them.

The truth is, Dylan hasn't changed much. He's essentially the same as he always was, it's just that partway through high school, he worked out how to speak to adults. Previously he'd been going about it all wrong: trying to make them laugh, saying the first thing that came into his head, interrupting, teasing – sometimes he hadn't done *anything* yet he still managed to rub people up the wrong way. Like back in Year 7 when he told Miss O'Donnell, his RE teacher, that he and James were Irish twins. Miss O'Donnell said it was offensive. Dylan initially thought she was upset by the maths of it, that she found it shocking to hear about the extent of his parents' shagging during the academic year in which he and James had been born. But she had meant it was racist. She basically called him a racist in front of the whole class during his first week of high school. It wasn't as if he and James were the ones who'd come up with the description, they'd copied it from Nan – it had seemed a convenient way of explaining that yes, the two of them were in the same school year and no, they weren't twins.

Peeved and embarrassed, Dylan felt it was only fair Nan be taken to task, as well. But whenever he saw her, he couldn't find it in himself to say anything. Grandad was still alive then, and he was the disagreeable one, making unasked-for pronouncements like, 'God has always been clear that marriage is between a man and a woman.' Dad would rise to the bait – 'What sort of marital relations are God's favourite? Concubines, polygamy, inheriting your brother's wife after his death …?' – while everyone sat in awkward silence and Dylan tried not to laugh.

It was easy to attribute Nan's silence to the secret adoption of Diet Coke versions of Grandad's full-strength views. But not long after Grandad died, Dylan remembers popping out to the caravan with Dad on some errand or other and mentioning to Nan that he wanted to get home in time to watch the football.

'Oh, that's fine. I like to watch the Olympics when it's on. Anything with horses. And that nice lady presenter. The one with the short hair. You know, I'm *sure* she could find a nice man, if she'd only *try*.'

It occurred to Dylan then that maybe Nan felt the same as Grandad but expressed herself with a greater degree of caution because, unlike Grandad, she wanted to be liked. It had already dawned on him that teachers wanted to be liked as much as he did, and he'd started to pay attention.

Mr Morgan (Drama) was forever mentioning his son, *our Jonnie*. Mr Adams (PE) was fanatical about Newcastle United. Ms Gatehouse (English) had started a lunchtime Writing Club.

'How's *your Jonnie* getting on …

'Good result for the Toon last night …

'Many people at Writing Club today?'

James laughs at Dylan's efforts and says he's probably a psychopath, going around memorising useful stuff about people and using it to his advantage. The thing is, Dylan *likes* people (except Miss O'Donnell). There's a lot of stuff he struggles to remember, but information about other humans sticks. He's a Sports Leader (Level 2) which means he occasionally gets to miss lessons to go to primary schools and help with team tournaments and sports days. Mr Adams lets him loose on the tricky kids. Awkward, uncooperative, stroppy – Dylan doesn't care; almost without exception difficult people need two things: a friend and a responsibility.

It's the same with the cousins now. Dylan is Sports Leader as they play the chocolate game, taking it in turns to scramble into a hat, scarf and gloves, and trying to cut squares of the big block of chocolate with a knife and fork before the next six is rolled. Sometimes the die goes under the bed and then it's up to him to retrieve it, awkwardly – he's wrapped in a sheet, after all – and announce the number. Depending on the state of play, he lies. Elijah has cried several times, which is par for the course, but he has yet to dash downstairs on a tale-telling mission. When it's not Elijah's turn, Dylan gives him jobs.

'Can you turn the gloves the right way out for me …

'Can you roll up the scarf …

'You're a great helper!'

Piece. Of. Cake.

When the chocolate is all eaten – a good portion of it smeared, handlebar moustache-like, across Amos's upper lip and cheeks – they begin their next game: Beanboozled. James decides it *must* be possible to tell the difference between the jelly beans. Stinky socks or tutti-frutti? Dog food or chocolate pudding? He observes everyone's selections and muses over his own – if there's a way to avoid the disgustingness of rotten-egg-, stinky-socks- and baby-wipe-flavoured beans, James believes he can discover it.

'There should be a stinky-cheese-flavour bean,' Nathan says as James flicks the spinner. 'Aunty Emma bought us this book called *The Stinky Cheeseman*. Instead of gingerbread, an old woman—'

'Makes a man out of *stinky cheese*,' Elijah interrupts.

'And no one chases him because he smells *so* bad,' Nathan continues.

Dylan remembers the book. It's possible the cousins were given his and James's old copy.

'And there's an ugly duckling,' Amos adds. 'But he doesn't turn into a swan, he—'

'Grows up to be an *ugly duck*.'

'Elijah! Stop butting in,' Amos says.

'Best of all is the Red Riding Hood poem,' Elijah adds, undeterred.

'That's from a different book,' Nathan says.

'*The small girl smiles. One eyelid flickers. She whips a pistol from her knickers.*' Elijah falls about, laughing. 'From her *knickers*. That is the *best* poem.'

Sometimes, when his dad is driving, Dylan's mum reads aloud in the car. It used to be the funny stuff the cousins are discussing, but now she reads things she liked when she was a teenager. There was this poem she read not long ago about a bloke looking at a painting of his dead wife. 'You *must* have done this at school?' she said to Dylan and James, but they hadn't. She paused to read one part twice, saying it was her favourite: '*Just this. Or that in you disgusts me.*' Afterwards, when Mum and Dad were busy, James said, 'Who do you think Mum was talking about when she read that bit?'

'What do you mean?' Dylan replied. 'It was the bloke in the poem, talking about his wife.'

'I *know* that.'

'But?'

James shrugged. 'Do you think they even *like* each other?'

'Who?'

'Never mind.'

Dylan watches as James flicks the spinner and the cousins crowd him, crouching on wobbly knees, robes tucked into their trousers. While James examines the contents of the box, Dylan thinks of his dad who likes to go on about his weird childhood and how hard it was to grow up believing Grandad and Nan's story of a God who was all set to come back and slaughter everyone He didn't like. Well, at least *that* story had rules. There were good guys and bad guys, and you could opt out of destruction by being holy. Dad's story is much worse. Everything's going to shit, and it's random. There's no protection; goodness won't save anyone. If the world could just hang on for a bit, Dylan would appreciate it: he doesn't want to die a virgin.

He saw something this afternoon. He hasn't told anyone, not even James, though he had the perfect opportunity to exchange confidences when, not long before the cousins arrived, James whispered, 'I kicked some nails into the road the other day. They were lying on the pavement, outside a house with scaffolding. I reckon Dad's puncture was my fault. What if he hasn't gone back for the beanie? What if he's gone for an argument with the people who dropped the nails?'

'Heavy,' Dylan replied, uncertain if his own secret would make James feel better or worse.

While scoffing a third mince pie, despite explicit instructions to the contrary, Dylan had seen something.

Mouth full, jaw working nineteen to the dozen, he'd glanced out of the window as his dad toppled his mum. Shocked, he ducked, raising his head again in time to see his dad stride into the garage. Then his mum locked the door and disappeared into the gap beside the fence. He did nothing, and it has been gnawing at him all afternoon. Dad is trapped in the garage like a wild animal and Nan thinks he's on his way back from town having done something heart-warming.

Dylan understands anger's trajectory, the way it fires straight to feet and fists. He's been in plenty of scraps. Once, he and Callum properly lamped each other: crack, smash, whack, thump, on and on it went until finally, circling between strikes, they saved face by allowing Toe-head and Jonesy to separate them. Dylan also understands less urgent compulsions to wound. He and Toe-head went through a stage of giving each other dead arms until a particularly hard thump resulted in Toe-head hurrying home in tears. For a while, the four of them would intermittently trip each other as they walked around school. There have been protracted episodes of kecking, benching and wedgies. But Dylan has never hit Jonesy who is slight and a good head shorter than him. And he has never hit a girl.

Finally, James selects his bean, and the cousins hold their breath.

James groans. It's not peach; it's vomit flavour. He crouches on all fours, pretending to gag as the cousins laugh.

Dylan watches dispassionately. He wonders whether it is cold in the garage.

*Just you knocking my mum over disgusts me*, he thinks.

# JANET, COME FORTH

Janet's heart, her personal metronome, the first of her organs to form and function, started as the fusion of two tiny tubes, and then bloomed into four chambers, beating for the first time in the damp, dark hollow of her mother's uterus. For decades this complex swirl of muscle, protected by a tough, double-layered sac, has been pumping blood to her lungs to receive fresh supplies of oxygen. Janet's heart has kept time through the many disappointments of her life. Subjected to unkind words and unwelcome events, it has taken feelings that are low in happiness and added a fresh supply of optimism, circulating newly aerated versions of the truth. Now, having beaten more than two billion times, Janet's heart slows.

Her head aches and, despite the fire, the room is newly cold. Never mind, it's Christmas. And what a Christmas it is! She could hardly believe the moment when the doorbell rang and, having hurried to answer it, she discovered Ruth and Rob and the boys, like the Norman Rockwell painting – though there was no snow and everyone's feet were covered in mud, and Ruth was soaked and not merry at all. But the children – three Wise Men, heads topped with crowns, robes tucked into their trousers, Elijah's mouth as chasmal as the boy's in the painting – were exactly as they should be, excitedly awaiting admission. And there were cries of 'Merry Christmas' as Janet, like an innkeeper, said, 'Come in, come in.'

Now her daughter sits beside her, while her son performs a series of good deeds in town: pushing a stalled car through flood water, placing a ring of stones around the lip of a close-to-overflowing pond to save the fish – Janet can picture it all. Though the pain in her head is blossoming into something thick and viscous, and she is assailed by waves of tiredness, she is lucky, isn't she?

Janet's eyes close as her blood pressure drops. The tide of her life recedes, and thoughts are left stranded like shallow pools on a beach.

Once, she was a little girl, running through the streets to feel alive ...

What a gift it was to learn to play the piano ...

How she loved Frank in the beginning, when love was unintentional.

Here she is, singing a solo in church ... Here she is in another church, directing the choir ... Here she is accompanying the Sunday School of a different denomination ... Here she is in the front room at Victory Avenue, playing hymns for the service Frank, having run out of congregations, delivers himself ... Having been sanded and polished by memory, each of these musical moments is now equally happy.

Here are the births of her children, agonies unremembered, her body parting like curtains to reveal first Chris, and then Ruth ...

Here are the children in the kitchen of the farm cottage, back door propped open, the warm smell of the fields blowing in on the ...

Here are the peaceful mornings in the caravan while Frank was out walking … email subscriptions for daily inspirational thoughts landing in her inbox like blessings. She knew the contents of the emails were the same for everyone, but someone wrote 'Dear Janet', didn't they? She always liked …

Here are the bedtimes when Frank, come to say goodnight, turned out the light for her, and she lay, covers touching her chin, like her younger, tucked-in self …

Janet opens her eyes. It's an effort to raise them but worth it, as there's Frank, waiting in the corner, beside Emma's ridiculous 'tree'. Where has he been all this time? A choir sings – what lovely music! She would stand and follow the sound but something strange has happened. Her legs are no longer hers. Neither are her hands. She can see her fingers splayed, motionless on the keyboard, yet they feel separate from her and, vision tunnelling, Janet decides she doesn't need them any more. Her inside parts, caught in the net of her skin, feel liquid and, as the world contracts, it seems she might leak through the latticework and follow the sound of the choir.

Her heart struggles now. There is not enough oxygen to meet her brain's demand and Janet is carried on a tide of oblivion, past thought and back to her beginnings. Her heart, her first organ, the simple, paired tube that folded and looped, separated and divided, then beat, and beat, and beat, is finally beaten.

She closes her eyes. This time, forever.

It is dark, now.

*In the beginning the earth was without form and void.*
In the end it is the same.

Sometimes Dylan's mum makes bread at the weekends and the smell creeps up the stairs and wakes him. He's got a nose for food. It's been a family joke since he was small, another label with which he's been tagged: 'Dylan, the sniffer dog'.

Now, as James kneels on the bedroom floor inspecting jelly beans, the cousins already laughing in anticipation of his imminent flavour-failure, Dylan smells something. He opens the bedroom door and inhales. Gingerbread. Not entirely pleasant: there's a toasted edge to it.

He emulates the cousins, tucking the bottom of his sheet into the waistband of his jeans before taking the stairs two at a time, one hand sliding down the bannister, the other palming the wall. The lounge door is closed. He can hear carols playing. Mum must have lost track of time.

'You need to …' Dylan begins as he steps into the room.

What a joke they are playing! Nan, slumped at the end of the sofa, keyboard on her lap. Rob and Ruth, fast asleep beside her. And Mum, sitting on the floor, back to the wall, legs stretched out, head lolling to the side. Sleeping lions, all four of them, no sign of movement or laughter.

Very funny, he thinks. Hilarious! He thinks this for longer than is reasonable because the alternatives are unthinkable.

'Ha-ha,' he says, his voice uncertain, so it comes out like a question: 'Ha-ha?'

No one moves and Dylan is afraid.

Have they been hurt? Is there an intruder in the house? His heart thumps as he scans the room. But there's nowhere to hide. He notes the plate of mince pies on the floor beside his mum's foot. But he has eaten three. And he's *fine*. Dylan crouches beside her. It's like a spell, he thinks: the princess pricked her finger and fell asleep, and the king, queen and servants all slept, too. He doesn't touch her in case, inexplicably, it is something infectious. He remembers James talking about refugee children in Sweden who lost the will to live and entered a coma-like state following the trauma of being told they were going to be deported. He thinks of what his dad did, earlier: the thud as his mum hit the ground.

His dad. His dad, outside.

Dylan skids into the kitchen and grabs his mum's coat from its hook, frisking it until he finds the garage key.

The back door slams into the worktop edge as he flings it open. His feet splash straight across the patio: trainers, socks and the bottoms of his jeans instantly soaked. He leads with the key, holding it out in front of him like a wand, as if there is magic in its notches.

## THE END OF THE WORLD

The world was always going to end. It ends now as Chris sits on the hay bale in a shallow, alcohol-infected doze, the tide of his breath drying furrows into the roof of his mouth.

He dreams he has built a house on the sand, near the pier. There is samphire growing beside the front door and the views from its windows are astonishing, yet he is filled with dread because he knows the water is coming and he has no idea why he has done this foolish thing.

He stands in the lounge of the improbable house, family around him, as he explains the gravity of their situation.

'In the coming years, one in nine people will be on the move,' he lectures, pacing, just as his father, in his house-church phase, paced on Sunday mornings when Chris was a teenager, his steps a percussion accompaniment to long, fraught sermons.

The boys aren't paying attention. Dylan wears head-phones; James holds a magazine in front of his face. When *my* father spoke, I listened, Chris thinks, momentarily forgetting his own escape, not via music or literature but a job at a garden centre since, in his father's mind, work was the only legitimate excuse for absence.

'By the year 2200 the sea levels will have risen by almost ten metres. And that's probably wrong – estimates are always too conservative.'

'We'll all be dead,' Emma says gently.

What rubbish, Chris thinks, 2200 isn't so far away.

'The whole town will disappear,' he continues.

'You can't know that.'

'You think they'll build a wall here to protect us? You think they'll bother? In the *desolate north*?'

'We'll all be dead,' she says again.

'Shut up,' he replies, as scared of her words as he is of the incoming tide.

If there were only cliffs, he thinks. But no. In East Anglia, the sea is eating the cliffs while the government adopts a strategy of 'managed realignment', and in Happisburgh, near Norwich, people are retreating from the earliest known human settlement in Europe. There's something portentous about that.

'Silly man,' Emma says. 'You can't stop the future.'

'Shut *up*.'

'If you can just retain some hope in the present—'

'I don't want *hope*,' he shouts.

A tot of dread, a nip of horror, a shot of anger – he isn't asking much. If Emma would only join him in a measure of *something*. It's all right for her; she doesn't spend her days outside, trying to shape the world in ways that are less and less possible.

'You're a hypocrite,' he says. 'That poem? *Rage, rage against the dying of the light*. "Ooh, I love it!" you said. But you're not enraged by *anything*, are you?'

And then he hears the water. He turns in time to see it charging towards his foolish house, waves rolling over each other like separator blades on a thresher. The boys – Dylan, deafened by his headphones; James, blinded by the angle of his magazine – haven't noticed. Emma sees though, and, placing her hand on his shoulder, murmurs, '*Many waters cannot quench love, neither can the floods drown it.*'

Chris shrugs her off and concentrates on the water, coming at them like the future. He is not a strong swimmer. He will struggle to save himself, never mind his family.

The water comes and comes. He is hypnotised by it: reeling, roaring, never quite arriving. Eventually, he glances back into the world of his house, his lounge. While he has been studying the water, time has passed. Emma is old. And the boys are gone.

It smashes him, then. An uppercut to his exposed jaw, chased by a full body blow, rendering him helpless as the house collapses and his lungs flood. He is gasping, struggling against the pressure when the garage door bursts open, and the darkness is divided.

Chris starts. He coughs, the inside of his mouth bone-dry and rippled.

It's not Emma come to liberate him. Though it could be an angel, he thinks for a moment, confused by the figure's bright torso. But no, it is Dylan, insensible and frantic, inexplicably wrapped in a sheet. The water must be in the house. Chris shoots to his feet, swiping strands of hay from his clothes. He should have filled the sandbags. But he was busy drinking, caught in a loop of *poor me*. Disgusted with himself, he staggers after Dylan, through the standing water that *hasn't* yet breached the back door – not that, then. But there is something else, something bad; he can hear it in Dylan's repeated 'Dad, Dad!'

The lights are on. Emma must have discovered the flipped switch. His stomach plummets as he wonders what she will say and, worse, what *he* will offer by way of explanation. Having grown and justified the idea in the shelter of his own thoughts, only now does he doubt its ability to withstand the blaze of her scrutiny.

The kitchen smells of burning sugar and Chris's concern eases as he pauses in front of the oven, twists the dial and opens the door. Smoke billows into the room. *There*, he thinks. But Dylan grabs his arm and pulls him on.

The scene in the lounge seems staged. Unreal. Chris curses his vodka-fogged thoughts. Four statues. Pillars of salt. As if they've been touched by something supernatural. The world has stopped, and he must start it again.

For a moment, Chris considers that this may be the second in a series of nightmarish dreams and there could, therefore, be a simple solution, a way of outsmarting his imagination and undoing whatever has happened. Naaman, touched by leprosy, and King Midas, by his own greed, washed themselves in rivers. Is water the key to this sickness, too?

But no – he is awake; the soles of his feet pressed to the floor, hands clenching and unclenching, stupefied by confusion. Christmas music streams from a phone on the floor beside the sofa. '*Who with his sunshine and his showers turns all the patient ground to flowers.*'

Chris looks again: Emma's daft tree is lit, and the room is toasty thanks to his mother's fire – oh, the fucking fire. He curses and turns it off before dashing into the hall where he opens the front door, wide, propping it with a heavy bin bag lying nearby.

As cool air rushes into the house he thinks he hears the sea but it's only his thoughts crashing against one another.

Back in the lounge he opens the windows. 'Get them out, get them out,' he says, while Dylan stands beside the sofa, as immobile as the others. Rob moans in response to Chris's voice and Chris shakes him, hard. 'Get up and get out.'

Rob tries to move and ends up on all fours.

'Call 999,' Chris says, suspending Dylan's shock.

There is no time to weigh anything. Chris must carry someone out first. The decision is born of instinct but also comes down to this: who can manage without their mother? And the answer is: him.

Crouching, Chris grabs the loops on the waist of Emma's jeans. Her face is flushed, and she is warm to the touch. He manoeuvres her so she is sprawled against his shoulder; then he struggles to his feet and, legs trembling, carries her into the hall like a sack of potatoes. 'Tell them about the gas fire,' he calls to Dylan.

His nephews appear on the landing, dressed as Wise Men, alongside James who, like Dylan, is wrapped in a sheet.

'Boys, get down here and go outside. Round the back, now.'

'I'll take them,' Dylan says.

'Just call 999.'

'What are you doing with Aunty Emma?' Amos asks, hesitating at the top of the stairs.

'Sleeping lions, for the grown-ups,' Dylan says. 'Come down, quick. Who wants to see some really burned biscuits? And who wants to stroke Girl Rabbit?' He herds the boys into the kitchen and Chris hears his nephews' muted responses to the burned gingerbread as he staggers out into the darkness.

Just put Emma on the drive, Chris thinks. It doesn't matter about the wet; it's the oxygen that's important. But he can't make himself do it. The vestiges of the dream

– his foolish house, the menacing water – mean he can't turn and leave her in the dark, on the remembering ground. What if he returns to discover she, like great chunks of the field opposite, has been reclaimed by the water?

Awkwardly, he tries the back door of her car. It's unlocked. He kicks it wide and struggles to manage her weight as he bends, attempting to lay her across the seat. Once she's in, he angles her on to her side and checks to make sure she is breathing.

As he skids back into the house, he hears James, on the phone.

'... that's right. The bridge is closed, though. Yeah ... The long way round.'

'I need help,' he says to James.

'No, I won't hang up,' James tells the operator, holding the phone with one hand and untying his sheet robe with the other. 'But I've got to help my dad ... Four. My uncle Rob's breathing ... No, he's crawling ... My mum, my aunty Ruth and my nan ... I don't know.'

Chris grasps Ruth under the arms. For some reason, she is wearing his mother's dressing gown.

'Grab her ankles,' he says as James stuffs his phone in his back pocket and his sheet drops to the floor. 'One, two, three, *lift*.'

Chris shuffles down the hall backwards, banishing thoughts of the young, bossy Ruth as he attempts to keep his emotions in check.

'Hang on,' James says.

Chris manages Ruth's weight as James adjusts his grip, heaving one sturdy leg and then the other, until each calf is tucked under one of his arms and her knees sit just below his shoulders, round and stippled like wheels of blue-veined cheese.

They shuffle past Rob who has almost managed to crawl to the door but is resting now, forehead on the floor.

'Where are we taking her?' James asks as they step on to the drive.

'To the car. If we can get her in the passenger seat, I can lie it back.'

'Are you driving them—'

'No, just getting them out here, into the fresh air.'

A washing basket sits on the passenger seat. There's something in it, wrapped in a towel. It strikes Chris as odd until he remembers Emma's earlier threat; she must have gone to the vet.

'Move that out of the way,' he says.

James relinquishes Ruth's legs, leaving them sprawled on the wet ground. He removes the basket and adjusts the seat. They manage to heft her into it and tip her towards them, facing the open door. Then Chris belts her in.

It hits James, as they step back. Chris sees the horror on his face as he looks at Emma lying on the back seat.

'Get your phone out and let them know what's happening. And talk to Mum,' Chris says. 'Tell her about those birds, the storytelling ones. See if you can get her or Ruth to wake up while I get Nan.'

On his way into the house Chris steps over Rob who is vomiting on the doormat. Good, he thinks. And then he's back in the lounge, lifting his mother's hands from her keyboard. He puts it on the carpet and, kneeling, manoeuvres her on to the floor. He places his hands under her armpits and, apologising, drags her first into the hall and then the kitchen. Kneeling again, he clasps her wrist and feels for a pulse.

Nothing.

He uses three fingers in case he has missed it.

Silence.

He presses them to her neck, and waits.

There are runner bean seeds in a drawer behind him. Smooth and shiny, harvested from the inedible too-thickened coats of last year's crop. All they need is a dark bed and a little water, and they will spiral skyward.

Death is a process, James says. Brain waves, like those experienced during sleep, can continue after the heart has stopped; brains and hearts may even have different moments of death.

In the face of further silence, Chris places the heel of one hand on his mother's breastbone and the other hand on top. If only he could open her up and harvest something he might place in a dark bed, with a little water, allowing her to emerge again in the spring.

He isn't counting; he doesn't know the right numbers. It's all compressions now, isn't it? He thinks he's heard that but can't be sure.

Already tiring, Chris is aware again of music streaming out of the phone in the lounge, a carol he's never heard before; a dirge, with no helpful beat to urge him on.

*And they did eat, which was a sin,*
*And thus their ruin did begin;*

296

*Ruined themselves, both you and me,*
*And all of their posterity.*

He swears – softly, in case his mother can hear – his strength briefly renewed as he pushes against the disagreeable words.

Dylan appears at the open back door. The nephews peep around him, faces pale, quiet for once.

'Thirty compressions to two rescue breaths, Dad.'

'Go away,' Chris huffs.

'We did it. At school. You need to lock your elbows.'

'Go. Away.'

Dylan disappears with the boys. Chris counts to thirty, and then to two; thirty, and two.

If he is very lucky, this may be the middle of his life.

Thirty blows.

Might it be the end of his mother's?

Two breaths.

She saw him into the world.

Thirty blows.

Is he seeing her out?

Two breaths.

He never asked what she *really* thought of her life.

Thirty blows.

Would she have even been able to tell him?

Two breaths.

Thirty, then two. Thirty, then two. Chris keeps going, shoulders burning, sweat gathering on his forehead. Until, finally, the choir's mournful singing is interrupted by the sound of sirens wailing across the Moss.

# PART 5

# You Are Here

# Christmas Eve, one year later

## AND IT CAME TO PASS

One orbit of the sun later, barely a beat in time, and bulbs that reached from their outer papery coverings as the soil warmed have since retreated. Crops have been planted and supplanted. Hibernating animals awoke, and now sleep again. The potholes on the other side of the bridge, finally repaired, are reopening as rain seeps into cracks in the bitumen. Global surface temperatures continue to rise, and the extent and thickness of Arctic sea ice continues to decline, exposing landscapes that haven't seen the sun for more than a hundred thousand years. Thawing permafrost releases ancient viruses and bacteria, while melting glaciers unveil the dead bodies of climbers. And Chris Abram parks his van on the drive outside his house.

He parks here briefly on weekday mornings to collect and return tools, and on Wednesday evenings and Saturdays when he comes to see his sons. He still has house keys but hasn't been using them.

Chris opens the driver's door and the outside air spears him. This winter is colder than last. There have been floods on the southern plains and in market towns further north. But not here. Not this time.

Emma hears the engine and steps to the window. The light is fading. Soon it will be dark. She glances at the cloud-forsaken sky; there will be a frost tonight. In the morning, she will fasten her coat, step outside and, hands wrapped around a cup of coffee, appreciate the cold.

On returning from hospital, plagued by headaches and dizziness, she'd felt like her grandparents: perpetually on a quest for fresh air. At first, the boys followed her about, as they used to when they were little. Chris made solicitous enquiries as to her well-being but otherwise said very little. He was grieving and she didn't feel up to confrontation; it could wait. He elected to sleep on the sofa bed so she wouldn't be disturbed by his snoring. After work and at quiet times, he made alterations to the patio, hoping to improve the drainage. Enclosed by a lid of grief, his long-standing misanthropy bubbled over when he was alone. Emma heard it in the crash as he unfolded the sofa bed each night and saw it in the furious way he wielded the pickaxe as he smashed a pattern in the flags. She suspected he was saving it up, for when she was better. So, when the park reopened and he said he would go to the caravan, she was relieved. The thought of him sitting in the house during the last blast of winter, dragging every breath of happiness from the air like an emotional dehumidifier, was enough to make her head ache again.

But at night, Emma wished him back. She had strange bereavement dreams. After her grandparents died, she searched for them in her sleep, knowing she would find them just around the next corner, or the next, or the next. After Chris left, she dreamed he wandered the earth like Gilgamesh, overcome with sadness and afraid of death, desperate to solve the puzzle of mortality. When she woke, she felt unnerved and confused; Chris wasn't dead, but in those first moments of the morning, lying beside his empty place, it fleetingly seemed as if he was, and she missed him. Then she remembered his snoring. His cynicism. His disregard of her opinions, and her feelings, and the wet thunk as he knocked her to the ground.

Chris steps on to the drive. He remembers standing here a year ago as the ambulances pulled away. He remembers standing here, weeks later, packing his belongings into the van.

When he first left, he blamed the rain. Its constant drub had worn him thin, eroding the person he'd cultivated since leaving home, and uncovering his old, credulous self. He blamed Emma for not having been as alarmed as she should; for the unwarranted consolations of wishy-washy gestures – refusing to upgrade her ancient phone, starting a second-hand uniform sale at the primary school, making vegetable broth out of kitchen scraps: so what? He blamed his mother for bringing the gas fire and his father for buying it. He blamed the pair of them for dying within months of each other before he'd had a chance to make peace with either. He blamed circumstances. If he'd made more money the previous year, he wouldn't have been so keen to turn off the boiler. If the weather had been cooler, he'd have been persuaded to turn it back on. If the caravan hadn't developed a leak, his mother would never have come to stay. If the rabbit had taken better care of itself, Emma wouldn't have locked him in the garage. If Rob and Ruth had stayed at home, Ruth wouldn't have fallen in the ditch and needed warming up.

And then there were other ifs. If Dylan didn't have a nose for food. If the lounge door had been shut not for twenty-five minutes, but for thirty, thirty-five, forty …

'What about *you*?' Emma had said, standing on the caravan steps, dropping off a canvas shopping bag containing tins of beans and bags of rice from his store in the garage. 'You're conveniently absent from this list. What if *you* hadn't faked the power cuts?'

'That was neither here nor there,' he replied. 'It made no difference to what—'

'It made – *makes* a difference to me. To know you were enjoying—'

'I wouldn't say *enjoying*—'

'—watching me struggle. Manipulating me by pressing a button, like I was a robot and you had a remote control. Spoiling things. Disrupting everyone. Ruining Christmas Eve. There I was, trying not to react, trying to keep calm because you were already so anxious—'

'*Anxious* isn't how I would —'

'—and all while it wasn't *real*. You were just trying to frighten me.'

Chris felt a strong urge to deny it; it hadn't been like that all. He'd only been trying to make his family feel a *fraction* of the worry he was feeling, to make them *see*.

He recalled that day: Dylan's and James's horror as their mum, aunt and uncle were loaded into ambulances. His own, as the paramedics stopped working on his mother. Finally, a communal fear.

Had there been comfort in seeing his sons terrified and attentive? Had he been glad?

'It was about preparation,' he parried. 'That's—'

'You treated me with contempt, and you're not accepting any responsibility for—'

'Are you saying it's all my—'

'*Listen*, Chris. I don't trust you any more.'

'OK,' he said heavily. 'OK.'

It wasn't so bad at the caravan. In the mornings, when he woke, the air had a fresh, outdoor quality, reminding him of the few occasions he'd been camping. He could feel his parents there, in the last of their belongings, and rather than veer away from old ideas and feelings, instinctively seeking opposing routes, he tried to examine other, less absolute courses.

Ruth called regularly, taking the temperature of his mood in brisk, nurse-like interrogations. She had left hospital with a high-frequency hearing loss which they hoped may improve, in time, and occasionally Chris heard Rob in the background, calling, 'Mummy's on the phone, the quiet game starts now!' In the meantime, Ruth happily took advantage of Chris's sympathy: would he come one evening and teach the women's group at Rob's church how to make compost? she asked. Would he come back and teach about tapestry lawns? About companion planting?

He knew what she was up to and his instinct was to evade capture. But she persuaded him and now he sees there are different ways of being caught: it's one thing to be seized by a lasso, another to be saved by a well-positioned net.

The church was applying for a Community Resilience Grant to fund a community garden – would Chris take charge of the project if they were successful? the rector wondered. Would he teach some gardening classes as part of a neighbouring congregation's Men and Mental Health project?

'I'm not religious,' Chris said, a heads-up in case the rector preferred to ask someone else.

'Yes, a lot of people aren't.' The rector smiled politely and waited for a moment. 'Was there something else?' he asked.

Emma watches as Chris steps away from the house and walks to the wall where he stops and looks along the road to the bridge. He said he would bake something for the party. She wonders what he has made. The house smells of cooling mince pies and the leek tarts and Brussels sprout and bacon pizzettas still in the oven.

In the spring, the leeks started their lives on the kitchen windowsill as, outdoors, the first bulbs nosed their way into the warmth and branch-tips gleamed green. Newspapers printed photographs of half-naked women lying in parks during another hottest Easter, and Emma sweated, draining the water butts so she could wet the soil around newly planted potatoes and the tiny first-threads of carrot tops.

On Saturday afternoons, the boys got themselves ready to run. It wasn't the same. The performance of reluctance, the sulking and recalcitrance, had been their main source of pleasure, and they were newly hesitant, unsure about the real-world impact of any disobedience. Emma concluded that Chris, too, had enjoyed *making* the boys do it, and their obvious humouring of him also took the edge off his pleasure. She pretended uninterest and then, once the three of them had left, she stepped outside and walked to the thin band of pavement at the front of the house. The boys' interactions with Chris had been sullen and monosyllabic since Christmas Eve but the moment he moved out, surliness was replaced by uncertainty and Emma, sensing they were assigning themselves a role in his departure, reiterated that it was just a break, a chance for Chris to spend some time on his own and have a think about things. She watched the three of them, long legs motoring as they disappeared into the distance, before walking round the back to check on the garden.

Girl rabbit, christened Mary Hoppins by the boys, bounded into her run as Emma passed. In the meadow, emerging tulip leaves were laced with holes, but the lilies were unharmed, though, their leaves fanning like pineapple crowns. She thought of Frank who, many years ago, having overheard a passing remark about favourite flowers, presented her with a bag of fifty bulbs he'd picked up for a couple of pounds because they had already sprouted. Emma had added them to the jumble of flowers in the meadow: the daffodil and crocus bulbs she'd planted; the crimson clover, forget-me-nots, and poppies grown from seed; and the gatecrashing ragged robin and bluebells. She usually left everything to fend for itself, but she always kept an eye on the lilies. She should have planted them in clumps, she realised, that first year as they shot up, head and pedicel above their neighbours, striking and lonely. Frank examined them when he visited and declared himself pleased. Sometimes, Emma had almost warmed to him. What must it be like, she wondered, to believe there was *one* right way to live? How to accommodate such a person? Janet opted for discipleship and pacification. Chris and Ruth each settled on a version of compartmentalisation, recognising, consistently in Ruth's case and erratically in Chris's, that a gamut of ideas and emotions were effectively verboten. Emma would not allow Chris to put his family in a similar position, she decided as she stepped carefully through the emerging vegetation, noting each of the returning lilies.

Chris reaches into the van and lifts his contribution to the Christmas Eve festivities from the passenger seat: a tub of brownies; dark chocolate slabs speckled by the first fruits of his mother's cherry tree – picked, pitted and frozen back in June. He has done a lot of cooking this year: easy, quick stuff for himself; but each Wednesday night, having accompanied James to hockey practice, he returned to the house where he prepared something decent for the family and, afterwards, the boys took to making themselves scarce as he washed up and Emma dried. Sometimes there was small talk. Sometimes, in late spring, when things between them began to feel a little easier, they sat at the table with mugs of tea and there was tentative big talk.

'What should I *do*?' he asked one evening.

'Reseed the lawn where the grass has died.'

'That's not what I meant.'

Later that week, he collected a postcard from the site office. On the back Emma had scrawled:

*It may be that when we no longer know what to do,*
*we have come to our real work*
*and when we no longer know which way to go,*
*we have begun our real journey.*

Wendell Berry

The next time he saw Emma, Chris said he would follow his mother's motto and, henceforth, say only nice things.

Emma said it was a terrible idea, particularly as niceness, in his mother's mind, equated to smothering words in a buttery icing of soft intonation and smiles. She understood Chris had been unhappy for some time, experiencing what she could only describe as an anticipatory grief, but she believed there *had* to be a better way of dealing with sadness than what he was proposing, a way that wasn't reliant on pretence. Keeping it all inside, attempting to change his skin from permeable to watertight, was not a solution.

'I don't want you to censor yourself,' she continued. 'Well, maybe a bit,' she added, and the skin around her mouth rimpled with the faint echoes of bygone smiles. 'But perfection is the enemy of good. I just want you to stop being … like a swimmer with cramp who ends up drowning the lifeguard.'

He looked at her, properly. Grey hairs flecked her temples and frown lines rode her forehead like breakers. Would she like to swap with him for a while now the weather was warmer? he wondered. Would she like the silence and evenings, after work, spent looking after no one but herself?

She said she wouldn't, but thanked him for asking, and for considering that she might.

He could see how tired she was. How she might not love him any more. How that, too, felt like the end of the world.

'Dad's here,' Emma calls.

The boys' feet pound the stairs, and she hears Dylan's hand palming the wall as he descends.

'Hand. Wall. Dylan!'

'I'll get my playlist on,' he calls, heading for the kitchen to connect his phone to the digital radio.

'Listen,' he calls again.

She does and, with some dismay, recognises 'Believe', an unfamiliar a cappella arrangement, sung by a male voice choir.

'All we need is some ribbon dancing, and Emma-Jane will be in bits.'

She wraps an arm around James's waist, half-hug, half-remonstration. He rests his chin on her head for a moment before breaking free.

'Can we have a mince pie?'

'Can't you wait a— Oh, go on then,' she says, stepping back to the window where she can see Chris, standing beside the wall, glancing down the road at the bridge.

In the summer, she began to walk him to the door when he left. They stood in the doorway, saying their goodbyes, her inside the house, him in the porch. It reminded her of when they were first seeing each other: one last kiss, followed by another, and another, until her father, unable to sleep while the front door was unlocked, appeared on the landing and despite Emma's reassurances and protests about her age, called, 'Goodnight, Chris, goodnight *now*.'

One evening, having let her feelings slide back to fondness, she almost kissed Chris. But, ice melting, she discovered a blast of buried anger under the surface.

'You knocked me over,' she said.

'You shoved me first.'

'You're stronger.'

'You're prettier.'

'Not funny.'

She stared at him until they were both uncomfortable.

'I'm really sorry,' he said.

'For what?'

'Knocking you over. All of it.'

For a moment she saw him as a stranger might: tired and lean, worried trenches digging his forehead, under-eye skin scalloped and smudged blue. And then, in a blink, he was Chris again. Just Chris. The young man with the chainsaw, the older man with the sandwich board, and every man between; her lips had covered all his ground. When love fails you, do you have to go on believing in it? She thought of her own body, altered by the before and after of childbirth and, lately, by the origami of age. She was the same, she had once joked, in the way a grape and a raisin are the same: underneath the changes, she remained herself. And she could see how easy it would be to love Chris – to continue loving Chris, if there was hope of him returning to himself.

'It won't happen again.'

'No, it won't,' she replied, and shut the door, softly, as if her father were upstairs, trying to sleep.

Not long after, Emma found a button from his mother's blouse on the floor under the sofa. She wasn't sure what to do with it and asked if he would mind her incorporating it into the quilt she was making. He nodded, and Emma went on to remind him of the time when Janet, visiting for Sunday lunch, had asked for a duster, presumably to clean their filthy house, though she was careful not to say as much; she had asked very politely – *nicely*, in fact. Chris laughed and mentioned the time his parents gave them a hundred pounds towards the kitchen, thereafter repeatedly referring to 'the kitchen we bought you'. Emma, softening, recalled Janet, after James was born, confiding that she had callouses on her knees from praying for Emma's recovery, and then lifting her skirt to prove it. Chris nodded. He remembered his mother taking him to one side to say Dylan would turn out fine in the end, she was sure of it.

At night, Emma sat in the sewing room, listening to audiobooks on her phone as she worked. She had orders for reusable Christmas gift wrap and bags, and bundles of washable napkins, quilted place mats and table runners. Once in bed, she swapped to a real book and as she lay on her side, thumb pressed between the pages, she was newly struck by writers' dependency on paper. On trees. On sunlight. On water. On carbon dioxide. The way every physical book is a product of thinking and forests. The instant she had the thought, she wanted to share it with Chris.

She told James, at breakfast, instead.

'Want to hear something I've been thinking?' he asked. 'You know you've got this immense ecosystem of bacteria, fungi, yeasts and viruses that weighs more than your brain living in your gut? And you know how when you read something or hear something that makes you feel anxious – like, say, *over a hundred species go extinct every day* – you feel it in your gut? That churning feeling. Well, this is what I've been thinking: we're in *our* world – Planet Earth, watching things go tits up; and they, the bacteria and all that, are in *theirs* – the gut, responding to the worry that's being introduced into their climate. How weird is that?'

Dylan appeared, face creased down one side, yawning.

'Is it all right if the lads come round after school?'

He'd started checking after Chris left, as if he didn't quite know how things worked any more.

'It's been a while,' Emma said. 'Has there been a falling out?'

'We're allowed round at Toe-head's now. His dad's left, too.'

'Yours hasn't *left* left.'

James made a show of looking under the table. 'Well, he's not here.'

'Is he coming back, then?' Dylan asked.

'He'll be round on Saturday.'

'Not an answer, Emma-Jane.'

The return of Dylan's mates and James's needling were annoying, yet welcome signs that things were getting back to normal.

Emma stood, stuffed her feet into her trainers and opened the back door.

'Snails are shredding the lettuces,' she said. 'I'm going to see if I can catch them at it.'

'You need hedgehogs,' James began. 'I read—'

'Dad could help,' Dylan said. Then he muttered something about adults. No idea. *Tut*. Everyone needs two things. *Pft*. A friend. *Sigh*. And a responsibility.

'What was that?' Emma asked.

'Nothing,' he said.

By the following Saturday, Dylan had found some chunky timber off-cuts on Freecycle. The woman even offered to drop them off after he complimented the rockery in the background of her photograph. Once they got back from football, Chris and the boys made a hedgehog house which they placed at the end of the garden, near the vegetables, hoping its future inhabitants would return the favour by eating the snails.

There's no waterlogging this December, just the dark soil on the other side of the ditch, waiting, its inhabitants alive and insulated under the frost layer. Before Chris knows it, there will be barley growing there; it will be summer again, and sweltering, probably. But he's going to have to get used to it, isn't he? Everyone is.

In the summer, he bought a sunblock stick and drew thick stripes under his eyes. And he made unsolicited suggestions to customers.

'Given the rising temperatures, I think it'd be a good idea to plant some tall annuals to act as windbreaks and stop soil moisture evaporating …

'Have you thought about finding a way to collect the run-off water from the drainpipes so you can water, next time there's a drought …

'How about shading the soil here with some vining plants to give it a little protection next summer?'

Occasionally someone told him he was in thrall to the Chinese or the Russians and accused him of getting his facts from the MSM. Once, he was charged with subscribing to a watermelon philosophy: green on the outside, Communist underneath.

'Oh, come on!' he said, laughing. 'I'm encouraging you to take *individual responsibility*!'

While working on the community garden, he picked up jobs from new friends and friends of friends: problem-solving, thinking-of-the-future work.

'I've been learning about biodiversity and don't want a lawn any more, what can I do instead?'

'I'd like a pond, but I'm worried about mosquitoes. Do you think it'll be OK as long as there's movement in the water?'

'I read this incredible novel about trees; I've got space to plant some, but I don't know what to get.'

Here was a way of activating his imagination in the service of preparation: running through worst-case scenarios and envisaging outcomes without upsetting anyone. And as he did this, it struck Chris that he was part of a ready-made network of people who might like to do something worthwhile. A group of them began to get together once a week on a Saturday or Sunday afternoon; Chris preferred Sunday, though it wasn't always possible – these were church people, after all. Sometimes he brought the boys and Emma with him. They planted trees, vegetables and fruit bushes. Built raised beds, attached diverters to downpipes, assembled a greenhouse – whatever labour each householder required during their allotted afternoon. Between them, they requisitioned used concrete fence panels, breeze blocks and pallets, old bathtubs, scrap sheet metal and discarded doors: repurposing broken objects and abandoned dreams.

July saw the hottest day ever recorded in the UK. And then came the downpours. At the house, the patio flooded, though not as badly as at Christmas. When Chris checked the online forecast, he tried, and failed, to ignore the news: huge swathes of the Arctic were ablaze, deforestation of the Brazilian Amazon was happening at a rate of three football fields per minute, government advisors declared the lack of climate crisis planning in the UK to be shocking. He started to feel restless again, utterly sick when he thought of the boys' future and inordinately irritated by the holey socks Emma was turning into fingerless gloves – it was all micro-consumerist bollocks, wasn't it? During a Sunday-afternoon garden blitz, surrounded by cheerful, optimistic people who laughed as they brainstormed 'punny' names for the group – Weed it and Reap, Strawberry Fields Wherever, Another One Fights the Dust – Chris felt himself withdrawing. Why was he encouraging a collective delusion that a few raised beds and fruit trees could make a difference to anything?

Before he'd had time to note or appreciate their absence, the old feelings rushed back, each day bringing him closer to a time when the convergent impacts of climate change would coalesce in nightmarish scenarios, supposedly beyond imagination, though he was giving it a good go. He thought of his father's obsession with Job, and the idea that a willingness to sacrifice everything might lead to Godly approval. Chris remembered a much younger Ruth asking whether he knew *the whole story*, and then listening as she whispered that God had *killed* Job's family and taken his money as a kind of test, only to give him more money and a *new family*, later, after he'd proved his loyalty. Can you *believe* it? she'd asked indignantly. What if, like Job, their father endured his life's test and was rewarded with a different family? Where did that leave them?

Chris lay in his father's old bed, staring at the ceiling. He might be living in a caravan, swamped again by the misery of his helplessness, but he'd keep his family, thank you very much.

He dragged himself out of bed in the mornings, forcing himself to speak to people. He had planned, in the autumn, to ask Emma if he might come back, but envisioning his despair as a tidal event, something that might recede again, in time, he decided to wait. He went to work, saw the boys, sat with Emma and made halting attempts at conversation. Then he returned to the caravan, slept, and began again. And again. Until the hole into which he had fallen seemed shallower, its sides less sheer, and he could see his way out.

As Christmas approached, Ruth wondered what he would do when the caravan park closed. He was welcome to stay with her and Rob. Chris thanked her but said he would be leaving for good at the end of the season – their mother had paid the year's site fees in advance, and he didn't have the money to pay for a second year. Ruth drew breath and he knew she was going to offer to pay. The caravan should be sold, he said quickly. It was old, and by the time the site owners had taken 10 per cent of the sale and collected their disconnection fee, there'd likely be nothing left, but if there was, it was their money and he'd make sure she got her share. Would he come for Christmas, then? Ruth wondered. He thanked her again and declined. He'd spoken to Emma and he was going home.

And here he is. Home. The last of his belongings packed in the back of the van. He turns and sees Emma, standing in the window beside the stepladder tree. A year is a dash and a distance; no time at all and five hundred million miles of travel around the sun. It is helpful to remember that each moment arrives on the crest of everything that happened before – the thirteen billion plus orbits that have already occurred. What can he do in the face of that? Inhabit the world by living well in his part of it. And if there isn't hope, there is hard work, and that may have to do, for now.

When Chris raises his free hand, Emma waves back, watching as clouds of breath swirl around his head. This winter is cooler than last. As autumn ebbed and the temperature dropped, Emma had thought about asking if he would like to come home. She knew it must be freezing at the caravan – he was sleeping in Frank's old bed, under a blanket and both his parents' duvets. But something wasn't right.

'Is anything bothering you?' she asked.

He shook his head.

'I'm proud of what you're doing,' she said. 'Lending yourself out to people, like a human library.'

She waffled on about shared spaces and culture: museums, parks and libraries – the importance of *everyone* benefiting from collective wealth. It must feel good, she said, to know that more than twenty families were growing food because of him. And wasn't it great that there was a waiting list long enough to keep him and the other volunteers going until spring, depending on the weather?

She awaited a response, and then, ill advisedly, perhaps, having told the boys to tread carefully, mentioned their participation in the recent school strike and their subsequent detentions, or time spent as 'prisoners of conscience', as James put it. She brought up the suspension of fracking and remarked on the council's declaration of a climate emergency. She asked where he would be volunteering on the coming Sunday.

'Yes,' he replied, absently, before trudging outside to winter wash the cherry trees.

What if his peripheral vision was forever occupied by this bleakness? And what if, each time he glanced at it, he temporarily turned to stone?

Let him try, Emma decided. The geese were on the move, honking as they split the sky in arrow formations. She had flown ahead throughout the previous year, cutting the drag in half. But flight is a journey of turns. She would help, if he asked. Otherwise, this time, it was up to him.

The weeks passed, and, eventually, he returned, restrained and weary. *There* you are, she thought, welcome back.

Is love a choice? Perhaps it becomes one, over time. Meanwhile, there is work to do and food to make. Revision to schedule and homework to supervise. The boys' exams loom large and college and sixth-form prospectuses wait on the kitchen worktop; personal statements must be finalised (in James's case) and written (in Dylan's) during the Christmas break.

Emma moves away from the window as the boys slope into the lounge.

'Remember the sheet costumes, last year, for Nan's nativity?' Dylan says, half a mince pie in his hand.

'Not many lads your age would have humoured their nan like that. I'm sure it meant a lot to her.'

'She asked if I'd "open proceedings".'

'With what?' James says, surprised.

'The first bit of the nativity story. I remember it, from school.'

'Really? Let's hear it, then,' James says.

'*And it came to pass in those days, that there went out a decree from Caesar Augustus, that all the world should be taxed.*'

Emma remembers the over-warm school hall. Dylan, standing on the stage, red-faced and fidgeting. *Those days*, she thinks.

'Why don't you both go and help your dad with his things?'

She rearranges the sofa cushions and lifts the unfinished quilt from the floor, where it sits beside her spot.

Captured in fabric, on a newly completed panel, is the moment when, north of the old mere, an elk ran from hunters, a barbed flint embedded in its ankle. Eventually, it stumbled and fell into an icy pool where its skeleton was preserved in pitchy quietude for thirteen thousand years, until it was uncovered following the introduction of steam pumping in the mid-nineteenth century. The central panel, also finished, features the present, drained landscape: an aerial view of flat fields, a winding road, a waterway, and a house, its roof dotted by three skylights. Behind it, a patio, now a chessboard of alternating flags and pebble-topped drainage. Other panels – renderings of ice, desert and ocean; treeless tundra, lake and forest – are works in progress. Invisible blocks of time hang between them, calling to mind other nows. The now when language gave people memory, allowing them to communicate with the future and preserve the lives of the already dead. The now when two thousand men tried to drain the mere. The now when Frank Abram sold his house at God's behest and bought a caravan and a gas heater. The now when water returns, and people do what? Bellow at it, like King Canute? Beat a hasty retreat? Or watch transfixed as it traverses familiar courses, sloping and twisting, stealing sediments and running with them, welcoming itself home. Emma can't know for sure, but she has language and memory, she has a past, and she can imagine a future.

And it came to pass, she thinks, as the front door opens, and the boys call out to Chris. And it came to pass in those days – or, indeed, *once upon a time*, which is not so different – that a man and a woman bought a house on the bed of a drained lake. In settling there, they demonstrated their conviction that deluges, and drought, and other calamities belong in old stories and faraway places. But the rain came down and the floods came up. And the man went away for a while, not in search of adventure or fame, as men in stories so often are, but in sorrow.

And it came to pass in those days that the man returned, thinner and older, without the blessing of the gods, or enlightenment, or magic. Just himself, and his sorrow, which he was learning to tend, not yet certain of its taxonomy or life cycle.

And then what? she wonders as the boys' voices return, bags are dropped in the hall, and Chris offers his thanks.

And they lived, she decides. Not always happily. But they lived.

# ACKNOWLEDGEMENTS

Thank you to several kind friends and professionals who shared their expertise with me as I wrote this novel. To Lisa Knight for talking to me about sewing and showing me how to make a tote bag. To Claire Finn for talking to me about working as a welfare assistant. To Jason Lawal for chatting to me about flooding. To Jeff and Eric Bray for answering gardening questions. To Dawn Peacock for answering questions about flystrike. To Susan Crosbie for providing detailed notes about Churchtown Library, and to all the lovely staff who worked there over the years – I will always remember your kindness and profession-alism. Any mistakes are mine.

Warm thanks to authors Terry Bisson and Dan Rhodes for allowing me to reference their stories 'They're Made Out of Meat' and 'Jam', respectively. If you'd like to ex-plore more of their work, I recommend Bisson's collection *Bears Discover Fire and Other Stories* and Rhodes' comic novel *When the Professor Got Stuck in the Snow*.

Thanks to Shelley Harris, Sarah Franklin and Stephanie Butland for their generosity, support and friendship. Special thanks to Stephanie and Sarah for reading earlier drafts of the novel and offering thoughtful feedback. Thank you to Professor Ailsa Cox for reading parts of the novel in draft and for a decade of mentoring and friendship.

Thanks to Veronique Baxter and Jocasta Hamilton for believing in the novel and encouraging me to complete it, and to Rose Waddilove and all at Hutchinson for publishing it. Thanks to Daniel for reading the manuscript and to Neil, Sam, Joseph and Alice for everything, particularly the long conversation in the car on the way to St. James' Park.

# ABOUT THE AUTHOR

Carys Bray's first novel, *A Song for Issy Bradley*, won the Authors' Club Best First Novel Award, was chosen for Radio 4's *Book at Bedtime* and was shortlisted for the Costa First Novel Award and the Desmond Elliot Prize. She was awarded the Scott Prize for her debut short-story collection, *Sweet Home*. She's also the author of *The Museum of You*.